Pursued

By Michael J Reiland

PURSUED

This is a work of fiction. All of the characters, names, incidents, organizations, and dialogue in this novel are either the products of the author's imagination or are used fictitiously.

iUniverse books may be ordered through booksellers or by contacting:

iUniverse
1663 Liberty Drive
Bloomington, IN 47403
www.iuniverse.com
1-800-Authors (1-800-288-4677)

ISBN: 978-1-5320-2487-0 (sc)
ISBN: 978-1-5320-2489-4 (hc)
ISBN: 978-1-5320-2488-7 (e)

Library of Congress Control Number: 2017908578

Print information available on the last page.

iUniverse rev. date: 02/06/2018

Paris
September 5, 2015

Prologue

It was cool and quiet. The only sounds came from the open doorway. The occasional car drove past the front of the café; otherwise, the night was still. Michael had washed the twenty wooden tables as well as the evening's dinner dishes. The café was ready for the morning crowd. The last of the regulars had started leaving three hours before. Francoise had left an hour after that, but there had still been some activity outside. It was when all the day's work was over and Michael was left alone to finish the cleaning that was the most dangerous for him. He couldn't hide behind the rush of customers in the crowded café. Cruthers's men were out there somewhere, waiting for him to make a mistake and expose himself. He had no idea how they had even found out he was in Paris, but he had seen two of Cruthers's men in the last week. That couldn't have been a coincidence. His looks had changed—his hair from a dark brown to blond, clothes from elegant and professional to casual and comfortable. Even his normally brown eyes had turned blue thanks to a pair of nonprescription colored contacts. Still, his face was visible and he had to be as inconspicuous as possible.

Michael ran the mop over the last few feet of tiled floor, although beyond the glistening wetness it looked no different now than before he had started. Years of foot traffic from tourists and Parisians alike had stained the white tile to a dingy gray. Satisfied that his job was done, he put on his coat and made his way out into the night. It was cooler than usual. However, the weather was nothing compared to the sixty-below windchills he had experienced in Minneapolis.

Yet, having been born and raised in southern Florida, he had never completely lost the want for constant warmth. He locked the door and started north along Rue Strasbourg.

His route through the empty streets brought him past a single newsstand, where he stopped to read the headlines of *Paris Match* and *Le Sport*. He reached behind a long crack in the plastic structure and grabbed the copy of *Le Monde* that Fabrice always left for him. His French wasn't perfect, but he could understand most of the articles. Besides, he wanted to appear as French as possible. Walking down the street, even in the dead of night, with an English newspaper wouldn't help out his attempt. The men Cruthers had sent after him most likely included some native French, and it was quite simple to distinguish the average American tourist from the local crowd. Michael had to distance himself from that tourist element.

******

The apartment building was completely dark except for a single light on the top floor, verifying that Stacy had stayed up late for him again. She would shut the light off after she heard him unlock the door, and then she would deny being up at all. Michael wondered how she was able to handle being cooped up all afternoon and evening waiting for him to return. The only time she left was during the mornings, when the two of them would go grocery shopping as well as take a short walk through the Champ de Mars. But at three o'clock, when Michael left for work, she would lock the door behind him and wait for him to come back home. He had tried to ask her about it, but every time he brought it up, she changed the subject. Michael walked up the seven flights of stairs and tried to unlock the door as quietly as possible. He had been trying to catch her with the light on for the last two weeks.

The bedroom was as dark as the rest of the apartment. He had failed again. Actually, he was happy that she was so alert. "It's just me, Stacy." She would pretend not to hear and feign sleep, but he knew she could hear him. He had given up trying to make her admit it; it only caused problems. If it made her feel better to pretend he was still in the dark, that was the way it would stay. Maybe someday she would move past this phase in her life. He wondered what would happen to them when that happened. Would she leave him again?

The apartment had four rooms. The main living room, which also served as an entryway, was sparsely decorated with an old gray couch that they had found at Le Marché au Puce. A short oak table with a tall antique lamp stood next to it, and nearer to the door was a comfortable leather recliner. The kitchen was separated from the living room by a chest-high counter. Its blue Formica top was peeling away from the edges, and numerous burn marks spotted its smooth surface with dark brown splotches. A table for two sat on the opposite side of the counter, with a single folding chair at each end. Michael noticed the blue notebook in which he often saw Stacy writing. Not for the first time, he reached for the notebook, curious what exactly what was written there. He stopped as he touched the rough exterior cover. Did he really want to betray her trust and read something she obviously didn't intend for him to read? *Of course not*, he thought.

The den was out back, beyond the bedroom, and was by far the most impressive room. With its tall windows on two sides, the room was never dark. Even in the early hours of the morning, the large windows filtered in the lights of the city and cast a dim yellow glow on everything. Michael closed the door and turned the lights on. After his eyes adjusted to the sudden brightness, he walked over to the far end, past three easels on which sat two half-finished paintings and a third that looked complete. Stacy definitely had talent before, but she had used this time alone to truly develop that talent into a near genius ability. Not that she would ever agree with him on that accord. He stood and looked at the last painting. The stark gray buildings of Paris stretched out forever alongside the sickly green of the Seine. In the distance was the Eiffel Tower, somehow made to look small and insignificant in comparison to the world that surrounded it. The painting was a portrait of the view that could be seen through the northeast windows of the den.

Michael's half of the room contained a desk on which sat his iMac. A large office chair and an oversize trash can, currently filled to the brim with crumpled papers, sat behind the desk. The papers represented the latest failed attempts to write about the occurrences of the last few months. The words would flow while he was writing, but they never seemed to convey the same feeling once he reread them. Michael didn't know if he would ever actually do anything with the text when he finished it, but his past life was something he needed to get beyond. He knew being an assassin would always mark him emotionally; however, he envisioned a time when it was a dull background thought. Writing down what had happened recently would be his start to healing. His targets may have all been very bad people, but he realized now that none of them deserved what he had done to them.

Michael sat down in the chair and pressed a key on the keyboard, and the computer came to life. The monitor displayed the Apple logo, and the printer whirred. He swung his chair around and turned on a second switch that controlled a coffee maker. He had never been a coffee drinker, but the machine did an admirable job of heating water and keeping it hot, which allowed him fresh—and, more importantly, hot—cups of tea whenever the thought occurred to him.

The computer had booted up, and the blank typing screen of Pages was staring back at him. He closed the empty document and opened the only file under Misc Documents. He wasn't in the mood for writing, so he decided to go back and edit what he had completed so far. The first sentence brought him back six months to the day—April 5, 2015.

It was cold and rainy that day, and his last card had been played in the game that was his old life. He had decided that working for Cruthers no longer held any kind of future for him—no kind of future at all, as in a quick and easy death. He was waiting for Cruthers to show up at a meeting that had been set only the day before by one of Cruthers's men. Michael knew there was a decent chance this was a trap; perhaps they already knew that he had taken the cash for the deal that was supposed to happen the night before. Yet he needed to see Cruthers one last time to try to convince Cruthers to just let him go away. Michael had no wish to die, but if this was the end, he would die with the knowledge that he finally took responsibility for his own actions. The empty warehouse echoed loudly with the sound of thunder and rain.

Minneapolis, Minnesota
April 5, 2015

Chapter 1

The sharp scrape of metal against metal sounded above the rain and thunder. Michael turned around and watched Cruthers enter through the same door he had used only a few moments earlier. Cruthers was dressed as was usual, with his long, gray London Fog trench coat swaying open to reveal a black double-breasted suit. His long black hair was soaked and clung to his head. His skin had a deep tan yet always seemed to carry a hint of gray to it. The lights from the warehouse ceiling cast a dim yellowish tint on him, causing his skin to look even less healthy than usual. A stark white shirt stood out against the otherwise somber colors. His right hand was embedded deeply into the pocket of his coat, and Michael nervously felt into his own. The smooth, cool metal of his Glock G19 reassured Michael a little more than it should have. Cruthers didn't like guns, and Michael never knew him to carry one, but he also knew that Cruthers might have already found out that the previous night's deal hadn't happened. In that case, Cruthers might intend to take him out. Michael suddenly wondered whether he had subconsciously decided to kill Cruthers. It wasn't as if he couldn't have done it. A lot of people would probably have even thanked him for it.

Cruthers took his hand out of his pocket, and Michael tensed for a moment, gripping his gun tighter. Cruthers's hand contained nothing more than a pack of Lucky Strikes. With a shake of the pack, a single cigarette slid from the package. "Michael, how are you?" He took the cigarette in his lips, reached back into his pocket, and pulled out a gold lighter. An orange flame flared as he took a long draw and then released a rush of gray smoke.

"I'm doing, Sticky. I'm doing." Michael had always called him Sticky—not for any particularly good reason.

Sticky took a deep breath and balled his left hand into a fist at the nickname Michael had given him, and then he relaxed. "Good. I'm glad, because I wouldn't want anything to happen to you."

Why are people always saying that to people they are just about to have killed? "Bullshit. You would have tried to kill me a long time ago if your father would have let you." His father, Domino, was the real leader of the organization. Sticky would have been shot down himself long ago if it hadn't been for his father's influence.

"Now, Michael, don't get hostile on me. I invited you here to have a quiet, friendly conversation." He took a long drag on his cigarette.

"Right. You invite someone to your home for conversation—not to an empty warehouse in the middle of nowhere." Michael shook his head.

"Look, Michael; I'm the one who hired you to do a job, and you blew it." Sticky pointed the cigarette at Michael.

"It's complete," Michael said nonchalantly.

"What?"

"Last night. I completed it."

Sticky shrugged. "Well, Michael, I'm sorry you did that."

"What do you mean you're sorry? I want my money, Sticky."

"No can do. I already paid someone else in advance to do it. I can't help it if you did it for him." Sticky took the cigarette from his mouth and blew two rings into the air.

Michael took the gun from his pocket and took a step toward Sticky. "Fuck that. You'd better do—and quick!" He was taller than Sticky by almost six inches, and he liked to use this to his advantage. With each step he walked, his six-foot-five height became more and more evident. Sticky fell away from Michael as he drew closer until Michael finally stopped only a couple of feet from him.

A line of sweat immediately broke from Sticky's brow—or perhaps it was just the rainwater from his hair. "What's that for?"

"Just keep your hands away from your pockets and tell me what I'm here for."

Sticky glanced at the huge truck entrance on the far side of the warehouse. "Nothing, like I said. Just conversation. Look, you can't just kill me. What do ya need the piece for? You know I don't carry one."

"I'm not going to kill you, Sticky; not right now at least. If we're here for conversation, then let's talk. Get down on the floor and lie on your back. And give me your cell." Michael smiled.

A slight smile broke onto Sticky's lips. "What? I don't have my phone on me." Sticky patted down his pockets.

"You heard me. Get down there, and don't move a muscle."

"Yeah, sure, whatever." He took one last pull on his cigarette, snuffed out the butt with his shoe, and smiled slightly again. He glanced at the truck entrance one more time and got down on his back. "What do ya want to talk about, Michael?"

"First, let's make sure of one thing." Michael stepped over Sticky and patted down his pockets himself. No phone. "How about the people you're expecting to come through that door at any minute? Better yet, how about travel plans?"

"Travel plans? What about them?"

"I'm leaving town today, and I won't be back."

"Doesn't bother me none."

"I'm glad you understand. I don't want to see your guys anywhere near me either. I'm out of this for good. Don't make me come after you."

"Like I said, doesn't bother me. Do as you like." He turned his head to look up at Michael. Michael could see that hate was still there, now maybe even stronger because Sticky knew what was coming next.

"Good bye, Sticky." Michael walked past Sticky's prone body.

Just before he reached the door, Sticky called out. "Leave Marta alone." His voice rose in volume and he started to get up. Michael fired a shot that ricocheted off the floor only inches from Sticky's hand.

"I told you not to move."

Sticky stopped momentarily and looked up at Michael. Dark brown eyes glared back at him from beneath thin eyebrows. Michael's hair was the same intense brown as his eyes; although he didn't keep it as long as he used to, there was still a thick mass of curls. Sticky's hand reached to his own head, where years of stress had dropped his hairline back from his forehead. "She's coming with me."

Michael watched as Sticky's eyes went to his gun.

Sticky's lip trembled slightly, and he lay back on the floor. "Where?"

He couldn't have thought I would tell him that, Michael thought. "I'm sure you'll find out soon enough. I'm going to walk out of here now, and I don't want you to move until you can't hear the sound of my car anymore."

Sticky remained silent. Michael knew he'd be on his feet and out the door only seconds after he heard the car start up, but then again Michael had the gun and Sticky was not ready to die over her. Sticky was counting on his thugs to do the job, and they would be coming through that truck entrance any moment now.

"Michael …"

The sentence stopped abruptly, and Michael turned around just as he reached the door.

"What do you want, Sticky?"

"If you're leaving with her, why did you come at all? How come you're still around? You knew I'd be here. You could have been long gone before I suspected a thing."

"That's a good question, Sticky. I should be at the airport right now, waiting comfortably for my plane. I wanted to look you in the eyes when I told you to stay out of my life. If you send just one person out looking for me, they will be dead, followed shortly thereafter by your death." Michael continued on through the door, pushing against it with his shoulder. The rusted hinges creaked against the strain of nonuse.

Michael's car was parked only five feet from the building, and he ran through the downpour to it, but before he got in, he looked over to the Lincoln Town Car that was parked beyond. He could gain some time by disabling it. Michael took one look back toward the warehouse door; Sticky would wait a little while before following. The Lincoln's door was unlocked, and Michael popped the hood. He reached into his pocket and retrieved a pocketknife. Michael sliced a couple hoses and cut the wires leading to the battery. He threw the remains of cut wires on the ground. Sticky wouldn't be going anywhere for a while.

Sticky's cell phone was there on the passenger seat. Michael grabbed it and dropped it to the ground. He stomped on it twice, heard the glass shatter, and then tossed it over the tall fence into the junkyard next door. With the last of Sticky's connections to his thugs thrown away, Michael ran back to his own car. His Pontiac Sunbird roared to life as he turned the ignition key. Through his rearview mirror, Michael could see Sticky standing in the rain, watching the car leave him behind. He needed to get to Marta before Sticky could.

******

Michael parked his car in the empty space that was usually reserved for Sticky's Town Car. His hands were steady as he reached for the bag in the passenger seat. The backpack contained a couple of essential items and, more importantly, a cashier's check made out to one of his aliases in the amount of $200,000. This would keep him going until he could get access to his Swiss bank account. Once he had safely tucked the bag on the floor in the back, he went through the archway that led to the front door. Tall two-story columns rose on each side of the entryway. Several deck chairs and lounges lined the brick porch, all of them facing out toward the front garden, where tulips and gardenias were flowering. He considered knocking first but decided against it. He needed to get in and out of the house fast. The door was unlocked, so he went straight in.

He took the stairs three at a time. Marta's room was at the far end of the hall on the right. The hallway was lined with numerous paintings, most of which were from the early impressionist period. Sticky had bragged that many were originals. While Michael had no doubt Sticky had the money to purchase such pieces of art, he seriously doubted that Sticky's father would allow him to display originals so prominently and without adequate protection.

A single knock on the door was answered immediately. "Just a sec." Michael opened the door despite the response and found Marta sliding a large suitcase under her bed. She looked up instantly, her face a flushed mixture of surprise and dread. She pulled a few loose black curls away from her eyes as she looked up. "Michael." She relaxed and retrieved the suitcase. "I thought you were Dean."

"Sticky won't be around for a while, and we've got to get out of here before he does."

"Tonight … now?" She opened her suitcase and continued packing.

"We don't have time to pack anything. I have some money that was supposed to go to bad people; we can get what we need along the way." The deal with the Moroccans wasn't any secret around here. Sticky had bragged about it often enough to both of them.

"Where are we going?"

Michael hadn't told her anything more than that they were leaving. He had even hesitated telling her that much. Sticky was an overpowering presence when he found himself with a physical advantage, and Marta had succumbed to his influence more than once before.

"Paris. Our plane takes off in four hours; we have to leave now. Get your small bag, stuff a couple of essentials into it, and we're gone."

While she had never been over to France, Michael knew it was the one place she would choose to disappear to.

"Can I call my mother?" Marta's eyes glistened in the bright lights.

Michael shook his head. "No, sorry. No one can know where we're going."

She began to cry in earnest. "You've done so much for me already. I just want her to know that I'm well and with someone that is honestly looking out for me."

Michael sighed. He really would have liked to let her make that call. Her mother had basically disowned her because of the choices Marta had made. She should know, in the end, that Marta had left all this behind. "I understand. Maybe once we get settled we can find a way to get a note to her. For now, keeping things quiet is for the best."

They left the bedroom and had just started down the stairs when Marta stopped. "Just a sec." She ran back up the stairs and disappeared into the bedroom. She came back with a second black bag. As if to verify his assumption, Marta questioned him before leaving the house. "Tomorrow's deal, huh?" He nodded in response. "Do you think it's wise to carry that much cash into France?"

"I converted it into a cashier's check. We can cash it once we arrive in Paris." He got into the car and unlocked the other door. She slid onto the seat and tossed her bag into the back. Michael started the car, and a live version of The Cure's "Boys Don't Cry" came on over the speakers. The screeching whine of tires against pavement sounded above the car stereo.

The rear window of the car exploded into a thousand shards of glass. The shotgun blast echoed in Michael's ears as he instinctively fell forward in his seat and reached for his gun. Marta ducked forward as well but returned her gaze to the back after the initial shock.

The morning was quiet again, and all they could see through the shattered remains of the back window was a dark brown car parked along the edge of the driveway. As Michael reached to pull her down, another shot rang out and Marta's body snapped back, her head landing against the dash. Michael didn't react as he looked across to her and saw the red circle of blood just beside her left eye. He only sat there staring at her, watching the blood pool up and finally drop down her cheek like a red tear. *She didn't deserve this*, Michael thought. Too many people he loved had died, and Marta was the most innocent of them all.

His body exploded into action. He flung his door open and rolled to the ground, coming to a stop behind the short brick wall that lined the entryway. Two shots followed his movements, and a third ricocheted off the top of the wall. Michael rose just as the sound of the last shot died away, firing his entire magazine toward the end of the driveway. His rapid analysis of the scene took in two men, both beside an old brown Chevy—most likely a stolen car. Sticky's men would never purposely drive a car like that. His aim automatically shifted to the men, and both fell before they could react. Michael fell behind the wall again, dropping the empty magazine into his pocket and reloading another. He sat with his back to the cold stone, waiting for additional shots or the sound of movement. His breath came in short, harsh rasps. He forced himself to slow down and regain his composure in order to think about what would come next.

Nothing happened. The nearest neighbors weren't far away, and gunshots in the affluent neighborhood would bring the police immediately. Michael crawled to the edge of the entryway and glanced down the driveway. He ran the short distance to his car and rolled into the front seat. He once again stopped and stared into Marta's open, shocked eyes. Michael couldn't believe she was dead. He had to make sure she was truly gone. He reached over and felt for any sign of life at her throat. All he could feel was the damp warmth of her skin; there was no trace of even the slightest of heartbeats. They had been so close. A couple of hours and they would have been on their flight. As if the thought of the flight propelled him into action, he reached into the rear seat and grabbed his backpack along with the black bag for which Marta had returned, still not taking his eyes off her. He wouldn't be able to move her, and he certainly couldn't drive with her sitting there. He would have to take a chance and use the hit men's car.

Michael was positive he had killed both men, but he wasn't taking any more of a chance than he needed. *No sense ending up in the same place as Marta. Though I would most likely not end up in the same place anyway.* He walked the distance between his car and the brown Chevy with his gun trained just above the car's hood. When he reached the far side of the car, he discovered he had been correct. In fact, he had connected with more shots that he would have guessed. Both men had at least three or four wounds. They were not the professionals he had assumed they would be. Sticky had hired these two to do some brutality work a few times. Michael stepped over the bodies and jumped into the front seat of the Chevy. Just as he had hoped, the keys were still in the ignition.

The car roared above the now distant thunder, and Michael pulled away from the house, leaving not only the two bodies in the middle of the road but also Marta in the front seat of his Sunbird. He hoped Marta's mother would finally forgive her and give her a decent burial. After all, it wasn't entirely Marta's fault that she had gotten involved with a man like Sticky.

******

Michael arrived at the airport only an hour before his plane was scheduled to depart. He hoped he would have time to get through security and to the gate. Having a first-class ticket would certainly help that. He parked the car at the upper entrance and left it there. Whoever owned the car would eventually get it back in perfect shape. The airport was busy despite it being a late Wednesday morning. The monitors just inside the main concourse displayed the departure and arrival gates for various Delta flights. "Flight 50 to Detroit departs from gate six," he whispered to himself.

Michael rushed through the corridor before impatiently waiting as they x-rayed his bag. The red light on top of the x-ray machine went off as Marta's bag was sent through. He hadn't even thought about looking to see what was in it. He anxiously watched as the two security people looked at the monitor, pointing to a couple of objects. Finally, they decided it was nothing important and continued with their checking. Michael grabbed both bags and made a mental note to check the contents of Marta's bag at the first convenient moment.

The attendant at the gate smiled as she took his boarding pass. "We're just about ready to pull away, so hurry on, Mr. Dupont." Michael almost balked at the name before remembering, obviously, he had used a new alias.

"Merci." Michael smiled back hardly knowing why; there wasn't much reason to smile. The rush in trying to arrive on time had allowed him to forget about Marta for a brief period, but now that he had made it, the memory of her face against the dash came back. The flight attendant personally led him to his seat and placed his bag in the overhead compartment.

"Fasten your seat belt. We'll be taking off soon."

"What?" Michael looked up at her, somewhat dazed.

"Your seat belt."

"Oh, yes, of course." Michael tightened the strap around his waist. He picked up the bag Marta had wanted to bring along. He was afraid to open it. They had examined it more carefully than the average bag at the x-ray machine, yet they hadn't seen anything important enough to make them open it up. Michael unzipped the long central zipper and looked inside. A smile came to his face. It was nothing more than an iPad and a mess of power cables. Marta could never go anywhere without her movies and music. He placed the bag under the seat in front of the empty seat next to him—the seat Marta was supposed to have. Tears welled up in his eyes and finally released down his cheeks. A small girl sitting across the aisle watched him cry and stuck out her bottom lip as if she too were trying to stop from crying for Marta. Michael couldn't help but smile at her, which caused her to instantly cheer up. Maybe that was all she was trying to do—just make him smile, the same way Marta used to do whenever he was depressed.

September 1, 2015
Paris, France

Chapter 2

It was early morning when Lawrence left the apartment. Stacy had had a bad feeling about him going, and she had told him as much. He was supposed to meet up with Michael Rudy this evening, but Stacy had told Lawrence she knew he wouldn't make it to Boulevard Montmartre and Poissonnière. Lawrence had to admit that her psychic ability did often pan out, but he believed this was more about her past entanglement with Michael. She had told him all about their past relationship and how their love had ended the day she found out Michael was an assassin.

Lawrence had no doubts about making that meeting. He was eager to meet Michael. Lawrence had provided weapons when Michael was doing a job in the upper Northeast of the United States; however, he had never met the man. Now that both he and Michael were out of the organization, though both were still being hunted by Cruthers, they could meet and plan an underground network where people could hide—not only from Cruthers and his father, Domino, but from any one of these drug rings. Good people who had been pressured to enter the world of Cruthers and his peers would have a way out: new identities, new lives. It would have to be small to begin with, but who knew where it could lead. His sister's death at the hands of a gun runner from Jamaica had led him to this new life. He was hoping that Marta's death would lead Michael to the same place.

Before meeting with Michael, Lawrence had to brief the small group who had already been working toward this same end. Alain Cordon led the group in creating new lives for people. Lawrence wasn't sure how much he could trust Alain at this point, but things had worked out so far. To date they hadn't been able to help too many outside a very specific group of trusted associates, but with Lawrence and Michael as well as their sources, they were hoping to expand.

The warmth of the afternoon sun beat down on the crowd at the corner of Tour Maubourg and Rue de l'Université. It made them long for the warm days of spring that were soon to come—the days between the cool, rainy afternoons of winter and the long, hot, busy days of summer; the days before the tourists arrived and unnerved the entire city. It was a welcome moment when the first warm wind blew out of the southeast, waking the flowers and the trees.

Lawrence waited for the light to turn and basked in the sunshine. He was no different from the others, although with his work the tourist season brought about a different reaction. It was much easier to move people through the system when there were throngs of tourists in which to hide them.

******

Lawrence stepped from the quay alongside the Seine onto a wooden dock. A dilapidated boat whose name was brightly painted across its bow was secured to the dock. *Le Belle Femme* hardly lived up to her name, although she may have at one time. The deck was a mélange of fraying ropes and rusting anchors. Nets in various stages of disrepair confused the entire ensemble, making one wonder whether anyone had set foot aboard her in the last decade. He weaved his way through the mess to a stairwell that led to the captain's quarters. With one last glance toward the shoreline both to the left and right banks, Lawrence went below.

The stairs were in no better shape than the deck. The glossy white paint that had at one time adorned the wood below his feet had long since been worn away by crewmen as well as bad weather. He pushed a light oak door open.

The room behind that door was in absolute opposition to the outside. A plush dark green carpet layered the floor with a soft cushion. To his right was a small antique rolltop desk that had been restored to its original deep mahogany luster. An armless swivel chair sat slightly pulled away from the desk's writing surface. Above the desk was a window, presently shuttered on the outside. Sunlight leaked in through the small divisions between the shutters. To both the left and the right of the window were bookshelves filled with books neatly arranged according to size.

To the left, two steps led to a comfortable living area. Two love seats and a recliner were organized around a TV and stereo. Three men occupied the loveseats. Joseph, Louis, and Etienne sat in silence, their hands folded in front of them. They had all once been involved in organizations that preyed on those who were easy to manipulate. They were good people who had become bad owing to circumstances but had since found their way out. Lawrence simply nodded to them and took a seat in the recliner. He followed their lead and sat staring into space without saying a word, waiting for their fifth.

Her heels clicked firmly on the wood as she made her way down the stairs. The door opened, revealing a tall brunette. She ducked through the doorway and stepped onto the carpet, her footsteps effectively muffled by the shag. She was Caroline, the leader of their group and a professional woman that had never been involved with the underworld until a man took her husband's life. She wore a fawn business suit with dark brown shoes. She took the elegant hat from her head and seated herself on the love seat. She smiled to each man in turn.

"Shall we begin?" Her gaze went around the table to each of her compatriots.

Lawrence was the first to speak up. "We have an opportunity to add a potentially valuable member to our ranks. I called this meeting in order to get your personal approval." He glanced at all the members of his assemblage so as not to exclude anyone from his comment. "His name is Michael Rudy. I'm sure you have all heard of him." They nodded in unison but still remained silent. He would have to prove that Michael was truly out of the organization before they would comment. "He has left Cruthers scrambling for help. From what I understand, a deal with a certain group of Moroccans has gone sour and Michael is solely responsible. A woman—whose name is Marta, I believe—has been found dead in Michael's car outside of Cruthers's home in Minneapolis. She was Cruthers's girl, and if rumor be true, she was readying herself to leave with Michael."

A hush of whispers sprang up from the group as they discussed possibilities. This information was all good if it were true. And even if it were, what proof did they have that Cruthers had not simply tired of this Marta and used her one last time as a pawn. The telephone rang, quieting the conversation for a moment. Lawrence walked across the room to the desk and answered the phone. The others continued their discussion.

Lawrence returned to the others. A smile played on his lips as he sat down. He watched the other four make their pleas for acceptance or denial. Everyone had his or her own views, even in cases where the decision was obvious; unfortunately, this one wouldn't be an easy one. Yet this final piece of information could turn the tide in their accepting Michael as a part of their group.

"Excuse me, gentlemen. And lady." He nodded toward the sole woman in the group. "Additional information has just been relayed to me from Minneapolis. It seems the Moroccans have fulfilled a threat they initiated. Cruthers was shot down outside the Guthrie Theatre yesterday at eleven o'clock p.m. local time. The woman's death may have been a ploy, but I don't believe Domino would have his son murdered just to get Michael into this group of ours. In fact, he has no idea Michael is even in Paris. He has sent word throughout the world to find the killers and has taken out a contract on Michael Rudy. They have no idea where he has gone."

"I would say that this should complete our discussion then," said Caroline. "We shall leave the decision to your personal choice on the matter. If he is clean, bring him here tomorrow at 2:00 p.m. We will see how he responds to our proposition. I must remind you he has not yet made his own mind up." She got up and started toward the exit.

Caroline was stopped as the man she had been sitting next to spoke up. "But if Cruthers is dead …" He turned to Lawrence. "By the way, is this confirmed by a reliable source?" Lawrence simply nodded. "Anyway, won't Mr. Rudy be hot? Not only with Domino but also with the cops. He did, after all, leave a dead woman in his car before he disappeared."

"The car was registered in Cruthers's name. The police now believe the two murders were connected. They think the Moroccans botched a primary attempt. And Domino has no idea of what Marta's intentions were. I understand that Cruthers tried to cover up the whole mess and told his father nothing of the situation at hand. His father may never know the truth of it."

"May."

Caroline continued toward the door, opened it, and turned back to the group. "Our work has finished then?"

All four men nodded.

******

It was just after midnight when Lawrence passed through the arched entrance to the courtyard where he was supposed to meet Michael. The night was cool and quiet even though he was only a couple blocks from the busy foot traffic of Boulevard Montmartre and Rue du Montmartre. Dozens of apartment windows looked down on the courtyard, but just as Michael had said, they were all dark and lifeless.

A car drove by the entrance, and Lawrence slipped into the shadows. His dark form moved silently, slowly. *Michael might not show up for hours—maybe not at all.* Lawrence took a cigarette out, and for the brief instant it took him to light it, the corner he had moved into brightened with the yellow-orange flame of his lighter. Stacy had wanted to come along, but she had understood when he suggested she bring news of the meeting to Arnaud, who had helped them a lot but had yet to be formally introduced to the others. It would please Arnaud. They had wanted to incorporate someone with Michael's connections for a long time.

Stacy would now be waiting for him to return home. She worried too much about her premonitions. Everyone had a time to die, and this was not his. Lawrence took a long pull on his cigarette and slowly released a cloud of gray smoke into the air. He had never smoked back home; in fact, he had abhorred the habit. Yet with the combination of stress and tension, as well as having all his friends smoke, he had begun himself. He didn't know exactly when he had started, although he remembered smoking a single cigarette every now and again.

A sharp whisper of a footstep sliding across the ground followed by a rock rolling to a stop broke Lawrence's mental stream of thought. The noise did not repeat itself. This bothered him. Only someone not wanting to be detected would caution himself after causing such a slight disturbance. It could be Michael, or a junkie looking for a fix. If it was Michael, he would find Lawrence. Their meeting spot had been specifically laid out by both men.

After five minutes and still no sound of movement, Lawrence wondered whether someone else was waiting for a second person to show—or, more importantly, waiting for Michael. He was a wanted man after all—not by the law, but he would have been safer had it been the law. Those looking for Michael would not have been instructed to locate and detain him. They were going to kill him. Not that they wanted to or were supposed to, but they were going to kill him. A fire began to rage deep in his gut. Why did a man like Michael Rudy deserve to die just because he wanted to rid himself of a dirty past?

A light from a top-floor apartment went on and just as quickly went dark again. This was the all clear, but what about the footsteps? Something was amiss, and Michael hadn't caught on. Lawrence slipped from his perch within the shadows and put himself in full view of the apartments. Their meeting would have to be delayed. There was too much at stake here. Footsteps sounded again in the entryway. Lawrence ran into the dark archway and followed the sound of shoes slapping against the cobblestone driveway. He exited to the south, and his eyes went blind for a moment while trying to adjust to the sudden light of street lamps burning on every corner.

Lawrence blinked once and made out the dark figure taking a

step toward him, a gun firmly held in both hands. Lawrence froze for an instant, wondering whether he should go for his gun.

The shot came before he made up his mind. A single bullet ripped through his shoulder, twisting him in a circle and throwing him off balance. He tried to reach for his gun as he fell to the ground, but it only tumbled out of his grasp and to the sidewalk. His whole arm went numb, and his shoulder burned with an intense pain. The fire in his shoulder quickly subsided into a dull ache, and he hit the ground without the benefit of bracing himself. His head bounced once against the concrete upon initial impact and fell again.

Lawrence couldn't move as he noticed the assassin walk slowly toward him, oblivious of the shouts and lights waking the neighborhood. Lawrence's view was obscured by a shadow of a figure, and then he saw a flash of light.

******

Before the shot had finished echoing off the gray buildings of the neighborhood, the assassin moved away from the body and down the street. Michael came through the doors of the apartment building only a block away. He approached Lawrence's fallen form hastily. Even though the blood was hidden in the shadows of his body, Michael knew Lawrence was dead, if for no other reason than the small hole between his eyes. Michael rose and followed the dark form of Lawrence's murderer.

The assassin had gone up Rue de Montyon toward Rue Montmartre. Once there, Michael knew, it would be next to impossible to follow him. There were at least two or three large metro stops within a block of there, including Rue Montmartre. The black outfit wouldn't make it any easier either. Michael had almost passed by the Theatre le Palace when he noticed the small form of the assassin moving quickly through a mass of people in the entrance. The play hadn't as yet started, and there were people still milling in the aisles. Michael followed as they pushed through the crowd one after the other and jumped up on stage. The assassin followed the exit signs to the back and finally went through a door into the streets behind the establishment.

They went west along Rue de Cité and back onto Rue de Montmartre, and Michael gained on her as they reached the mostly empty streets. Michael grabbed the assassin's jacket and pulled her small form back into the archway they had just exited. Her hood fell away, revealing a smiling face.

"Bonjour, Cava?" The assassin's question was casual, almost as if she were actually wondering how Michael was doing.

Michael slapped her once. Her smile slipped away instantly, her eyes burning a dark black. He threw her to the ground and pulled out his gun. She scrambled against the wall. "Pour qui travaillez-vous?" Michael had to know who had sent her to kill Lawrence. *Who does she work for?*

Blood trickled from her mouth, and she wiped away the wetness, but she didn't say a word. "Pour qui ..." He didn't finish the question. The woman was now smiling again and looking past him, back toward Rue Montmartre.

"Qu'est-ce qu'il se passe?" A voice from behind Michael asked.

Michael turned, keeping his jacket between the gun and the policeman who had wandered into the courtyard. "What?" he asked, stalling for time.

"Vous êtes Americain?"

"Oui." He couldn't waste any more time. Michael threw the assassin at the cop with as much force as he could. Michael then turned and ran through the archway and back into the Theatre le Palace. The play was just about to begin, and he jumped from the stage to the empty aisle. The crowd, confused by the sudden turn of events, didn't know whether this was a part of the play or not. The policeman was so shocked he didn't react immediately; Michael was through the entrance and starting south along Rue Montmartre before he gained the stage.

* * * * * *

The lights on the patrol cars turned methodically, giving the scene an eerie blue glow. There were too many of them to get any closer than she was. Stacy hid in an enclosed doorway two blocks down from the crowded intersection. The loud, repetitive siren of an ambulance exploded in the night air and only seconds later came to a sudden stop just outside the ring of police cars. The paramedics moved through the crowd with a stretcher.

Stacy strained to try to see the body as they put Lawrence into the ambulance. *Do they have the sheet up over his face?* Of course, it might not have been Lawrence at all. She couldn't tell; there was too much activity going on. The rear doors were closed, and the ambulance pulled away from the scene. It was moving too slowly; weren't they in a hurry? And the siren didn't ring; didn't that mean he was already dead? No, not dead—just not in critical condition. *Is dead a critical condition?*

She slid down the wall and sat on the floor, her knees up against her chest. Lawrence was dead. She suddenly knew that and wanted to somehow accept it. Tears ran down her face and dropped from her chin, continuing their journey along her calf and finally evaporating into the night air.

A door opened on one of the upper floors, and the footfalls of a tenant sounded on the stairs. Stacy knew she should really leave before they saw her. She wouldn't be able to explain what she was doing here, curled up in the corner, sobbing. She was on her feet just as the man reached the bottom floor. He hadn't noticed her at first, but when he did, his eyes quickly looked out through the glass doors and to the crowded intersection two blocks away.

"You knew Lawrence."

Stacy took a step back, nervously glancing toward the scene beyond the glass. Was he a cop, or perhaps one of the guys who had just murdered Lawrence? She quickly searched the surroundings for a way out. The only way seemed to be through the front door, in which case she would have to get through him in order to leave. Her hand tightened on her purse. The Rhino 20DS was still there. She didn't want to have to shoot him; there were too many cops still around. She was almost as afraid of them as she was of this new stranger.

"Je suis desolé." His words carried truth of sorrow, and Stacy noticed for the first time his eyes too were full of tears. Those eyes seemed familiar—friendly—but it was still too dark to see his face. The police cars were beginning to leave the area, and one by one they went in different directions. "We need to get you out of here before they start coming around asking questions. And you probably have questions for me. It's been far too long."

She followed him up the stairs. It wasn't that she trusted him—not yet—but she did feel safe with him. She couldn't explain the feeling; it was just there. As with many of her psychic thoughts, this one defied common sense, but she knew to trust it. Their footfalls echoed in the otherwise quiet stairwell. She still hadn't said a word to him, yet he trusted her. Had he really known Lawrence? Even if he had, Lawrence had very few friends she would have trusted. He hadn't even told her his name.

Michael reached out and pushed a lock of her hair behind her ear, and it came to her before he had unlocked the door.

He had changed more than she could have imagined anyone changing. His hair was shorter, and his eyes glowed an intense blue. But she was positive it was Michael Rudy: the man with whom she had once been in love—the man she had left because he had refused to stop killing. She had wanted nothing to do with a professional assassin.

And now he was suddenly back in her life. She had almost forgotten how much she loved him, how much she missed him. If there was one man in the world she shouldn't trust, it was him. Her feelings would get in the way. They always had. Nothing had changed. She found herself following him up the stairs. His hand was warm, and perspiration ran down his arm to their grasp. He let go of her hand to unlock the door. They were inside before she could refuse. She didn't want to be there. He knew her weaknesses. Yet there was nothing she could do. Her mind was telling her it would all be all right.

"Have a seat. I'll make some tea. Or would you prefer coffee?"

"Tea." It was the first word she had spoken to him, and she saw his body relax. Michael's smile came easy and full. She sat down in an old recliner. The chair was so comfortable that she closed her eyes. As emotionally exhausted as she was, she couldn't sleep; the anxiety of seeing him again and wondering just what his end game was, it was too much. This was a man who had fooled her for years, killing people for money while pretending to be a public affairs specialist. She didn't trust him when she left him so many years ago, and she still didn't trust him now.

Chapter 3

Stacy left Michael's apartment shortly before eleven the next morning. Michael had gone earlier, and she had woken in his bed alone. She couldn't remember having moved from the recliner to the bed, and it made her wonder whether she had done so or if Michael had moved her.

She hadn't wanted to leave without thanking him, despite the possibility of what he might say to her, but she waited as long as she could. There was business to attend to, even on the morning after such a devastating loss. This was especially so because there were people who had to be informed of Lawrence's death. Otherwise, more deaths would occur. Someone had infiltrated their organization. Such a leak was potentially lethal to them all. So she held back the emotions that tried to pour their way out and headed toward Rue Strasbourg. It was better this way. The temptation was gone as soon as she walked out his door.

There were always taxis waiting along the stretch of road, as busy as it was. Stacy could have taken the metro; it would have, in fact, been quicker, but she still felt uncomfortable about using any type of mass transit so close to the location of the previous night's murder scene. If someone had tagged Lawrence, it was also likely that that person knew who she was. It was easier to think as well. She relaxed against the well-worn cushions of the rear seat and let her mind flow with the soft chant of African rhythms playing on the radio.

The night's activities were only a blur. She could remember little between arriving at the scene and waking up in the morning. The only clear visions she had were of Michael's soft, understanding face when he first discovered her as well as when he offered her tea. But that was it. Otherwise the night was a random mixture of flashing blue lights and sounds of policemen moving about, trying to control the small crowd while still doing their investigative work. Now, in the light of day, she began to wonder. Michael hadn't told her what exactly happened. In fact, he hadn't said anything at all about the murder. Lawrence had been positive Michael was out from underneath Domino's control, but wasn't it possible that this was all a ploy to take out the group? Of course, if that was true, why was she still alive?

The taxi pulled to a stop outside her apartment. She became aware of the driver staring at her and broke from her thoughts. "Ah, desolé. Combien?" Just as she asked how much it was, Stacy suddenly wondered whether she had any cash.

"Vingt-trois euros cinquante."

"Twenty-three euros and fifty cents," Stacy mumbled to herself while digging through her purse. She found a couple ten-euro bills folded into the side pocket. She didn't remember putting them there, but she probably had for just such an occasion. She found a five-euro coin among the tissues and stray sticks of Hollywood gum. She placed them, along with the two ten-euro bills, in the driver's hand and murmured "Merci bien," before sliding out of the cab and onto the sidewalk.

The driver watched her cross the street and whistled. "Ça bien," he called out. He smiled and pulled away from the curb.

Stacy heard the whistle as well as the comment, but she ignored both. She was too tired to turn around and start anything; besides, she had heard worse. It was also good to know that someone thought she looked good even dressed in clothes she had worn for two days and slept in for a night. She hadn't even had a bath or shower for two days.

All she wanted was to strip off her dirty jeans and T-shirt and soak in a cool bath. The bare white concrete steps of her building were a welcome sight. She walked slowly up, taking a deep breath with each step. Once at the top, she pressed the four-digit code into the security box and waited for the door to unlock. A solid click followed by a terse buzz told her the door accepted her code. She opened it and went inside.

The coolness of the hallway made her realize how hot it had gotten outside. She was sweating, and the cool, dry air quickly made her uncomfortably cold. The elevator took her to the third floor. The doors opened, and she exited to the left. She went past Mr. Dubois's and the Lennoxes' door without a glance. They wouldn't be up yet anyway. Nobody in this neighborhood seemed to get up before noon on Sundays. She remembered the first week she had moved in. On Sunday, she had stayed in bed until nine thirty, which was uncommonly late for her. As was her custom, she took a quick shower and made breakfast to the melodies of her favorite jazz ensemble. Just as she was sitting down to eat, there was a soft, tentative knock on her door.

Waiting for her outside were Mrs. Lennox and Mr. Dubois. They curtly informed her—in their best English, so as to make sure she understood them—that it was a policy that people be allowed to sleep until a decent hour on Sunday morning. They asked that she please turn off—not down, but off—her stereo and try to keep the noise to a minimum if she insisted on waking up so early. They returned to their respective apartments before she could say anything in response. Since then, she had made it a habit to use her iPod Touch on Sunday mornings.

The door to her apartment slid open with the slightest touch of her hand. Her other hand went to her purse. The gun was there. She pushed the door open further, letting it swing until she heard the solid thud of it hitting the doorjamb. Light flooded in through a series of windows along the north and west walls. Her first thought was to wonder where, exactly, Michael had gone that morning.

Her apartment was in shambles. Drawers had been pulled out and thrown along with their contents on the floor. The furniture was torn apart and the cushions sliced into long, slim strips. The window, which had been painted shut, was broken, and the small flower box outside had been plowed through with a fork and spoon, which still stood upright in the dirt. The roses that had once occupied the box were nowhere to be seen.

The kitchen was in no better shape. Dishes, boxes of cereal, and pasta were all over the floor. A can of tuna was even half opened in the can opener, as if someone had realized his or her stupidity before completing the job. If the intruders knew where she lived, maybe they were still watching the place. "Oh, please, no," she whispered as she ran into the hall. Sure enough, the safe was open and empty. She let out a long sigh as she noticed her black leather appointment book lying on the floor. At least they hadn't had the sense to take it with them. A great many people could have been compromised if that book had fallen into the wrong hands.

She still needed to see Arnaud, but she couldn't risk anyone following her. One of the reasons she originally chose this building was its underground access to the building behind it. It would allow her the opportunity to get out of the area unseen.

The central stairwell led to an underground garage that served the four buildings on the block. She walked across the open lot. The lights glowed a dim yellow-orange, making the room appear to be in a permanent sunset. No one was around. In fact, very few cars were parked in the garage. Only a BMW and two Peugeots lined the far wall. The red BMW was the manager's. Carole was proud of her recent acquisition, although she hardly ever drove it. The two Peugeots were familiar as well. At least they couldn't have left a watch here. To her left, the main drive led to a ramp which exited onto Rue St Michel. They would most likely have someone watching there, but she didn't have a car. Stacy had never found it a practical expense.

She continued across the lot to the stairwell that led up into the other apartment building. She entered the four-digit code that allowed her into the building. It was a number she knew thanks only to a few well-placed bribes and a greedy landlord. At the time, she thought herself lucky to get it. Now she realized that if she had gotten it, anyone could do it the same way.

The first flight of stairs ended in an entrance hall with two sets of elevators, one serving each wing of the building. She went past the elevators and into the doorway. Before leaving the building, Stacy watched the street for anyone who seemed to be loitering. The block was empty besides one old lady yelling at her kids. Her voice was muffled by the glass doors, but Stacy concluded the woman wanted her children to return to the apartment. The two kids, however, refused to budge and followed her along the street.

Once they were out of view, Stacy walked out the door. She tried to appear as casual as possible. Just because the intruders knew where she lived didn't mean they knew what she looked like. However, she had a feeling they did. Whoever had murdered Lawrence had taken the time to do their homework. She was sure they knew all about her. There was only one place she would feel safe. First she would meet with Arnaud and apprise him of the situation, and then she would return to Michael's. She still had a bad feeling about the coincidence of all this with Michael's reappearance in her life, but if he had wanted to kill her, he would have done so already. An old saying came into her head: "*Keep your friends close but your enemies closer.*" If Michael was really out, she could use his help. If not, she needed to keep him within sight to know what his end game was.

Chapter 4

The Louvre is a huge building and is always busy from open to close. It is one of the best public places in Paris to hold a private meeting. Stacy entered through the little-used Porte Jaujard. Farther to the east, a long column of tourists had wound its way around the outside of the pyramid. The sun was high above in the cloudless sky. It was as hot as Stacy could remember it being in early May. She had worked up a sweat just walking from the metro at Palais-Royal to the entrance. It was on days like this that she wondered why more people didn't use the alternate entrance. Sure, there was some sort of mystique about entering the old museum through the ultra-modern pyramid, but one could exit through it as well—and with much greater ease.

It was cool inside but not overly so. Much of the building was climate controlled to preserve the works of art. Stacy made her way through the section of the museum known as Denon. Much of this section was dedicated to Greek and Roman sculptures, including the *Winged Victory of Samothrace*. The *Venus de Milo* was located in the Sully section, which was where she was to meet Arnaud. Stacy wandered around in the room directly to the east of the statue. She pretended to examine a sculpture of the tomb of Philippe Pot, grand seneschal of Burgundy, in which eight cloaked pallbearers were carrying his body. The work was not distinctive in any particular way, yet Stacy actually found it was one of her favorites. She came to examine it quite often, and thus it wasn't odd that she now spent time looking at it.

Arnaud showed up a short time later. He was shorter than Stacy, but his muscular physique made him seem bigger than her. His smile and generous hug were normal, but Stacy knew something was bothering him. "I heard about Lawrence. I am sorry. I did not know if you would show up."

"I could not let you worry about me," she whispered. "Besides, I need to discuss a new development with you. Michael showed up after Lawrence was murdered. Shall we go somewhere we can discuss our options with more privacy?" She glanced around at the tourists, who continued to shuffle through the halls oblivious to their conversation as well as much of the artwork. Many of them came only to see three things: the *Mona Lisa*, the *Winged Victory*, and the pyramid.

Stacy took Arnaud's hand and led him into the new Medieval Louvre and finally to the Hall Napoleon. They found an open table at the Cafe du Louvre and sat down. Stacy looked through the small orientation guide she had picked up until the waitress came to help them.

"Bonjour." Stacy thought it must be the beginning of the waitress's shift. Nobody could look as happy as she did after dealing with customers, half of whom couldn't even speak her language, all morning.

"Bonjour." Stacy smiled back. "Cafe au lait et du pain, s'il vous plait." Sometimes she felt as if she lived off coffee and bread, but in the middle of tourist country, it was the cheapest thing to eat. Even water tended to be just as expensive as, if not more than, coffee.

"La même," Arnaud said, ordering the same.

"Merci." The waitress smiled again and left to fill their simple orders.

"Arnaud, someone went through my apartment last night. I don't know what they were looking for, but they tore the place apart."

"Mon Dieu. Are you okay?"

"Oui. I wasn't there; I was ..." She hesitated a moment, wondering whether she should tell him she had been at Michael's. "... at Lawrence's, waiting for him."

If he had caught the hesitation in her voice, he didn't show it. "That is fortunate, but your apartment—you cannot stay there if they are after you as well. I will find a place—a safe place. For tonight, you stay with me."

"No, I appreciate that, but I believe my friend will put me up for a while." She suddenly wondered whether Michael would mind her staying with him. They had barely even spoken the night before. She had only assumed he would be willing to take her in. She reminded herself she should really be more worried about Michael's role in all this than whether he would house her. But she had already decided to "keep her enemies closer." She then said, "But if he can't, I will leave a message for you. You needn't worry though."

"I understand. Could they have found anything that could eventually jeopardize us?"

"No. They got into my safe, but they didn't realize the significance of my appointment book. I found it lying by the door."

"But they looked through it?"

"Yes, I suppose so, but I have it coded. They couldn't have understood what my entries were."

Arnaud rose from the table, looking around the café. He dropped two twenty-franc bills on the table and grabbed Stacy's hand. "On y va."

"Why? Where?"

"How much do you put in your book?"

"What do you mean?" She was flustered now. Why was he in such a rush? "Just dates and times of my meetings. No names. And the rest is coded, like I said."

"Is this one in there? Did you have this meeting time down?"

"Yes," she answered; then she came to a realization. "You think they didn't care who I was meeting with but only that I was going to be here, and that they tossed the book only to make it look like they hadn't cared at all."

"Exactement. We must leave separately. Call me: we will talk again soon." With that he rushed through a crowd of people headed back into the Louvre.

Stacy waited until she couldn't see Arnaud's small black cap anymore. Then she too thought about exiting the Louvre. Her best bet was to attach herself to a large tour group and try to lose herself with them for a while—at least until they were well clear of the museum. *They certainly aren't here to kill me*, she thought. *But what else could they want, and why wait until now to act? Are they simply watching me?*

"We will now be leaving the Louvre and walking east through the Tuileries Gardens. Our bus will meet us at the Place de la Concorde. Is everybody here?" The voice came from behind Stacy. She turned and noticed a group of twenty-five or thirty quietly counting among themselves. *Perfect*, Stacy thought. She waited until they had started up the escalators toward the exit. It was easy enough to mingle in with the group on her way up, and even though nobody paid much attention to her, it would have been difficult for anyone to distinguish her as not belonging.

They traveled up the three sets of escalators and finally out through the rotating glass doors. The sun was still hot, and the cool interior of the museum ended abruptly at the entrance. Stacy fanned herself with the paper guide she had. It was a long walk across the Jardins des Tuileries, but she didn't want to yet risk separating herself from the group.

A shot rang out in the calm afternoon air. A clear glass panel in the pyramid just to Stacy's left shattered. She was on the ground with her own gun out before the second shot exploded into a second pane. Havoc broke out. Half the people hit the ground just as she had. The other half ran in every possible direction. The cries of confusion sounded out from every corner of the Carre Napoleon.

Stacy crawled behind one of the smaller glass pyramids, away from the sound of the shots. Once again she wondered at their motive. They couldn't just want her dead; they could have killed her much easier at her apartment. She decided to get up and follow a group moving toward the archway in the north side of the Louvre. From there she could find a metro stop and lose herself in the crowds. Besides, she didn't need a confrontation with the police. She was far from legally in the country. As much as she had helped others create new identities, she had never done the same for herself. Staying around any longer would only increase that possibility.

She got up from the ground and ran north, toward the archway. There was a metro stop just beyond the gardens, but she had to cross quite a bit of open space to get there. Without another thought, she passed under the Porte Dauphine and turned again to the west. Nobody fired at her. She reached the stairs that led into the metro without an incident. People were staring at her and moving away. She realized then that she was still carrying her gun and put it back into her purse.

She decided to go east to Cité, which was one of the larger stops in the area. From there she could go north to the Gare du Nord. Train stations were one of the best places to lose people. The next metro train came just as she reached the platform. A crowd of people exited the car, and she followed a group, going in after them. Her eyes swung around the car, searching for anyone who seemed out of place or was paying too much attention to her. All was normal—whatever that meant. She found an empty seat in the rear next to an old man who was tapping his cane against the window to the beat of the train on the track. He smiled and nudged closer to the window as she moved to sit down. She relaxed against the cool metal of the train's interior wall and tried to ignore the rough jostling of the ride. It still wasn't over. In fact, this whole episode brought up far more questions than answers.

Chapter 5

Stacy found herself outside Michael's door almost two hours after the gunshots at the Louvre. She had circled through the Gare du Nord before once again taking the metro to Place Pigalle. It being too early for the night traffic, the area surrounding the world-famous Moulin Rouge and Paris's own version of Amsterdam's Red Light District was quiet. Few people roamed the streets; they were mostly tourists who wanted to view the area but had been warned away from the nightlife there. The sun was just disappearing behind the multitude of dark buildings when she entered through the front door to Michael's apartment building. She followed the stairway to the third floor and turned to the right.

Her first knock was followed by silence. The entire building felt deserted. After a second and third knock went unanswered, she gave up and started back down the stairs. She hadn't considered what she would do if he wasn't home. She couldn't wait in the hall all night for him. Somebody would eventually see her and begin to wonder. Outside, the night had completely overcome the day; yet the warm spring air refused to give way. There were more than enough cheap hotels in Paris, but that would mean using her credit card. If it was Cruthers's men who were pursuing her, they would have access to the type of equipment that would track her accounts. His people were well versed in all sorts of reconnaissance throughout the world.

No, she would have to spend the night on her own. Perhaps she could stay in the neighborhood and catch a glance of Michael returning home. There had been a park only a few blocks to the south. She could stay there even until morning if necessary. Stacy looked down the street both ways before exiting the building and heading down to the street.

The yellow-gold burst of headlights lit up the street and temporarily blinded Stacy. She edged to the inside half of the sidewalk and tried to keep her face away from the street. They couldn't have tracked her down so quickly—unless "they" included Michael. Her heart began to beat even faster, and her breathing quickened. What could she do? The car went past, and she breathed a long sigh of relief. Then she froze as the car screeched to a halt.

She heard the sound of a car door opening. It did not shut; nor did the engine turn off. She had to do something fast. A solid concrete stairway leading up to another building was no more than five feet from where she now stood. She decided she could make it to the far side before the man could react—unless he already had his gun out, in which case she was already dead.

She took three long strides and dove for the grass square just beyond the stairs. She rolled to her stomach and reached into her purse for her gun. It was the second time that day she had had to pull her gun. She hoped the outcome would be the same, with her getting away unharmed without having to fire it.

"Stacy." Her name rang out in the warm, humid air. She tried to place the voice but couldn't. The only thing she knew now was that it wasn't a complete stranger. "It's me, Michael." She wanted to look in order to verify it was indeed him. She couldn't risk it though. They had already missed once that day; she wouldn't be that lucky again. Once again, thoughts of Michael being a part of the "they" filled her mind.

"Et moi, Arnaud." That voice she knew. Even muffled by the steady hum of the car engine. It was Arnaud. *How did they meet up?* She now felt a little safer but more confused. No one found Arnaud; he found others when needed. Had he searched out Michael, or was there more to Michael than she knew?

She cautiously raised her head to peer through the rusted iron grillwork of the stairway. Arnaud had turned the lights off. There, standing in the semidarkness of the Paris night with Arnaud, was, in fact, Michael. She rose to her feet and ran to him and hugged him. She pulled herself away within a moment though. She scolded herself for being so needy. She hadn't needed anyone for years, and now, all of sudden, Michael was back. Besides, she couldn't be sure about what he wanted yet. She felt safe around him, but she hoped that it wasn't just old feelings clouding her mind. "I didn't know what to do. I figured I needed to go someplace they didn't know; then you weren't home." A part of her still wanted to go back to his embrace, but she didn't want to give in to that. They had barely even talked about the past, let alone the future.

"We were afraid it was you at the Louvre. The reports said nobody was shot, but we couldn't be sure." His voice shook with relief. "Let's get off the street." Michael walked down the street past Arnaud's car and up the stairs to his building.

"Wait," Stacy called out. "I didn't know you knew each other. How is it that you ended up here together?"

"Maybe we can talk about this upstairs?" Michael motioned toward the front door to his complex.

"*Mes amis*, the two of you talk while I do some research," Arnaud called out, smiling. "We first need to find out who … and then why the interest in our meeting." He returned to his car and drove back the way he had come.

"Yes, of course. I'll be here tonight. We can find something more permanent tomorrow." Stacy walked to the stairs.

Arnaud got into his Peugeot and left.

Michael turned to Stacy and said, "I was afraid you were dead."

"They weren't looking to kill me," she replied.

* * * * * *

The apartment was cool and comfortable—a welcome relief from the humid evening. Stacy sat down in the same recliner in which she had fallen asleep the night before. She closed her eyes and tried to let the tension drain through her body and out her feet and hands. It was no use. The day's events had wound her up too tight. They were still out there, and without knowing why they wanted to watch her movements—and more importantly, why they would just shoot at her. It was worse than if they just wanted to kill her. She was determined to figure out who they were and what their motives were.

Smooth, warm hands gently massaged her tense shoulders. He moved from the joints to her neck and back again, all the time softly pressing his fingers over her tight muscles. Soon she began to relax, and Michael moved his fingers up to gently rub her temples. The headache that had been with her all day mysteriously disappeared, almost instantly.

He brought his lips down and caressed the deeply tanned skin of her neck. She sighed softly and turned her head, reaching for his mouth with her own. Their tongues united with desperation, unwilling to release one another. His hands slid down her body, and his fingers grasped onto hers; he then helped her rise from the chair. It was as if the last five years had disappeared. They were lovers again, and she had never left him.

Their mouths unlocked for a moment but quickly found each other again after she turned to face him. She could feel the warmth of her slim body against his. Sweat beaded on his brow and slid across his face, mingling with the lush taste of his tongue against hers.

She pulled away and looked into his eyes. *What is happening here?* she wondered. They stayed like that for minutes before she grabbed his hands from around his waist and pulled them in front of her. "I can't do this. Not right now."

Michael frowned but nodded. "I understand. It has been a while, and we've both been through a lot since the last time this happened."

"I just need some sleep right now." She let go of his hands and turned toward the bedroom. She could feel his eyes on her as she went. She hoped they could once again know each other as they had so many years before, but she had hoped for so much more than that then. Until she could trust him fully again, she couldn't give in to temptation.

* * * * * *

Dawn crept through the open window, throwing golden rays of sunshine across the room. Stacy rolled away from the light, and her hand slid across the bed, reaching out for Michael. Then she remembered how the night before had ended. He wouldn't have joined her, even just for sleeping, after that exit. The apartment was quiet and still. He must have left her alone again. The only sound was from the apartment above. The slow repetitive pleading of a single trumpet sounded out in the morning air. Stacy listened to the music until it died away and the morning was quiet again.

She put her feet on the cool hardwood floor and forced herself out of the bed. Somewhere in the distance, a dog barked. Donning one of Michael's robes, she went to the window. A comfortable breeze came through the opening, and she could already tell that it wouldn't be as hot as it had been the previous couple of days. The sky was still a clear, brilliant blue.

The two buildings directly opposite the street were still dark in the early hours. Many people were just getting up, and the street below was empty. The busy traffic from Rue Bonne Nouvelle whispered faintly above the silence. In a few hours, the neighborhood here would be just another noisy section of Paris.

The squeal of tires as a car braked was immediately followed by the honk of a horn. Stacy jumped at the sudden disturbance. The dog barked again twice, and the car horn blared a second and third time. Stacy laughed quietly to herself. Someone had once told her that it was against the law to honk your horn in Paris except in emergency situations. Unfortunately, Parisians found almost every traffic situation an emergency.

The apartment door opened and then slid shut. Stacy moved from the window and started into the hall. Her footsteps stopped two feet out of the room. *What if it isn't Michael? They could have gotten to him. Shouldn't he have called out to me by now?* She contemplated saying something to him but decided not to. It wouldn't do her any good either way. The doubts circled in her mind. She returned to the bedroom. Her purse was in the living room; and in it, her gun. She would have to make do without that gun—unless she could find one in here. She considered perhaps Michael kept one in the bedroom for emergencies.

She began with the nightstand, carefully pulling out the drawer and searching the contents for a gun or something else she could use as a weapon. Every moment Michael didn't call out to her made her more nervous. Certainly he would come in and check on her. The nightstand was empty except for a box of tissue and a bottle of Sudafed. The dressers contained only clothes. He was very neat. All his shirts were folded and piled squarely in the drawers. Even his socks were paired together and placed in straight rows.

"Looking for something?" The voice came out of nowhere as Stacy was bending over a box containing old magazines. She hadn't even heard anyone come down the hall. She slipped on a magazine and tried to right herself. Michael laughed as she stumbled and fell to the ground, ending up in a pile on the floor. "It's only me."

"You scared the hell out of me."

"I'm sorry." He helped her up, and they went into the hall.

"You could have said something when you came in."

"I said I was sorry."

"Yeah, I know you are, but that's twice in the last ten hours that you've sneaked up on me without saying a word. I wish you would at least let me know you're there."

"I promise, from now on I will." He kissed her lightly on the cheek.

She swung and connected with a blow to his gut. "Don't patronize me."

He doubled over and fell to the ground. His surprise quickly turned to laughter. "I'm serious. Really, I am." His words were interspersed with bouts of laughter.

Stacy smiled but did not laugh.

"What?" Michael's laughter died away.

"I'm serious too. It's bad enough not knowing what or who is coming next, but you sneaking up on me doesn't help. You know how much I hate that." Stacy sighed.

"Okay, okay." Michael's tone turned serious. "I can understand that. I'll make a point of that in the future. Sorry."

"Thanks." Stacy hugged him. She still felt ill at ease for some unknown reason. Why did he have that effect on her?

******

Michael left early the next morning. He had been gone most of the afternoon. He refused to tell her where he was going, even implying he didn't know where he was headed. Stacy waited for him at the apartment—patiently at first, as if he would be gone only an hour or so, but soon with anxious pacing. She walked from one end of the hall to the other, passing the bathroom and the bedroom time and time again. The hardwood floor echoed dully in the enclosed space.

A photograph of Michael standing beneath the Arc de Triomphe hung at one end of the hall. From time to time, she would stop and examine it. Each time, she would take in a few more details. Michael was waving an American flag while two men, one on each side of him, were waving French flags. Arnaud was one of the men, his bright smiling face always present for a picture. Stacy did not recognize the other man, although she had a feeling they had met before—not recently, and maybe not even within the last few years, but she had seen him before. Maybe it was his big, bushy eyebrows. At least that answered one question—Michael and Arnaud had a history. The photo had to be ten years old.

The door to the apartment opened and closed in a rush. There was a momentary pause of silence, and Stacy took her eyes from the photo and looked down the hall. A dark shadow spread across the red throw rug at its end.

"Stacy? Are you here?" Michael called out.

"Down here." She walked up the hall.

"I have a surprise for you."

He was sitting in the living room amid a pile of papers, many of which looked like brochures. Was he planning on sending her away? She wouldn't go. Not now, no matter how dangerous it was for her in Paris. She didn't care if someone was trying to find her. She wasn't running like some little girl from the bogeyman. The person who killed Lawrence was still out there—not to mention the work that still needed to be done to help those who wanted a new life. While perhaps Paris was not the best place to be, it was where these things were, and she wouldn't leave.

"Come look at these." He looked up and smiled at her. "I think you'll like some of these places."

The anger began to rise within her. He was going to send her on vacation. She was not the kid he might have known so many years before. She could take care of herself. He was not going to treat her like that again. "I'm not going!" She suddenly blurted out.

His smile disappeared into confusion. His mouth moved as if he were about to say something, but he stopped. He looked down to the brochures he had spent the afternoon collecting. "I just thought that we …" He trailed off, collecting the papers into a single pile.

"I don't have to run and hide. I can't. There's too much here that needs to be finished. Lawrence's killer—who you let go, by the way."

"But we can't stay here. They have a lot of people on their payroll, and it only takes one of them to see you on the streets. Once they find out you're here, they won't wait long. If they have to come in and get you, they will."

"We?" she asked, wondering if he would be going too or if they were both going to run. That didn't sound like the Michael she had known.

"Yes, we. You don't think I'd just let you live on your own after what happened. You need someone to help you, but if you don't …" He stuttered and coughed. "I mean … if you have someone else, I understand. It's been a long time. Whatever." He turned away from her.

"No, that's not what I meant. I mean I don't need you to help me. I can take care of myself, but I would be lying if I said I don't want you around. I loved you when I left Minneapolis, but you know I couldn't be around that lifestyle. You were so casual about it all." For the first time, she really examined the brochures on the table. They were listings for apartments in Paris. He wasn't going to make her leave. He just wanted them to move to a new place in Paris. She felt the warmth of embarrassment rise in her cheeks. "I thought you were going to send me away."

"No, never. Stacy, I love you. I always have." The words came out naturally, almost as if he had said them a thousand times before in practice for this moment.

"Oh, I'm sorry I didn't trust you. I wish I could say that I love you still too. I don't know. I worked so hard at forgetting about the possibility of us. I can't just—"

Michael rose from the couch and hugged her tight. "You don't need to love me right now. I know that I want to help you. I'm glad you can take care of yourself. But know this: I am done with that part of my life. I will never again kill, except to protect you."

"I don't want you to kill for me. I don't want you to kill *period.* Can we try to resolve this without that?" She reached up and kissed him on the cheek.

"Well, I'm not going to let anything harm you. If that means killing, I will. I can't promise anything more than that. For now, we need to strategize. How can we help Arnaud get information on the reason they are targeting for you?"

They spent the next few hours detailing the information they needed to move forward without having to worry about someone—anyone—targeting either of them. That meant Domino and anyone associated with his organization. Arnaud, and possibly Alain, could help with that. They didn't want to move much beyond them, as it would attract more attention than either of them wanted. Michael would go to Alain, and Stacy would talk to Arnaud.

September 6, 2015
Paris, France

Chapter 6

The smell of freshly brewed coffee filled the morning air and broke Michael's deep sleep. He may not have been a coffee drinker, but the aroma of the strong French brew was still a pleasure to his nose. The sun sparkled through the dusty windows in the den and marked the bedroom floor with a dim golden triangle of light. *Those windows really need to be cleaned*, Michael thought. He'd have to talk to Ludivine again. While she wasn't exactly a procrastinator, she didn't get things done too fast either.

Stacy was already hard at work on one of her paintings when Michael walked into the den. Her back was turned toward him, and she stared intently at the canvas depicting the scene outside the window. She delicately added touches of color to the painting in various spots, deftly switching from one paintbrush to the other. She held one brush in her mouth while she used the second. "Morning," she murmured through the brush.

Michael walked over to the window and looked across the skyline of Paris. Actually, there wasn't much of a skyline to see. Only the Eiffel Tower stood above the otherwise regular landscape of the city. Most of the buildings in this part of Paris were built to the same height and style. A mass of black roofs shaded a dark lavender from the sunrise spread out across the distance. A gray shadow marked the Seine's route once it disappeared around the bend to the northeast. It looked as if they were in for a sunny day—somewhat of an oddity over the past week, which had been filled with early fall storms.

"When did you get home last night?" Stacy had finished her touch-up and turned to face Michael.

"Early. The late crowd wasn't as bad as usual. I looked at your paintings last night. They're really good, you know."

"Thanks." That was the only comment she ever allowed herself when he complimented her work.

"I especially like this one." He pointed at the landscape he had noticed the night before.

She smiled and looked at the painting. It was her favorite as well. "I just finished it last night."

Michael walked across the room and stood behind her. "Yes, I really do like it." He brought his hands up the length of her body and began to gently massage her shoulders.

"Do you think we could bring it to Alain? Maybe he could find a buyer. I wouldn't have to depend upon you buying my supplies for me if I could sell one of these." She looked up at Michael with a hopeful smile on her lips.

He didn't like her to be out in the city any more than she was willing to venture out, but she couldn't stay inside for the rest of her life. "I'm not sure that's the best idea."

Stacy's smile disappeared. "And why is that? You're afraid they are going to say that my work is crap?"

Michael shook his head. "No, of course not. That's not what I meant. I just don't want to risk your safety out there until we know what's going on."

"Really?" Stacy said sarcastically. "And what makes it so safe for you out there? You're the one living your life like nothing's wrong, but it's too dangerous for me."

Michael didn't know what to say. She had a point. "You're right. Neither one of us should be out there, but we also shouldn't let them shut down our lives."

"So what are you saying?" Stacy asked.

"Let's take your best work to someone. Let an expert tell us what we already know."

"Okay, great. I'll pack it up."

******

Michael made the bacon and eggs while Stacy packed up her painting. She came into the room with her portfolio and set it beside the door. Michael could tell she was anxious to go. The kitchen was smaller than either of them liked, but they could sit fairly comfortably together at the table. Breakfast was a quiet time for them. And even on this morning when there was a little excitement in the air, neither said a word.

Stacy let her mind wander to possibilities of future fame. Perhaps one day she could make a real living off her work; then she could move into a house somewhere on the outskirts of Paris. She didn't know where Michael fit in. For now he was a comfort, and she did care for him, but she couldn't again commit to anyone who might end up dead the next day. When this was all over, if she found that they were indeed still in love, he could always quit his job at the café and go to the country with her. He would have more time to explore his writing talent. He had been investing quite a bit of time in it lately. That is all some people need—some kind of break that allows them to concentrate on their craft. It was only that she missed the freedom of movement. There was still the unanswered question of how far she could trust him. It wouldn't have been the first time he had told her a lie. He had changed; there was no doubt about that. He was quieter and less intense, yet at the same time he was the same person with whom she had fallen in love. *And left*, she reminded herself. She had told him that she would never forgive him, but now it was one promise she couldn't guarantee to keep.

"I think it would be good if you went out more often. You don't need to imprison yourself here just because I'm not around." Michael ran some hot water to wash the dishes in.

Stacy wanted to tell him that she could take care of herself and it had nothing to do with him not being around. "I'm not ready yet. I just don't feel comfortable. I tried the other day, but I turned around and came back before I reached the corner." She lied in saying this.

She hadn't gone out without him for a while, but it wasn't because she didn't feel safe without him. No, there were people she'd rather not see until Arnaud and Michael found answers. Even her friends would have too many questions. It had been a long time since she had been dependent upon someone; not even Lawrence had had that luxury. That was why she was afraid to commit. She didn't want to do it just out of self-protection. That's how it was the last time they got together. But if it really was love, what then? Had he really left his past behind? Was he through with the killing? She had to know the truth before she could allow herself to love him again.

"I understand. Whenever you're ready."

But he was so damn perfect. How could she help but love him?

******

They left the apartment shortly after ten. Stacy held the painting in a leather portfolio case. She grasped the handle of the portfolio in one hand and Michael's hand in the other like two prized possessions. A bright smile lit her face, and her eyes sparkled in the sunlight. She had never been so happy. The worries of Cruthers and his men were put aside for a while, and they could live life as she had always hoped they would. When she was young, she had often dreamed of living in Paris. It was the reason she had wanted to learn French. And her father hadn't disappointed her. She had had a French tutor, Maurice, for three years, and then she spent every summer at a foreign-language camp.

Even after living in Paris for the past three years, she had never felt quite like it was home. Lawrence may have been out of the business of transporting drugs, but in order to put together new identities for those they were trying to help, he was routinely delving into the underworld. She never knew when he might not come home. Her worries were obviously not unfounded in the end. And that day she lost Lawrence, she found Michael again, with whom she had found a home. Sometimes she missed being a part of helping those people, but it was time for her to just be happy.

"Happy?" Michael asked. He wore a long black trench coat loosely bound around his athletic body. Even in early September, the mornings could be cool and unpredictable. Yet later in the day, after the sun rose completely above the city, he wouldn't need it. Dark gray loafers systematically peeked out from beneath the hem. His long, comfortable strides pulled him at an easy pace, and she had to hurry to keep up.

"Very. It sure is a beautiful day. I didn't think the rain would ever end." They followed Boulevard Exelmans along to the east and across Pont du Garigliano. On days like this, the dark mossy green of the Seine turned almost fluorescent, as if someone had turned on a bank of lights just below the surface.

Michael stopped halfway across the bridge and looked to the north. The Eiffel Tower stood in the distance, its black frame still dull even in the morning sun. "You know, this bridge is the first place I saw the Eiffel Tower from. And it was from this very bridge that I vowed to move here someday. It's too bad it took something like this to happen before I actually did it."

"But you're here, and so am I. We both made our dreams come true. That's all that's important right now. Let's go. I want to see what Alain thinks of my painting."

Michael had never seen her so upbeat, what with Lawrence's death and then having to be hidden all day inside that apartment. He returned his hand into hers and continued across the bridge. The RER station at Boulevard Victor was just across the bridge and down a concrete stairway. It wouldn't be long before they were in the north of the city, where Alain kept his offices.

As far as Stacy was concerned, Alain's occupation was that of art dealer. It had surprised him to find out Stacy knew nothing of his other life. Michael knew him on much better terms and under different circumstances as St. Clair. They had involved themselves in each other's affairs more than once during Michael's career with Cruthers. Alain's St. Clair alias was known in the crime world as the man who could get any type of hardware for anybody, as long as the money was right. Michael had used him numerous times to acquire handguns while in Europe. He refused to take the risk of carrying his own gun across the border; besides, he much preferred the newer and lighter models Alain was able to provide him.

Alain's international headquarters, for both careers, was in a late nineteenth-century building just to the north of the Hotel de Ville on Rue Turbigo. With the American Express offices just to his west and the Banque National de Paris, commonly known as BNP, to the south, Alain had access to his two major money sources within walking distance. While banking by phone and computer was more than adequate for his art dealership, he sometimes needed substantial sums of cash for his other vocation. Since he was dealing with the often whimsical natures of artists, the banks never questioned why he would want so much cash for them.

Michael and Stacy walked into the lower level of Alain's office, which doubled as a mini studio. Marsha sat behind the long marble-top desk. Its gray-and-white pattern created a subliminal sobering effect. "May I help you?" Marsha stood up and walked around to the front of the desk to meet the couple. She wore a long red dress pulled tight about her slim waist with a wide black belt. Her long black hair was pulled back into a complex braid, and a pair of oddly shaped earrings hung from her earlobes. One was a mix between an aquamarine ball and a yellow square. The other could only be described as a purple pyramid that had been bent out of shape. She smiled easily and extended a hand to first Michael and then Stacy. Her handshake was delicate yet firm.

Alain said she was fluent in three different languages and could spot an American from a French or German with ease. While she had correctly guessed that both Michael and Stacy were American, Michael decided he would test her further. "Alain, S'il vous plait." Michael responded in his best French accent. He noticed that her eyes were nearly the same color as the marble desk. He wondered whether they had planned it that way. Of course, that was probably as likely as Marsha wearing the shade of red she was because it matched to perfection the LaCose on the far wall.

"Avez-vous un appointement?" She asked him, switching to French with confidence. He had fooled her into believing he was French with only one simple phrase—or perhaps she just accommodated his wish to speak French. He liked to think the former though. She reached behind the large desk light for an appointment book.

Michael switched to German, dropping his French accent and styling a southern German accent without hesitation. "Nein, aber sagen, Alain, dass Michael Rudy hier ist, ihn zu sehen. Er wird wissen, wer ich bin. [No, but tell Alain that Michael Rudy is here to see him. He will know who I am.]"

He had definitely startled her. She no longer knew how to answer. "Yes." It seemed that she wanted to say more, but instead she put the appointment book back on the desk and picked up the phone. "Alain, Michael Rudy est là. Il m'a dit que tu le connais." She repeated Michael's request into the phone. Whatever response Alain gave her, she looked at Michael in a curiously quizzical way. "Oui." She answered after the brief examination. She put the phone back and walked toward the stairway that led to the next level. Only when she reached the bottom of the stairs did she say anything. "You may go up now." She looked somewhat annoyed, as if they should have guessed her intentions. She obviously didn't like people who played games with her.

The stairway was a circular metal frame with wooden steps, each covered with a thin layer of different-colored carpeting. It seemed everything in the place was some type of art object, from Marsha's earrings and her desk to the stairwell.

Compared to the lower level, Alain's office was empty. A rectangular black desk held only a phone, a tablet of paper, and a laptop computer. Two filing cabinets stood out of the way in each corner of the far side of the room. Other than that, there was only a wastebasket and a hat rack that held no hats. Alain sat in a chair facing the windows. He wore his blond hair long even in the heat of the Paris summers. His blue eyes might normally have been the first thing people noticed if it weren't for the long scar that ran from his chin to his shoulder. The busy Rue Turbigo was crowded with tourists as well as foreign and French businesspersons. "Bonjour, Michel."

******

Nikoli nudged Fabrice as he saw Michael and Stacy enter the offices of Art International. They took up watch across the street on the corner of Rue de Turbigo and Rue Réaumur. Nikoli sported a T-shirt with the University of Paris–Sorbonne logo on it. Faded jeans and a pair of well-worn Nikes added to his look, as did the Minolta Maxxum hanging from his neck. He had even dyed his hair a lighter shade of brown. Fabrice took a less traditional approach, yet one would hardly guess he was any more French than his partner. He wore a green polo appropriately wrinkled, straight from the suitcase, and a pair of Avia high-tops. His jeans were newer but fit him as he thought an American would like.

"Perhaps we should split up and check the rear entrance," Nikoli whispered. They used English whenever on a tail. Nikoli's accent was slightly tainted with his native French but was for the most part Midwestern.

"No, he does not think he is being followed. He would expect us to take him immediately."

"Yes, I believe you are right. Besides, Domino did say Michael was never very good at detecting a tail. I guess he always thought no one would tail a hit man. I mean, you arrest him or take him out, right?"

"Yes, true."

Chapter 7

Alain greeted Stacy with a kiss on each cheek as well as a hardy handshake. "Michael has told me much about your talent. He believes you are a genius."

Stacy blushed and smiled faintly at Michael. "I do okay." She pulled the canvas from the portfolio and placed it on an easel Alain had retrieved from the closet.

Alain stood back from the painting. His eyes searched the colors and detail while he turned the light switch, adjusting the track lighting to various intensities. He nodded slightly and took a step forward. After another step forward, he moved to the right and stood silent for a moment, once again nodding. "Yes." He finally said and smiled. "I do like it. It says something to me."

Stacy smiled back and asked, "May I ask what it says to you?"

"Yes." Alain returned his gaze to the painting. "Loss—especially a cultural loss. The Paris that once was is no more." Alain laughed as he saw Michael's reaction. "You did not see that, did you?"

"I can't say that I'm an expert at art, but I do think it's a great piece."

"So, the answer is no?" Stacy asked, prodding him.

"Yes, no is the answer. I'm sorry. I guess I'm just not a deep enough thinker." Michael ran his hand through his air, looking a little closer at the painting.

"I think we should hang this here now. Do you have a title for it?" Alain asked.

"Yes. *Ayant Perdu La Ville.*"

"Good. Very good. Bring it down to Marsha. She will find a place for it, as well as a suitable frame."

"Great!" Stacy grabbed the painting and practically ran down the stairs to the gallery.

When she had disappeared through the circular stairwell, Alain returned to his desk and sat down. "I am sorry I cannot offer you a chair, but I find dealing with customers is easier when they are forced to stand."

"You wear them down physically as well as psychologically in your negotiations that way?" Michael laughed.

"Yes, something like that. Speaking of which, there must be something I can do for you. This isn't just a visit to show me a painting." Alain stood and went toward the window.

"No. Can we do some friendly business?"

"Sure. She really is good. I think you should continue to encourage her. She is still unsure of herself." He held up a finger as Michael was about to speak again. "Un moment." Alain picked up the phone and dialed Marsha's extension. He told her where to hang the painting and to keep Stacy occupied for the next twenty or thirty minutes.

"It's not about her painting."

"I suspected as much. You are being followed?" Alain gazed intently out the window.

Michael turned away from the window. "No, they wouldn't follow me. They want me dead."

"What can I do for you then?"

"A favor. One I hope you will never need to act upon." Michael looked out through the window again and watched the crowd. There seemed to be more tourists than businesspersons. It seemed odd in such a commercial district, although many Americans used the American Express offices down the street, as well as the numerous banks in the area.

"Which is?"

"If anything happens to me, I want you to make sure Stacy doesn't get in too far. I don't want her going after anyone on her own. Don't get me wrong; she is a very capable woman. Really, that's the problem. I don't want her trying to take revenge on her own."

"Michael, you know I supply only. No action involved."

Michael paced across the room. He had long suspected there was little truth in Alain's commitment to not engaging in action. St. Clair had a twin brother—a dual personality, or whatever it should be called. With those he supplied, he had no direct intervention; but with others—a threesome of French radicals in particular—he led the action. Michael wasn't sure of the exact cause for which these three fought, but he did know they were not originally from France. He made a mental note to check into this. If he was out of the business, he didn't want to associate with terrorists. This made him think twice before continuing. "For me, as a personal favor."

Alain stared at the phone as if waiting for it to ring. "For you, because we are like brothers, I will make sure she does not go it alone. And I guarantee you will not go unavenged if they do anything to you." Alain walked over to Michael. "But personally I would put money on you before them."

"Are you sure she doesn't know who you are?"

"Yes. Lawrence was very careful of that. She knew Arnaud, and that is all."

"But she has a great number of contacts here in the game. She is an active participant in the group."

"That is true, but she knows no one at the top of our group. Only Lawrence knew them."

"Okay, good. I would like to keep it that way."

"It will. You are one of the few that know me personally."

"It is good that I do. You've saved me more than once, my friend."

"And you, me. Shall we go down and see how they're doing with the painting?" They shared a smile and started down the staircase.

Chapter 8

The possibility of selling a painting did wonders to lift Stacy's mood. She was no longer depressed and sullen. It had been only two days since they left her painting at Alain's gallery. In only that time, Stacy had finally begun to not seem so sullen, and she increased her time finishing the paintings that she had already started. Michael's feelings about her sudden turnaround were mixed. On the one hand, he was glad she was becoming more herself, yet he was afraid that she would eventually let go completely and disappear just as she had years ago.

They had met in Minneapolis in 2006 after a play at the Guthrie Theatre. She had been there with a friend of Cruthers. That was back when he had been happy, despite the killing. His job hadn't begun to wear on his nerves. He was still able to fire without thinking about his actions. That summer day in 2006, he thought she was nobody more important than a one-night stand for a rich playboy. He had never been more wrong about anyone in his life.

* * * * * *

Snow fell against the glass walls of the Guthrie Theatre. The first two acts of Hamlet were over. Michael was happy for it. In fact, he wished all five acts were complete. Shakespeare was his favorite, but he was a traditionalist. Hamlet wearing a blue Georgetown University sweatshirt and Ophelia dressed in nothing more than a bikini did not fit that mold. The dialogue, while Shakespearean, was cut and pieced together in a modern hodgepodge that caused meaning and symbolism to leave the words as if they had never belonged there in the first place. Michael wished, perhaps for the first time ever, that he had not agreed to attend the play with his friends. Then she appeared. First she was nothing more than a wisp floating among the Guthrie faithful. She glided from place to place, revealing herself to his gaze only when she wanted. He tried to follow her, and she knew it.

One month later, after a romance that gave them both reasons to look forward to the future, he was lying next to her as the sun rose above the trees along Lake Minnetonka. He knew then that he needed to tell her, let her know, what he was. She would leave him because of the truth. She had been hurt more by her own feelings, which would not go away despite his admission, than by his profession itself. However, she finally left more as a result of his lack of desire to leave his career. He wanted to continue. It was what he was.

The questions he had had for her were endless. He wanted to know everything about her. She had engrossed him like no one ever had. One month—that was all it had took to end his future happiness with any other woman.

******

The day after she had shown up again in his life at his apartment entry, he had returned from a morning conference to find the apartment empty. He was overwhelmed with a sudden depression. He had thought that she was once again lost to him forever. He spent the afternoon sitting in her recliner—the one she had fallen asleep in. Finally, when the sun hit the tops of the buildings to the west, he had gotten up and went to find Arnaud. If anyone could find her, he could. And sure enough, he had just met with her, but then Arnaud told Michael of the break-in and the shots that he had heard at the Louvre.

Michael had blamed himself for a death that hadn't even occurred. When they returned to his apartment and found Stacy walking the streets nearby, his heart jumped. Tears came unbidden to his eyes, and his ears hummed with the blood flowing through his body.

But all of that was months ago. She had returned then, yet now she was becoming more and more independent. Michael didn't even want to venture a guess at what he would do if she indeed did leave him. He imagined coming home from work, just as he was doing now, and finding their bedroom light off. She would be gone, and he would once again be alone.

He turned the corner at Rue Exelmans and Quai Saint Exupery. His eyes went straight to the top floor and their apartment building. There, shining a distant yellow, the third window from the left, was proof she was still there. Michael's feet pounded against the pavement as he began to jog, and then run, to the front door. He was so anxious to see her that he had to input the security code three times before he finally got it right.

The stairs echoed with soft creaks in the quiet night. He followed the staircase to the top floor, and in three steps he was at the door with his key out. He swung the door open. The handle sounded dully against the wall. The bedroom light was still on. Something was wrong. She always had the light off before the door opened. Maybe she wasn't there. Maybe she had left the light on when she departed. No, she was there. Not only was she there, but he would catch her staying up for him. His smile opened into a full smile. He went to the bedroom door and slipped around the corner.

The room was empty. The bed was sill untouched. He looked to the corner of the room where Stacy always left her nightgown on the chair. It wasn't there. His heart pounded against his rib cage in ever-increasing thumps. Perhaps she was working on a painting. He went quickly to the den. His body was tense in anticipation of being relieved when he found her sitting on her stool in front of a painting.

The den was devoid of life as well. The two paintings were gone from the room. Three empty easels stood staring at him, mocking him. She was gone, and he would never see her again. He would not cry. She was her own person. If she wanted to leave, it was for the best. "Stacy!" Her name exploded from deep within his throat. The single word reverberated against the windowpanes. He dropped to the floor and released his tears. "Why did you have to leave me?" He whispered the words, his hands further muffling them.

"It was only for a couple hours."

Michael's head shot up and turned to the door. There she stood, her black hair drooping in front of her eyes as it always did. She wore a black dress with white lace trim. Her dark eyes glowed beneath long lashes. He rose and went to her. His arms wrapped around her waist, and his lips brushed against her neck just below her ear. "I thought you left me." He didn't expect a response, and the only one she offered was to tighten her hug. When he faced her, she kissed him hard. Her tongue parted his lips with intense desire. Michael lifted her from the ground and carried her to the bedroom.

Stacy unzipped her dress and let it slip to the floor. Michael undressed as well and grabbed her. He felt her petite breasts press against his bare chest. His lips traveled across her body from her lips to her neck and down to her nipples. Gently, he ran his tongue along the edge of each nipple. They collapsed to the bed together. Her hands massaged his shoulders and lower back. He rose up and caressed her lips with his. "I love you," he whispered into her ear.

"I know," she responded with a short giggle.

******

The crisp ringing of eleven chimes woke Michael from a dream. He stretched his arms and legs past the edge of the bed. The ceiling fan swung silently in a never-ending circle, throwing a cool breeze toward his half-covered body. Beside him, Stacy still slept. He let one hand stray across the length of her side and then follow the curve of her hips to her thigh. A yawn sounded from her mouth as she turned over and smiled at him. She grabbed his hand and gently brushed her tongue across each finger.

"Morning," he finally said, breaking the sılence.

"Good morning," she returned, taking the last of his fingers from her mouth. She rose from the bed, dragging the sheet into the bathroom.

"I don't have to work tonight," Michael called out to her as he too got out of the bed and put on a gray robe. "I thought maybe we could go someplace and eat tonight."

"That would be nice. We could have a real meal for once."

Michael could hear her laughter float in from the bathroom. "What's that supposed to mean? You don't like my cooking?" Her response was drowned out by the shower. Michael walked over to the bathroom door and opened it. "What did you say?"

"Nothing." But her laughter told another story.

"Bitch," he hollered, and he was rewarded with a splash of water. He laughed and shut the door. "Life is good," he said, smiling, and he went down the hall to the kitchen.

******

The bright neon light of the Paradis du Fruits brightened the quai. Stacy and Michael stood outside the restaurant amid the full tables on the sidewalk. One of the waitresses finally came and led them to a table in the far corner. Michael squeezed between the tables where a group of women were all eating the same meal—toast pacific. This just happened to be Michael's own favorite dish: two large halves of tuna fish sandwich flanking an enormous helping of shaved carrots.

Michael took his seat and smiled across at Stacy. "So what do you think?"

"It's interesting," she said, looking around the room. Tables were arranged along each of three walls, with the fourth being the glass-front entrance. Another group of tables surrounded a centerpiece stacked with a multitude of fruits and vegetables. "How's the food?"

"Excellent. Everything is fruit, vegetable, or seafood." He lifted the menu and started scanning the various plates. He did this every time and always ended up ordering the toast pacific.

"What are you getting?"

"I don't know."

A waitress walked over and set down a carafe of water and two glasses. "Bonsoir, Michel. Çava?"

"Oui, çava bien. Nicole, c'est Stacy. Elle est americaine."

"Eh, ça bien. Hello, my name is Nicole." Her accent was undeniably French.

"Bonsoir." Stacy nodded politely.

Nicole smiled again at Michael and slipped away from their table.

"Why did you tell her that I was American?"

"What? Shouldn't I have?"

"No. I mean … it's not important, but why did you?"

"I don't know. She likes speaking English. So I supposed I would let her know you were American. I don't see the problem."

"No problem. It's just that you don't normally go around introducing me and qualifying it with the fact that I'm American."

"Whatever."

"You know I hate it when you say that."

"Look, like I said, she likes speaking English, and like you said, it's no big deal. Right?"

Stacy took a deep breath and looked down at the menu. "What are you getting?" she asked again, trying desperately to change the subject. She felt lost and a little confused. Over the past months Michael had been able to continue his life as hers had come to a screeching halt. He had friends that he saw every day, keeping relationships alive and beginning new ones. She, on the other hand, had only him. Michael had been her only constant. More than anything else, Stacy felt the need to escape from the shell she had created. It was time to change the flow of action. Instead of waiting for someone to recognize her, she would find them first. Michael said that Cruthers had most likely paid upfront for someone to get them; he was probably a professional that would complete the job even though Cruthers was dead. After all, they would have to contend with Domino if they didn't finish it. Her instinct told her that becoming the aggressor was the only way to end it. Michael needn't know what she did with her own time. Besides, he would only refuse to let her go after the hit man alone.

Chapter 9

Despite her denial, Michael could tell Stacy was wrestling with a particularly difficult problem, and he decided to give her some space by keeping clear of the apartment for the rest of the day. He suspected the problem was in the form of Domino. He wondered whether Domino knew Michael was in Paris with Lawrence's group. A month ago, he would have seriously doubted it. But after Lawrence's death, he suspected Domino's influence was much farther reaching than he first thought. Cruthers may have paid someone to kill Michael, but he would never have spent the money to try to disable Lawrence's group. He almost certainly knew nothing about it. No, this had Domino's hand all over it. That meant that even with Cruthers's death, there would be no stopping it.

The sky was a brilliant blue, and the sun had tilted just slightly toward its westerly decline. Michael stood still for a moment and let the sun warm his face. It was perfect weather for Paris, and Michael was one among many enjoying it. Every café along the southern bank of the Seine was packed with tourists and Parisians alike, most enjoying their lunches outside. It was mid-September and that meant an almost complete end to the tourists moving into the city by the thousands. Still, he would certainly be busy this evening at work. Chez Julian was not a normal tourist haunt, but it was in the heart of the university campus nightlife. September in the Quartier Latin was the worst. Not only were some tourists still arriving, but the students were beginning to be in full force after finishing up their summer vacations in August.

Michael headed to the north across Pont Alexandre III, its cornerstones topped with the golden statues that had been refurbished for the bicentennial. He remembered back to that year with a little distaste. He was in Paris completing a job for Domino. Michael had been trailing an ex-runner for Domino. The man had completely bungled a job, which left $300,000 in the hands of two dealers with nothing received in return. A suitcase holding over ten kilos of pure cocaine sat in the back of an abandoned car for two days until the police found it. Domino was subsequently out both the money and the cocaine. At the time, Michael found it to be quite generous that he was sent to disable the man instead of to kill him.

That day had started out much the same way this one had. Clouds and rain had quickly given way to sun and clear skies. Michael broke from his daydream just as he took a step to cross to the Place de la Concorde. A car sped past, and the horn sounded a continuous shrill. He had almost made the fatal mistake of any big city pedestrian—not paying attention when there was a car anywhere within sight. This was particularly true in Paris, where even the sidewalks were used as parking spots.

He waited until the light changed, allowing him to cross in somewhat safety. Even then one had to be certain a wild motorist was not in a hurry. Instead of crossing again, Michael took a left and headed west along the Champs Élysées. The refurbished boulevard was now a haven for pedestrians—even more than it had been before. Thousands of people could easily line the wide sidewalks, and there were actually few to no cars parked along the way.

He continued his stroll up the entire boulevard, past numerous auto dealerships, the McDonald's and KFC, and the Office of Tourism, where nearly a hundred students and other tourists had conglomerated. This was one of the few places in Paris where backpacks, tennis shoes, shorts, and T-shirts prevailed over standard French dress. Michael could only smile as he remembered his first trip to Paris almost twenty years before. The trip had been a disaster, as he either lost or had stolen almost everything he had brought with him. Somehow that had not affected the way he saw the city though.

Love at first sight is a rare thing; but between him and his city of Paris, it was real.

After a quarter of a circle tour around the Arc de Triomphe, Michael went north and then west again, passing the Quick, which attempted to pass itself off as a French McDonald's. It had been mostly successful, as it had helped to run Burger King out of the country. The streets were quieter here, and the sun was effectively blocked out by the buildings. He eventually wanted to get to La Defense, which was much farther to the west, but he also wanted to take his time.

"Monsieur?" He was tapped on the shoulder and turned to find a man dressed in rags. The man held out an old cardboard box that jingled with several coins. Usually Michael shied away from such beggars, but he was in such good spirits that he reached into his pocket for a euro. His hand had just reached a coin when the man dropped the box and punched Michael square in the face. Another man caught him as he fell backward, his hand still in his pocket. The pungent odor of chloroform filled his mouth and nose. Before losing consciousness, Michael felt them drag him a short distance and toss him into a vehicle.

* * * * * *

"Monsieur Rudy, it is time to wake up." Someone slapped him in the face once, and then again, as he was slow to regain consciousness. The hand came down again, but Michael blocked it, turning his hand to grab the wrist and twist it backward against the attacker's arm. The almost silent cocking of an automatic weapon followed by the sensation of cold metal against his cheek caused him to release the wrist and look up at his captors. Three men stood before him, and at least one with a gun was behind. The pressure of his own gun against his back was gone.

"Bonjour. How are you feeling, Mr. Rudy?" the man in the middle said. His voice carried a hint of an accent on his French. He was the shortest of the three, and his sandy brown hair contrasted against the black hair of the other two; however, all three had the same dark black eyes. His tight-lipped smile did nothing to make his face seem pleasant.

"A little dazed, and I think I might throw up," he replied honestly.

A smile pressed across the man's lips. "I hope it is not due to the company."

"I'm sure it's not. Now, since I'm not already dead, may I ask what I can do for you?" Michael wondered who might want information from him. *One of Domino's competitors. Perhaps someone that works against Alain?*

"I'm so glad you offered. I'd hate to presume that you were being forced into anything."

"How kind of you." Michael sighed. He really hated men who played games like this.

The man's smile disappeared, and he looked up to the man who held the gun. A third blow to Michael's head included the automatic's metal handle, and Michael fell to the floor. "I don't enjoy sarcasm, Mr. Rudy."

Michael didn't respond, lifting himself back into the chair. He wiped away a line of blood that had run down his cheek. A hand appeared over his shoulder, and with it a handkerchief. He took it and held it to his forehead.

"We brought you here so that you might do a job for us. I would be lying if I told you that it was a quite simple one, but a man of your ability has certain talents that make it, shall we say, much more likely to be a success."

"I'm no longer in the business."

"Yes, that is what we've been told. But I think we can convince you to change your mind. You see, we need someone who is not very active in Europe and at the same time has contacts enough to fulfill the contract. You are most qualified in both respects."

"I'm glad you feel that way. But as I said, I no longer work in that field. You can kill me if you wish, but my associates will not rest until they have avenged me."

"Ah, threats I can deal with. It is not you who will be harmed. Do you know this woman?" He handed Michael a picture.

"No, why? Is she the one you want killed?" Michael instantly regretted never having gotten good at spotting a tail. He always worked under the assumption that no one knew who he was and he could work in the open. That had worked for him for fifteen years. Now it was playing against him.

"Michael, please give us more credit than that. Perhaps you recognize this one, or this … or perhaps this?" He kept handing Michael photos of Stacy, Michael and Stacy together, and Stacy outside their apartment. "You see, she is the one who will be harmed. Not killed—no, not at first; she is too valuable for that. Just harmed."

"If you lay one hand on her—"

"That is up to you."

Michael took a deep breath. "Who is the target?" If he had done it before for money, he could do it again for something ultimately more important—Stacy. Agreeing to the hit did not mean he would need to fulfill the contract. He did find it odd how easily he considered killing again, and that disturbed him more than anything.

"That's much more agreeable. You see, this is not exactly extortion. We will gladly pay you for your efforts."

"Yes, yes. Who is the target?"

"Nazeem Basrath."

That was a name he knew. Nazeem led an extremist group out of Northern Africa. He never advocated violence, preferring politics instead. He would need to learn more about his captors to find their motive. "That will cost you."

"I am ready to pay whenever the job is complete." The man clasped his hands and smiled. "So we have a deal?"

"I usually work under a half before, half after contract," Michael responded casually.

"Yes, but as you can well understand, these are unusual circumstances."

"I will need something up front for materials," Michael bargained further.

"Josephine will provide you with whatever is needed." Michael turned to face the woman who had handed him the handkerchief.

She pushed her red hair away from her face, smiled, and offered her hand. He took her fingers and softly brushed his lips against her knuckles. "Enchanté, Mademoiselle." He looked up into her green eyes and smiled back.

"Enchanté," she returned.

"Now, you are free to go, but remember: you are going to have a tail. And I have it from a great source that you are not very good at avoiding those. If you by any chance make contact with Stacy or even attempt to evade your tail, Stacy will be harmed. And with each consecutive action along this line, the harm will be greater. Do you understand?"

Michael narrowed his eyes. *This man has been in contact with Domino, so why isn't he already dead? There will be no payment—only death. That is the exchange he had worked out with Domino. He must be thinking I will do my job, and he is planning to kill me when I come to pick up the money.* "Yes, I will need some time to get set for this."

"I will have Josephine show you where the hit will take place. From there, we will meet again on Tuesday to finalize your instructions."

"Okay, but after this you are not to contact me again."

"If our paths cross again, it will be your doing—not mine." The man's mouth formed into that same tight-lipped smile that he had shown when Michael first saw him.

"Little chance of that."

"Sarcasm, Mr. Rudy, I do not enjoy it. I thought you understood such minor details are important."

Michael ignored the comment and turned to Josephine again. "Lead the way out of here." He lifted an arm for her to take. She slipped her hand over his elbow, and without a word they passed through a door and onto the street between two warehouses.

******

Josephine had taken them by car, with Michael blindfolded for the first twenty minutes, back into central Paris. The Eiffel Tower loomed high above them as she parked underneath the metal structure. She left the car there with the keys still in the ignition. They made their way across the gravel pathway under the tower and down into the Champ de Mars. The green expanse of the park spread out before them toward the Ecole Militaire. Josephine took a left at the first opportunity and then took another into a small park centered with a pond. A group of tourists lined the fence around the water, throwing bread crumbs at the waterfowl that rested on the clear surface.

Josephine stopped before a chain-link fence that had been erected before the path to Rue Université. "He will be residing at this location." She pointed to a building on the right. "On the morning of the sixteenth, he will go by car to an important meeting with the French officials. He will not make it to that meeting. Understood?"

"Your boss was right when he said it wasn't going to be easy. There will be state security here. I've never done anything like this before."

"But you will this time."

"Yes, I will, but I want you to understand I'm doing this only to keep Stacy from harm. I want no news of who did this. It is not to be known that I am in Paris. Although, since your boss knows, I'm sure the people I don't want to know do already. Still, is that understood?"

Josephine shrugged. "I will relay it."

"You will make it a necessity." Michael took a step toward her.

Josephine did not back away as Michael came toward her. "Yes, it is done."

"So now I need some time to figure out what I'm up against. Two days?"

"Two days. Call this number." She handed him a slip of paper. "Ask for Josephine. They will respond by asking who it is that's calling. You give them a time and location to meet."

"I will be there." Michael wondered how much this woman knew about the organization's plan.

Josephine reached out a hand. "Sounds good."

Michael took her hand and shook. "A bientôt." He would be seeing her soon, he hoped. She just might be the person who could give him the information to pull this off.

"A la prochaine."

Chapter 10

Stacy had waited all night the first night Michael was gone and had fallen asleep despite efforts to stay awake during the second night. She had long since been afraid of the worst. It was not like him to just disappear for days. It was true that there were times when he would be gone from the time she woke until long after his work hours. Still, two days and no news was not good. She quickly took a shower and dressed. She put a cup of water into the microwave and set it for two minutes. While the water warmed, she called Arnaud.

"I'm sure it is. Let me get his calendar." The silence on the other end lasted only a few seconds. "Sure, no problem. I'll let him know you're coming."

"Thanks. A bientôt." She hung up the phone just as the microwave sounded the shrill beep announcing its completion. While she drank her tea and watched the clock move ever slower, she wondered what could have happened to Michael. She didn't think about the bad things that could be; she considered only the simple commonplace reasons why he had not contacted her or returned home. She knew it would take her only twenty minutes to get to Arnaud's. How she could pass the next hour and a half without going out of her mind, she didn't know.

Finally, after tapping her fingers on the card table for ten minutes, she got up and poured the rest of her tea down the drain. Leaving the apartment, she headed for Sacre Coeur only to return back into the city once the brilliant white stone of the basilica was in sight. After winding her way through the back streets, trying to avoid as much of the traffic as possible, she finally entered a small café and took a seat. The walk had done nothing to keep her mind off Michael and the possibilities that might have surrounded his disappearance.

She envisioned him lying in some dark alley with a line of bullet holes across his chest and another between his eyes, just to make sure the execution had been done correctly. She was tired of worrying about him every day of her life. Then and there, she vowed that if he was somehow miraculously alive, she would convince him to leave Paris and find some secluded place to try to start a normal life together. She loved him, though. Admitting it for the first time since she had left him five years before made her feel better and gave her some relief from something that had been plaguing her ever since she had seen him again. Deep inside, she had known that she had refused to love anyone else, hoping he would one day find her. And to now know that she had not been wasting her life away was the release of a burden. She had been faithful, and Lawrence had understood how she felt even before she could admit it to herself. Yet Lawrence was gone, and there was a good chance that something had happened to Michael. She didn't know whether she could take another loss.

All of this was good, but there still was the matter of trust. She may have finally decided to admit to her feelings for him, but that didn't change the fact that she still didn't trust him. Something about all this smelled wrong. There was definitely something going on that he knew about and was hiding from her. The only way she could find that out was to use Arnaud to help her investigate Michael. Between the two of them, they could find the truth.

* * * * * *

Stacy arrived at Arnaud's office shortly before eleven. He still had not returned, and Cécile had left her in Arnaud's office with a hot cup of peach tea. Stacy wandered through the room. She had been in the office before, but never for very long and always with Arnaud to occupy her. The books that lined the shelves at the rear were a diverse group that displayed Arnaud's odd taste in literature. Everything from *Frankenstein* and *David Copperfield* to Harlequin romances in both English and French were neatly arranged according to author, just as one would find them in the bookstore—except, of course, for the fact that every book was creased and smudged from use. The wall behind Arnaud's desk was covered in framed photos, many of which included Arnaud's smiling face. Among these photos was the one Stacy had seen in Michael's apartment. Arnaud, Michael, and a third man with bushy eyebrows who looked oddly familiar stood beneath the Arc de Triomphe. She would have to remember to ask Arnaud who he was.

Stacy went to one of the leather-backed chairs and sat down. She was beginning to worry that he too was missing. Yet, Cécile had been confident he would show up. Just then the door opened. "Bonjour, Stacy. Çava?"

Stacy rose from the chair and greeted him with a kiss on each cheek. A smile did not answer his though. "Non, pas de tout." She did not like that Michael was missing. Truth be told, she did not trust what he might be doing—perhaps another job to get them the money to live comfortably behind all this.

"Qu'est-ce qu'il s'est passé?" The smile left his face as well, and his tone shifted immediately to concern. He rounded the desk and sat, gesturing for her to do the same.

"Michael's been gone for over two days. I haven't heard a single word from him."

"Two days. That's not like him, is it?'

"Not at all. I don't know what to do. They haven't seen him at work, not at Françoise's place. Arnaud, I'm afraid they found him. He could be anywhere. They wouldn't do it out in the open either. They would make sure he wasn't found for a few days. They would want us to come looking for him."

"No, don't think that way. I will check around. I must admit I couldn't guess at one, but there must be a rational explanation. Be an optimist for me."

"I can't. I'm sorry, but I know something's happened to him. I have the same feeling I did when Lawrence went out." She wiped away a single tear from her cheek.

"Don't talk like that. You know you're always getting these premonitions. Remember what Lawrence always said to you."

"Don't hope for the worst."

"Exactly."

Lawrence had said that same thing just before he had gone out. Stacy refused to tell Arnaud this. *Let there be at least one optimist.* She would let Arnaud do his checking. If Michael was alive, Arnaud would find out where he was.

"Okay, can I help in any way?"

"Just think positive thoughts. Contact Cécile if you hear anything."

"I'll be at my place then."

"No. Under the circumstances, I think it's best if you stay away from your place until I can get some answers. I have a studio near the Bois de Boulogne. Get the keys from Cécile. You can even try to relax by walking through the *bois.* It is a very nice day for it."

"But what if Michael returns?"

"I'll have someone watch your place. I'll know where to reach you."

Stacy sighed deeply. She hated not being able to do anything. Perhaps she could after all. Maybe Alain had seen him. Yes, that's what she could do. Besides, she needed to bring another painting to him. Going back to the apartment for one second couldn't harm things. *Yes, think positive, as Arnaud said.*

"Okay, let me know as soon as you hear anything, no matter how trivial," Stacy said as she began to leave.

"Bien sûr. A bientôt."

"A bientôt."

Chapter 11

Michael called the number Josephine had left with him. The phone rang twice, and then a man with a deep voice answered.

"Allo."

As requested, Michael asked to speak to Josephine. "Je voudrais parler avec Josephine, s'il vous plait."

And as she had told him would happen, the other party asked who he was. "C'est qui?"

"L'entrance du Jardin du Shakespeare, trois heures et demie." He made the appointment for an hour later than it was at present, despite the fact that he was within a fifteen-minute walk of the Jardin du Shakespeare. He wanted to be there early so he could spot any tails that were behind him. He could ask for the equipment to be delivered that night, so he could disappear for a few hours without his blackmailers worrying.

The walk through the Bois de Boulogne was a pleasant one. The park was filled with families having picnics and strolling through the multitude of paths. Michael took his time and enjoyed the weather as well as the sense of calm that lay over the wooded park. He knew it might be the last day he could feel so comfortable for a month or even more. He needed to get Stacy and him out of Paris and away from the pursuit. He no longer had just Domino to worry about; there was this new group as well. But there was definitely a connection there that he hadn't been able to figure out. Perhaps it was just as he had thought, and they had agreed to kill him for Domino if Domino backed off long enough for Michael to complete this job. He cared little why they wanted Basrath dead; to him it mattered only that it would give him time to get plans set to disappear with Stacy. The only thing that worried him was that he wouldn't be able to go through with it. He had to make a contingency plan and ensure Stacy's safety before the hit. If someone was going to be hurt, it was him, not her. He reached the Jardin du Shakespeare forty-five minutes before the meeting.

Michael paid the ten euros to get into the garden and strolled just past the entrance. Stopping just around the corner of a large hedge, he set watch on the entrance, both for Josephine and anyone who might have been following him. Fifteen minutes passed by, and still no one had entered. He began to wonder if indeed they had anyone following him. It could have been a tactic to keep him in line. Of course, there was always the possibility that they were just watching the entrance. It was, after all, the only way in and out of the garden. Michael shifted his attention to the paths that surrounded the entrance. There were no benches, and anyone staying near would need to loiter on foot.

Josephine arrived exactly at three thirty. She stopped at the entrance and looked to her right. Almost imperceptibly, she nodded. Michael quickly looked in that same direction. An old man who was quietly talking to a young boy nodded in return. So he had located at least one tail. He hoped it was the only one. Josephine paid her fee and entered. Michael stepped away from the hedge and approached her.

"Salut, Josephine," he called out casually.

"Salut." She returned the greeting without a hint of surprise.

"Let's walk." He led her into the gardens, silent until they reached the bubbling stream that crossed under their path. "I will need very little. First plastique—no more than two hundred grams. Also a remote radio fuse and two feet of lead wire with a gold contact."

Josephine handed him a sheet of paper. "This is a list of time and dates of meetings along with approximate departure times. They encompass the next three days. It is at your discretion when this is done, but if it has not been accomplished by Friday at 1:00 a.m."—she bit her lower lip and looked away from him before continuing—"both you and the girl will be hunted." She paused again and returned her gaze to him. "A package will be delivered to you this evening at the address on the list. It will contain what you need. It was a pleasure meeting you." Josephine walked away.

"Aren't you forgetting something?"

"Excuse me?" She stopped but did not turn around.

"The payment. Your boss did mention payment."

"Yes, of course. It has already been deposited in an account in Amsterdam. The necessary papers will be mailed to the American Express office in Copenhagen the day after the job is completed and verified."

Michael watched as she left the garden and headed away into the bois. He delayed following straight behind her, looking for the old man and the child. Only two women walking arm in arm were within sight of the entrance. He could hear others beyond the garden on all sides, but he would need to exit to see them. Any further delay would begin to look suspicious as well. Perhaps they were satisfied, now that he had made it to this meeting, that he was going through with it. He could not leave that to chance. Starting toward the entrance, the old man and boy passed by him and exited. *So they followed her in.* Michael exited and started to follow them, only to turn in the opposite direction after the old man turned to check on him. He followed the path along the edge of the garden and got out of sight as quickly as possible before finally breaking into a run. He was down the path and over a rise toward the Lac Inférior when he turned.

The path behind him was full of walkers, but none resembled the two who had been trailing him. Yet this was not his area of expertise. He had no idea how many people were behind him or even if the man and boy were actually following him. He had always worked on the assumption that people had no idea who he was or what he looked like. That had all changed now that he had exposed himself to people. The fact still remained that very few people knew what he looked like, yet this strange man had somehow picked him off the street with veritable ease. Paris was no longer safe for him or Stacy;

they would need to leave under the cover of his assassination attempt in two days. The plans were already set in his mind. It would not be as difficult a job as it first seemed. The car was not well protected; nor was the entrance to the residence. Only a simple chain-link fence guarded the rear entrance. This man did not seem to be an important enough official to warrant full security.

His route had taken him to the Palais de Chaillot, where he descended into the depths of the metro. He returned to the Arc de Triomphe and went on to the Champs Élysées. A short walk to the east brought him to Rue Balzac. A sex shop, only a block north of the main boulevard, displayed a glowing neon light in both blue and red. The length of colored tubes was formed into the words "video, magazines et gadgets." It was here that Michael entered. The man behind the counter immediately greeted him with a simple "Bonjour."

"Bonjour, je cherche Anne."

"Oui, monsieur, et vous êtes qui?"

"Susie."

"Susie?" The man smiled.

"Oui, comme j'ai déjà dit."

The man continued to smile and disappeared down a stairwell in the back of the store. Michael gazed around at all the magazines and sex toys that surrounded him. He sometimes wondered why Arnaud worked out of such a place. Certainly, Stacy had never set foot in this place. She would have immediately disassociated herself with Arnaud. Not that Michael necessarily approved of what surrounded him. He did, however, find it less offensive than she did.

Chapter 12

The two men began to follow Stacy at the apartment, where she had quickly gone upstairs and come back down, with an artist's portfolio, to Alain's studio. Just as they had done when following Michael, they neither followed her into the art studio nor strayed far from the entrance. They had, however, changed their mode of dress. Nikoli wore gray slacks with a silk white button-down shirt and black loafers. Fabrice had jeans and a plain white T-shirt with brown loafers. They had no worries about blending in with the crowd. They were there only to observe and, if noticed, to end the pursuit.

******

The inside of the art studio had changed little since Stacy had last been in it. Marsha greeted her with the same falsely pleasant smile and showed Stacy to the stairwell only after another concise call to Alain.

Stacy went upstairs without hesitation. "Alain, Bonjour. I know you must be busy, but I brought another painting."

"Great. I always have time for my promising artists. But where's Michael?"

Stacy's smiled faded and her mood shifted, becoming noticeably darker. "That's another reason I came, in fact. I was hoping you would know where he was. I haven't heard from him in two and a half days."

Alain rubbed his forehead and let out a slight sigh. "No, I don't know where he is. In truth, I have been looking for him as well."

"Oh, about what?"

For just an instant, Stacy could have sworn she saw a worried look on his face, but if it was there, a smile quickly replaced it. "Nothing important; that's why I wasn't worried. But he hasn't contacted you at all?"

"No, and I was just at another friend's place, and he knew nothing either."

"That's very odd. This other friend—what's his name?" Alain asked.

"Arnaud Duchateau. Do you know him?"

Alain stared out the windows of his office, seemingly lost to their conversation. He then answered quickly. "Non, pas du tout."

Stacy didn't believe that for a moment. Still, she did believe Alain didn't know where Michael was. "Well, I am truly worried now. No one seems to know a thing about his disappearance. Arnaud is doing his best to find out what could have happened."

"Arnaud is looking for Michael at this moment?"

"Yes, I just left him." She instantly regretted telling Alain about Arnaud. There was definitely more to this man than being an art dealer.

"Well, I'm sure he'll find him." Alain waved his hand.

"I hope."

"I'm sorry I couldn't help you more. Shall we discuss a more pleasant topic? Perhaps your painting will take your mind off it for a while."

"Oh, yes, sure." She lifted her portfolio onto his desk.

Discussing her painting and the ensuing discussion of the modern art world did little to keep Stacy's mind off Michael. And as she left the art studio, her mind never strayed far from thoughts of possible outcomes. He was in some kind of trouble; she knew that for certain. It meant he was either already dead or that he was afraid of contacting her and thus exposing her to a dangerous situation. *That would be just like him. Even if it meant saving himself, he wouldn't endanger me.* Stacy also knew that no matter how much she tried to persuade him to change, he would never knowingly bring his problems to her.

It was well past seven when Stacy finally arrived at Arnaud's apartment near the Champ de Mars. She unlocked the front door and set the empty portfolio down in the entrance. The entryway was a mixture of deeply polished mahogany paneling and oak shelving. Each shelf prominently displayed trinkets from around the world. Directly in front of her, two glasses from the New York Hard Rock Cafe sat alongside a plastic replica of the World Trade Center towers and a ceramic Statue of Liberty. On the next shelf were three wooden masks, painted an ivory white and pale blue. The photo of Nelson Mandela giving a speech to a crowd in Johannesburg suggested the masks were South African. The list went on to include countries in all parts of the globe, including a photo of Arnaud next to a flock of penguins.

She left the entryway and went straight to searching for the bathroom. What she wanted more than anything else was a hot bath; then she thought Arnaud had been exactly right about the walk. She only glanced into the living room, which was decorated in black and white. A large Mickey Mouse phone sat on top of an answering machine half hidden by the arm of a white sofa.

* * * * * *

Fabrice and his associate sat outside the entrance to 12 Alboni. How convenient that there was a park there where they could sit and relax, eating their ham sandwiches and drinking wine. It was still quite warm, and they hardly looked out of place easing their feet after a long day at the office. Fabrice's pager sounded. "Merdre." He reached into his pocket and looked at the number listed on the liquid crystal display. "C'est lui."

"Il y a un téléphone au coin de la rue, just là." Nikoli pointed to a telephone booth just down the street.

"Okay. Si elle part, suivez-elle. Et puis téléphone moi quand tu peux." Fabrice hated leaving Nikoli to watch the apartment alone. Worse yet, he hated thinking she might leave. He cursed his boss for paranoia. The man wouldn't allow cell phones in their communications.

"Oui, bien sûr." Fabrice walked down toward the booth, and Nikoli returned his gaze back to the apartment.

He placed his phone card into the slot and waited a moment until the remaining balance appeared on the LCD screen. He then dialed the number he had been asked to memorize. As always, a woman answered.

"C'est Sophie."

"Un moment." It was the only thing he had ever heard her say. Never an "Allo" when she answered. Never a "please wait." Always the simple "one moment."

"Fabrice?"

"Oui, c'est moi."

"Disappear." That was all. "Disappear," and the phone went dead. Yet that single word gave him all the information he needed. They were through with simply following her. Someone had disobeyed orders, and this woman was going to pay the price.

Chapter 13

The sun began to drop below the buildings in the west of Paris. The period of semi quiet during dinnertime was coming to a close. It was, for Paris, a second awakening each night. The morning brought about the business day, but in the city that never slept, evening was a time for play. It was one of the best things about big city life; no matter what time of day or night it was, life was boring only if one wanted it that way or needed it to be that way. Stacy lay on the bed, stretching her legs to their fullest extent. She wondered whether it was worth getting dressed and going for a walk. She could hear the movement of people up and down the road, taking advantage of the Paris nightlife. Yet she had no desire to be around people or pretend to be social. Besides, Arnaud could call at any time with news. On the other hand, the news could be good or bad, and she would only sit wondering about why he wasn't calling. Finally, slowly lifting one leg over the other and then off the bed, she got up and dressed in the only clothes she had with her. She needed to find out what was going on, and perhaps it was only her contacts that could tell her the truth.

* * * * * *

Nikoli and his buddy still sat below the single shining light in the apartment. They would wait all night if necessary. The code word had been given and could not under any circumstances be revoked. They were just about to move to a third bench when Stacy exited.

They moved in behind her without a hitch. Now it was only a matter of timing.

******

For Alain, the night was far from boring. His work accelerated with the setting of the sun. He had contacts to make, deals to complete, and deliveries to ensure had been made to satisfy clients. Yet, on this night, he was sitting alone in his office, wondering if all that he did was worth it. The end result was indeterminate wealth, but in order to obtain that wealth, one had to avoid friendships. Only business associates were allowed in his work. Still, he had promised to protect Stacy if anything happened to Michael. Perhaps it was nearing the time when he himself would retire. Michael had tried to do just that and now was forced to return one more time to the world he had learned to hate. Alain did not want to end up like that. If he retired, it would be away from all this. However, the world was full of dealers, arms, drugs—whatever could be sold, including people.

That was really why he sat alone, contemplating retirement. He had sold someone's right to live unharmed. He had done so without so much as a thought otherwise. He was, on the one hand, promising to protect someone; and on the other, he was ensuring a lack of protection to someone else—whatever suited his needs. This world of his was filthy, and he was ready to leave it. While some part of him despised his own actions, there would always be a last—and the disposal of this group of associates that knew him far too well would be his last. He would rid himself of them and be done with it all.

Chapter 14

Stacy got off the metro at Porte Dauphine. She took the stairs to the walkway that crossed the Boulevard Périphérique. The sun was disappearing below the western horizon, tinting the mass of trees with orange-and-red glitter. A small pond glowed a bright yellow, and the soft gurgle of water fountains filled the air. Not many people were around during the night in the Bois de Boulogne—not unless you were looking for some action, that is. There were more than enough prostitutes and dealers. Stacy kept to the main path, where the globes of light would offer some protection from the lowlifes who inhabited the park after hours. She enjoyed the walk despite the potential downfalls. It really was beautiful despite its nighttime inhabitants.

She wandered aimlessly through the bois, following the paths to the southwest. She passed along the shore of Lac Inférior, where the Châlet des Iles was located. The restaurant was the solitary sign of life. Lights illuminated the grounds surrounding the restaurant as well as the far lakeshore. People laughed and joked inside the comfortable confines of the dining area.

Stacy wondered how many of them knew of the transactions taking place only a short distance away from their eatery. Probably most of them—not that they paid any mind to it. At least not until it touched them. A couple times a year, some rich local would get assaulted—or worse yet, murdered—within shouting distance of the front doors of Châlet des Iles, and then all hell would break loose. The cops would keep a close eye on the activities within the bois for a while until the heat died down.

Soon after the lake ended, the path forked to the west, and Stacy took this route, going deeper into the woods. Her world had turned upside down. Michael was gone, and Lawrence was long dead. If they killed Michael, she didn't know how she could continue to be strong. Fighting against people like Domino was like surrendering all possibility for hope. She knew that the work Lawrence's group was doing helped a great many people, but it had taken one man permanently from her, and a second could be just as gone.

She heard voices coming toward her on the path, and she looked up to see two men walking toward her. They were holding hands and laughing quietly to each other. Stacy slowed and looked around; no one else was within sight. The last building she had passed was the Garde Républican A Cheval. She felt a shiver rise in her back and trickle down her arms. It was that feeling of dread she always got before something bad was going to happen. Most people didn't believe her premonitions, and it had cost Lawrence his life. She wouldn't let others make her disbelieve herself, but they didn't seem to be paying any attention to her. Stacy felt the fear come anyway. She had spent her entire life being wary, and she knew this wasn't a time to stop. They went by her without even a glance in her direction. Stacy let out a huge sigh. She was being torn apart by this anxiety—this fear. Once again, she resolved to go on the attack. She needed to end this now.

A hand dropped to her shoulder, turning her around. She saw only a blur as the man slapped her face. "Slut." His accent wasn't quite French. She couldn't place it. Tears ran from her eyes as she tried to focus on his face. *Do I recognize this man?* Someone grabbed her from behind, and she screamed. The first man slapped her again, this time catching her cheekbone flush. It stung, and tears filled her eyes, further blurring her vision. "Ferme-là!" he shouted.

The man behind her stuffed a cloth into her mouth and wrapped another around her head to keep it in place. She struggled as the two men dragged her into the bushes. She felt a kick to the back of her knee and helplessly fell to the ground. One man grabbed her dress and tore a sleeve away from her arm. He tossed it aside and looked down at her. His eyes burned a dull whiteness in the ever-increasing darkness.

The first man threw her to the ground. He dropped onto her, pressing her into the soft mud with his full weight. She could smell the wine and garlic on his breath. She tried to fling him off, but the soft ground offered no resistance. She thrashed about for a moment, and his face hung just inches from her, breathing hard.

He shifted his weight and reached behind his back. He placed a length of cold steel against her throat. She stopped moving. "Bon," he said. "Tu me comprends."

He reached up his free hand and grabbed her hair, pulling her head further into the mud. "Restez ici," he whispered.

What is he going to do? Stacy could feel her heart racing in her chest. *Is he going to kill me?*

The man ran the knife down her dress, slicing the fabric between her breasts.

Oh, God! He is going to rape me. The words flowed through her mind, but she couldn't accept the reality of it.

She renewed her struggle, twisting her arms to break the grasp of the second man. One hand slipped free, and she felt a surge of joy pass through her. She lashed out with her fist, but she lacked the leverage to do him any harm. The blade of the knife had slipped to the side, but she felt something equally hard pressing against her thigh.

She screamed, but the gag muffled the sound.

He slammed a fist into her face, and a shower of pain exploded across the bridge of her nose. The sudden assault temporarily robbed her of motion.

He pressed his lips against her ear. "Ecoutez-moi. Disez ton ami. C'est ca que se passe quand il ne suit pas nos instructions."

The man sat up.

Dazed, Stacy just sat there despite the sudden removal of his weight. *My friend didn't follow instructions? Was he talking about Michael? What is Michael into?*

She stared up at her assailant. He grinned beneath the mask, and she caught sight of a row of broken teeth. Before she could move, he reared back and slammed a fist into her face. The world sank into darkness.

Chapter 15

Michael lay awake in bed, listening to the rain and thunder. Although it was nearly dawn, the sky was still dark. The window above his bed was half open, and the smell of sticky warmth flowed across him. He couldn't sleep; it would not be a day for much action. He stretched out and let stray sprinkles of cool water ease the warmth. He realized that if his face was catching some of the rain, the sill must be soaked, but for now it didn't matter. He needed time to think. Stacy had disappeared. Was she safe now? He wanted to believe she was, but something inside him told him that wasn't true, after the pain and unexpected fear he had felt yesterday. No matter what, she was still lost to him, though. He would need to find her before anything more could continue. They had threatened her, and he had played out what he thought was their bluff. Had she now paid for that? He hoped they didn't know where she was any more than he did. At least that would allow him the time to formulate some sort of escape. If he could find her before they did, the whole situation could be avoided.

The possibility forced him from the bed. He went across the room to the bathroom. The floor was strewn with clothes, only because she hadn't been there. He wondered at how such a simple thing could make him sad. She was always there for him. Every time he needed her, she found some way to be at his side. "Please be safe," he whispered. Somehow, the words spoken aloud made him sense that there was no truth to his thought.

A woman's voice answered the line. "Allo."

"Cécile, s'il vous plait."

"Oui, Madame." The line clicked once, and a moment of a Bee Gees song came on before it rang again.

"Allo, c'est Cécile."

"Bonjour, Cécile. It's Stacy. I'm looking for Arnaud."

"Oh, hello, Stacy. Arnaud is gone. He'll be back by eleven, though."

"Is it okay if I come by to see him then?"

* * * * * *

Michael missing—that was difficult news to take. Arnaud knew of nowhere to start his search. He would sit and wait to hear something, good or bad. Michael would show up, either alive or dead. If something had gone wrong, a message would be forthcoming. Either they had taken him out or he was in a safe house for a while. The possibility that he was safe was not a good one, though. The news should have already reached him through one of various sources. Michael had made sure of that.

"Arnaud," the intercom sounded.

"Yes, Cécile?"

"It's the shop; they said a man named Susie is waiting for you there. Shall I tell them you're busy?"

"No, no. I'm on my way. I'll be there in five minutes."

"I'll let them know."

So Michael was safe. It turned out that he had been right to tell Stacy to be optimistic, despite the fact that he himself hadn't followed that same advice. *Now, should I call her or wait and have Michael do it?* It could wait. She wouldn't be at the studio yet anyway. She might have taken him up on the suggestion to go for a walk in the Bois de Boulogne. He was through the back door and headed toward his Champs Élysées shop without another thought.

* * * * * *

Arnaud arrived at his shop and went straight to the back. The clerk barely rose from his seat before noticing who it was and returning to read his Le Monde. Arnaud opened the door to his office, and there facing the wall was Michael, just as promised.

"Ah, Michael. You are safe."

"You know I have this same picture hanging up in my apartment?"

"Which?" Arnaud entered further and looked over Michael's shoulder. "Yes, I remember that. It was quite some time ago now. Perhaps even ten years."

"Yeah, at least that, I think. Have you seen Gérard lately?"

"No, it's been almost what—three … no, four years."

"Is he in Paris?"

"Probably. He never strayed far once he retired."

"Do you think he still keeps his contacts?"

"One never truly retires completely from the spy game."

"Yes, I suppose not. Just as one never completely stops being an assassin." Michael picked up a glass ball inside of which was a replica of Cinderella's castle at Disney World. Flakes of white snow danced around the castle as he turned it over.

"You are found then?"

"No. I was with some old associates," Michael lied. He wasn't sure if he could trust Arnaud yet. "One thing led to another, and I couldn't extract myself until now. I was trying to get information on Domino—verify that he is somehow involved in all this."

"And this is why you've been missing?"

"Yes. Stacy hasn't been around for the last day at least. So I figured you would know where she is."

"She was here almost eight hours ago. I gave her the key to my apartment on Rue de Lave. I told her to stay away from your apartment. With you missing, I didn't want her to get mixed up in anything."

"That's good news."

"Yes. We should call her now." Arnaud dialed the number to his apartment. The phone rang five times before the answering machine took the line. "Bonjour, Laissez un message après le ton. Je vous téléphonerai plus tard."

"Allo, Stacy. It is Arnaud. Michael is here. Telephone me when you return."

"She wasn't there?"

"No, I told her to take a walk through the Bois de Boulogne. Perhaps she did that this morning."

"Oh. Well, it's better this way. I can't go to her now anyway. I have a job to do."

"You have a contract?"

"No, it's something else. Just preparation for getting past our current predicament."

"Tell me."

"Can't yet. I haven't worked out all the details. I need to find Gérard. He is the only man who can answer some questions I need answered."

"Have you tried Etienne?"

"Yes. He said Gérard would find me, but I don't have time for that. Etienne doesn't know—and how ironic is this—of our relationship with Gérard."

"Maybe Alain—"

"My thoughts exactly. I am on my way there now." Michael turned to leave the office.

"Michael, what do I tell Stacy?"

"Nothing." He stood facing the door, hand on the green handle. "Tell her I'm safe and that I'll get in touch with her. Make her stay in that apartment. I'll call her there." He left the room before Arnaud could argue that she had a right to know what was going on—especially if she might be in danger.

Arnaud might have argued that had he gotten the chance. *But she is already in danger, isn't she?* he reasoned. It was not long ago that someone had taken shots at her at Le Louvre. No, a threat to one's life was not a thing to take casually. Stacy would be on guard. She knew how to keep herself safe.

* * * * * *

Michael exited the shop and headed directly for the metro at George V. From there he went east to Cité and then north to Beaune-Nouvelle. In under fifteen minutes, he was standing before Marsha's desk, impatiently waiting while Marsha called up to Alain.

"Please, go on up," Marsha finally said sarcastically.

"Thank you." Michael returned her sarcasm with an "I told you so" look. He wondered why she constantly felt the need to call Alain before letting him go up.

Two men raced down the stairs and shoved past Michael, nearly toppling him over the railing. They went through the front door, eyes averted and hands to their faces. Michael followed their movements through the front glass window as he stood with one foot on the first step.

"Michael, come on up. You had us scared for a while. Thought I was going to have to make good on my promise." Alain stood at the top of the stairs.

Michael waited until the two men were out of sight. He could have sworn he had seen them before. Of course, if they were associates of Alain's, it was distinctly possible. Yet he knew very few of Alain's art people. Finally he shook off the thought and headed upstairs. "Do I know them?"

"Who?" Alain hesitated. "Those two that just left? No, I wouldn't think so. They run errands for me."

"In a hurry, were they?"

"What? Oh, yes, they were supposed to be gone an hour ago."

"Odd."

"What's odd?"

"It just seemed like they didn't want to be recognized."

"Michael, I've never known you to be paranoid."

"I'm not. I could have ..." Michael shook his head. "Maybe you're right."

"Stacy was here earlier."

"She was? When?"

"Oh, shortly after one yesterday. She told me you were missing. I'm afraid you gave her quite a scare."

"So she came looking for me?"

"Yes, and she brought by another painting."

"She had a painting with her?"

"Yes, why?"

"That means she had to go back to the apartment after leaving Arnaud's. Can I use your phone?"

"Of course."

Michael pulled the phone over and dialed Arnaud's private extension.

"Allo."

"Arnaud, it's Michael."

"Oui, have you found out anything?"

"No, not yet. Listen, was Stacy carrying her portfolio with her when she was at your place?" *Please say yes*, he thought to himself.

"No, she wasn't. Why?"

"I don't have time to explain. Just find Stacy as soon as you can. They have tailed her. Keep her safe for me, Arnaud."

"Michael, what's really going on? Why is she not safe?"

"I can't talk right now. Just let Alain know as soon as you hear anything."

"Oui, toute de suite."

Michael hung up the phone and tapped his fingers on the receiver.

"Something is wrong."

"Yes. Look; it's a long story. For now I need to find Gérard Delion. Do you know where he is?"

"Gérard? No, it's been years. The only man I know who might be able to help you is Etienne, and he is easy enough to find."

"At Carole's. I've already tried him. He was as mysterious as ever."

"I'll call him if you'd like."

"Yes, okay."

"It's *fini*."

"I have other things to do now."

"Keep in touch."

“I will, although it might be some time before I see you again in person.”

“You’re leaving Paris?”

“It’s a distinct possibility.” Michael started down the stairs.

“When?” Alain called after him.

“I don’t know. Two days?” And with that, Michael was gone.

******

Alain stood at his window, watching Michael head south on Boulevard de Strasbourg. Michael had never just run from trouble before. There was a time when he would have rather died than run from trouble. Perhaps it was possible that he truly wanted out of the game once and for all. That could not be helped. If Michael had wanted to disappear, he should not have come to Paris. There were too many people and too much action. Domino was the least of his problems. He should have told that to Michael months ago, upon his first arriving in Paris. But then, Michael had not expected to see Stacy again. She had changed the whole sequence of events. Lawrence’s death had allowed that to happen—an unfortunate incident that necessitated what would follow. Alain wished it hadn’t been so. Not that he condemned death; he in fact sold it. Without a doubt, much of the hardware he sold was used to injure, maim, and kill innocent people. That was not his worry, as long as it did not touch him. He laughed sarcastically to himself. He was not going to retire because he was losing friends. No, he was going because the effects of his work were wearing him thin. All he cared about was retreating now, before he began the inevitable fall from the top. Gérard had done so. Gérard could have done anything—and been paid well to do it. Yet he chose to leave the fighting to others. His sudden absence had created a rush to fill his void, ending the lives of at least six men and women. Alain knew his own departure would create just such a vacuum that would not be filled until a bloodbath came about that could conceivably last months before it ended—or even years. Six or seven people would seem small compared to the number that would fall trying to fill the void that he would leave behind. Again, that mattered very little; Alain would move on and be no more. If that caused problems for Michael and Stacy, or even their deaths, so be it. Alain knew that in order to exit this world, he needed to remove the connections between him and it.

Chapter 16

It was eleven thirty, and the sky had turned to an ugly gray. The clouds had rolled in from the north; that meant rain—and lots of it. The heavy smell of humidity had been present all morning, but until now no one was sure when it would start raining. A heavy darkness had fallen over the inside of the café where Michael was waiting for Etienne. The man was over an hour late. There was a chance that he had dropped out of sight for the third time in the last month. He hoped that wasn't the case. This time the meeting was not casual. Michael needed information, and Etienne was the only one who could provide it. Everyone went to Etienne for information. Paris was a big city, but he always seemed to know everything that was going on, or at least he could find out in a short time.

The first large drops of rain began to fall outside. The breeze came through the open doorway, bringing the damp, humid air with it. Jean-Claude and Marie moved from their usual place at the bar to a table in the far back in order to avoid the wetness. Personally, Michael enjoyed the feeling of heavy air flowing across his body. Carole worked behind the bar, serving the various regulars across the wooden service with a flair for conversation that only she could deliver. She wore an immaculate white apron across her wide waist, and a tan scarf tied her long black hair into a ponytail. At forty she had looked half her age. Now, only three years later, time had begun to catch up. Still, with her long, thick lashes, brilliant hazel eyes, and slim, smooth hands, it would have been difficult to guess her age to be much over thirty.

Marie, who now sat alone in the back of the café, was Carole's daughter. She had inherited much of her mother's beauty. The rest was a gift from her father. Her long hair and small hands were her mother's, but her eyes, instead of the radiant hazel of her mother's, were the deep black of her father's. Jean-Claude, the ever-cautious suitor, must have returned to work. Marie herself would be leaving soon. Michael knew from experience that she had class at noon. The café sat on the edge of the Quartier Latin, and the closest buildings of the Sorbonne were only two blocks down Avenue St. Germaine.

"Où est Etienne?" Marie placed another glass of water in front of Michael. Her fingers left a long strip of dampness against the clear glass.

"Quoi?" Michael asked unnecessarily. Michael had heard her question the first time, but his thoughts brought about his question anyway.

"Où est Etienne?" she asked again.

"Shais pas." Michael had no idea where Etienne was—or when he would arrive, for that matter.

Marie got up and walked to the bar. "Au revoir, Maman." Her mother smiled and waved. "Au revoir, Michel." She kissed Michael on both cheeks. The soft smell of her perfume drifted past his nose. Obession. It was what he had gotten her for her birthday only a week ago. Jean-Claude had confided in Michael that it was her favorite. Secretly, Michael knew it was really Jean-Claude's favorite and by buying it Michael was pleasing not only her but him as well.

"... classe?" Etienne's voice flowed into the café on the breeze. Michael turned around just as he walked in the door. He was wearing dark gray jeans and a short-sleeved white dress shirt. He ran his fingers through his brown hair once, only making it more unmanaged. It was more of an unconscious habit than an effort to fix his hairdo. He did not need to fix his hair to attract looks from the women around him. He was tall, with dark skin and a face that seemed to melt women's inhibitions.

"Salut, Carole. De l'eau, s'il te plait." Even when ordering a water, his ever-present smile never left his lips.

"Salut, Etienne. Cava?"

"Oui, Cava bien."

"Tu es en retard, n'est pas?" Michael wondered how she knew he was late. He certainly had never told her when he would be coming.

"Non, pas du tout. Il est midi." He always denied being late. Whatever time it was, was the time he was supposed to be there. He looked to Michael, and his smile fell away. It was the first time Michael had ever seen a serious look on Etienne's face. "Let us go in the back."

They walked to the rear and took the same table that Marie and Jean-Claude had occupied. The couple's half-drunk bottles of Evian were still there; condensed water had created a small pool around each. Carole was directly behind them with Etienne's water and took away the other bottles, wiping the table clean with a damp rag. Etienne smiled as she walked away, but he became serious immediately upon turning back to Michael. "You want to know about Gérard Delion. As I mentioned the last time we talked, he would find you. However, I understand you need information quickly. I do not know why, but this is what I hear."

"And it's true. Do you have anything?" Since he already knew what Michael wanted, Michael hoped he would have the information. Perhaps that was why he was late.

"I have much. He is a difficult character. Despite the fact he was born in Tunisia and raised in Morocco, nobody seems to know who he works for."

"That doesn't concern me. I only need to know where to find him."

"That, my friend, is easy. As I said, one only needs to let it be known that one wants to see him and the meeting is made. So why the urgency?"

"I want it on my terms, not his."

"That is impossible. Besides, he now knows that you wish to see him. I think the meeting will take place soon." Etienne glanced over at Carole. She was staring at them as if she had something to say but didn't want to bother them. "I believe someone wants you." Eitenne nodded in her direction.

Michael smiled. "I'll be right back."

Michael headed back to the table and sat down in a rush. "It seems you were right."

"Gérard?"

"Yes, he's meeting me tomorrow." Michael said his goodbyes and left the café.

******

Etienne watched Michael. He began to wonder just who these people were. In the past, they had seemed like simple American gangsters: "kill this man, kill that man." Yet now they seemed to know much more than they should. Worst of all, he learned that Michael and Alain had a history that went beyond guns. And now other American gangsters had followed them to Paris, leaving blood in their wake. He trusted Michael in only one way—the man would never betray his identity to anyone. Of that he was sure, but that didn't mean Michael didn't use the information provided to do bad things. Word on the street was that there was an American assassin in Paris who wished to be retired after one last job.

Etienne guessed that was Michael. Since Lawrence was already dead, perhaps that was the job that Michael was here to complete. Perhaps not. He needed to know more before helping Michael beyond what he had already offered. If Michael was truly here to collect one last body, and that was not Lawrence, then it was important to know both the who and the why. Michael had worked for Domino for too long to just disappear without repercussions. Either Domino was making him kill someone one last time or Michael was killing someone to help him get away from Domino. He would find out, and Gérard would know the answers to both of those questions after tomorrow.

******

Michael arrived at Arnaud's apartment before he decided that even if Stacy were there, he would be risking her. So he walked past the block without stopping. Only one glance in the general direction of the apartment told him that no lights were on. Of course, that could mean almost anything. She could be in there, asleep or hurt. She could be gone. It was possible she had never gotten there. At the end of the block, he entered a café and ordered some tea. The parcel would have been delivered by now. He needed to pick that up before the night was over. From there they would certainly pick up the tail again—that is, if they hadn't already. If they had found him, they most likely knew about Arnaud and Alain now. He hoped he hadn't compromised either of their organizations. His mind also kept returning to those two men who had rushed past him at Alain's studio. They hadn't wanted to be recognized. Michael knew he wasn't being paranoid, as Alain had suggested, but why were they afraid of Michael seeing them? Did they know who he was? And if so, how? Had Alain told them, or had they already known? There were too many questions that needed answers before the next forty-eight hours expired.

He left the café and went straight to 128 Rue de la Pompe, where he could pick up the package from Josephine. He still had doubts as to whether he would carry out the plans. He had vowed to both himself and Stacy that he would never kill again for profit. He wished that he could have promised to never kill again, but he would do so to protect either of them. And wasn't that what he was doing—protecting her? That was not a reasoning that Stacy would accept, and in all honesty, neither would he. This man had done nothing to threaten or harm either of them. He deserved to die no more than she did. No, there had to be a way to create enough of a diversion to harm no one but at the same time make the contract appear to be fulfilled—at least long enough for both him and Stacy to get out of Paris. In an hour, they could be in Lille. The TGV went directly there with no stops. Stacy knew people that could get them new documents necessary to start new lives.

The address brought him to a block in the southwest section of

Paris. The condos were a part of a renovation project in this part of the city. New deep-red bricks, untouched yet by the smog and filth of the big city, stood out against the aging, soot-covered buildings that were only a few blocks away. Soon this entire section would be rebuilt into luxury homes, and the people living in the existing buildings would be moved farther out into the suburbs. Michael knew the same thing was happening in Lille. He rang the bell at 128 and waited. There were no lights on in the house; nor was there any sound of movement. A solitary man walked the sidewalk with a backpack. He moved down the street, looking up at Michael once, and then twice. Michael rang the bell again. He looked at his watch. Surely the package should have arrived there by now. The man had stopped at the bottom of the stairs. Michael reached into his jacket for his gun.

"You looking for a delivery?"

Michael hesitated. "Who is it for?"

"Don't know." The man was American. He shifted his feet nervously. "The woman said to deliver it here when a man showed up."

"And her name?" Michael kept his hand on the gun but didn't draw.

"Josephine."

"It's for me then. Just set it down on the bottom step and continue your way down the road."

The man followed Michael's directions. Michael waited until he was out of sight down one of the side roads before going down to the backpack. He didn't bother looking inside, only stooping down to pick it up and slinging it over a shoulder.

******

Michael returned to his apartment before looking inside the pack. All that he had asked for was present along with a note. He set the note on the table and stared at it for a while. He knew it contained bad news, and he was afraid to confirm his thoughts. First he called Arnaud, but Arnaud had heard nothing from or about Stacy. She had been at the apartment earlier that day but had never returned after leaving sometime around eight. Someone was watching the house, and he continued to try to call her. Michael hung up and returned once again to the note. It would not go away, and he needed to know what was going on. He opened the envelope and pulled out a single sheet of paper. It read as follows:

> Cher Michael:
>
> You do not follow directions very well, do you? It was not wise what you did at Le Jardin du Shakespeare. We had to follow through with our threat, and Stacy was not treated very well. Yet she will not die from her wounds. No, they go much deeper than that. You may have some difficulty finding her, since even we have lost track of her whereabouts. But not to worry; I'm sure you'll find her sometime after the job has been completed.
>
> Love, Josephine

The note fell to the floor. No tears appeared in his eyes, and no noise escaped from his mouth. What had he done? Without even knowing why, he went to the telephone and automatically dialed a number. It was only when Arnaud answered that he woke from his dream state. He reread the note to Arnaud.

"I didn't think. I don't know." He couldn't say anything more.

"Michael, they say she will be okay. I will find her. Trust me. If they hurt her, she is probably in a hospital somewhere, or perhaps she just saw a doctor. She'll either get in touch with us or I'll track her down."

"Yes, okay. I'm going to find this man and kill him." Michael regretted having come to Paris. True, he would never have seen Stacy again, but then this wouldn't have happened to her. He thought back to when she thought he was sending her away. He should have gone away with her then; instead, something in him had insisted that he finish this. Now it had cost her more than him.

"Michael, don't do anything rash. The best thing to do is to continue as you were. If they find her first and you slip again, they won't be so generous. Besides, you have only two days to complete the job."

"But I can't let him get away with this." He wondered whether this was that same instinct again—to finish this. He considered that maybe just finding Stacy and taking her away was the best move.

"We won't. Listen; get some rest. You were going to see Gérard later?"

Michael wondered how Arnaud knew that. Despite their history, he had never known Arnaud had so many connections. "Yes—I hope so, at least."

"He may know who this man is."

"Yes, of course."

"Okay, get some rest and go see Gérard tomorrow."

There was only silence on the line. Arnaud waited a moment. "Michael?"

"Find her, Arnaud. Find her."

"I will."

"A bientôt."

"A bientôt."

Michael dropped the phone onto the cradle and walked down the hall. His mind was numb. His actions were slow and methodical—done only because he had done them thousands of times before. The water rushed into the tub, throwing steam into the cool air. He edged himself into the hot water and relaxed against the back of the tub with only his head above the water. He felt nothing, thought nothing. Sweat beaded up on his face and ran down into the water. The tears would not come, though. He had done this to her. He was the one who deserved the punishment. But first he would find Gérard and then kill the man who had ordered this upon her. Then Josephine—such a cold woman. How could she write such a pleasant note announcing such horrid news?

******

Michael spent the rest of the morning hours searching hospitals and care centers for Stacy. Outside of her regular contacts, these were the only places where she might be. He was convinced she was unconscious, and without documents, no one could identify her. Arnaud's initial information held nothing hinting at a Jane Doe with her description. His meeting with Gérard was not until 2:00 p.m., and there was nothing he could do to help Arnaud. Arnaud's contracts were both more numerous and better informed than his own. By noon he was back home and sitting at the wooden table, staring at a hot cup of tea. With each sip, he counted off the seconds that had passed by since the last. He had already gotten up to leave twice and sat back down. Sitting at Carole's and waiting for Gérard held little incentive for him. The man was notorious for being late, although he usually made up for it with the information he had. The truth was that Michael did not want to answer any of the questions Carole would pose to him. She would mean well, he knew, but he did not have the kind of answers she would be looking for. It would be better, he felt, if he spent as little time in the café as possible—and as much of that as he could with Gérard. If there was one thing Carole knew, it was when business was being discussed. It was not as if she lost her curiosity when it came to those matters; it was only that she knew when it was better that she didn't know what was going on.

She would not be the only one in the café with questions either. He had not been there for almost two weeks, and now twice in two days. People would wonder what he had been up to. In that arena, no one but Carole knew Michael was anything but a dishwasher from another café. Even Carole had no idea what went on beyond the doors to her café; she knew only that something did.

It had finally reached 2:00 p.m., and his tea was cold, so he dumped what was left in the sink and left for Carole's. He would still be there early, but if Gérard had heard what was going on, he would be early for once. Michael hoped he at least knew where to find the bastard. Another day trying to find him would be too late. He needed to see him before he met with the group again. Michael needed some sort of backing, and knowing whom he was dealing with would help him find that.

Chapter 17

Stacy opened one eye. The bright white of a street lamp burned her vision, and she quickly closed it again. Her whole body hurt, and she was cold. She felt a pain that went beyond simple physical torture. Memories continually pounded against her skull—memories of the night, of the laughter, of the crying. Nobody would help her. No matter how hard she tried to forget, the memories returned with greater force. She began to cry again. Why had they done it? She wasn't one of those women. Leaves and branches rustled with movement near where she lay. Were they returning? Hadn't they done enough already? *No, not again.* "I'll be a good girl. I didn't want it to happen; just don't hurt me." The words slipped from her lips, barely audible but nevertheless filled with sorrow. She heard voices coming nearer, getting louder; they hadn't said a word the first time. Her own pleas began to increase in volume. "No! Stay away. I'm not a whore!" She rolled away from the voices. Damp, cold leaves clung to her naked body.

Two men with flashlights broke through the shadows of the trees, holding the remains of her torn dress. Stacy screamed louder than she would have thought physically possible. She wanted to run as well, but she couldn't even get to her feet. She barely had enough energy to roll, which she did. When the two men finally reached her, she was covered in wet grass and leaves, curled up in a ball beside the trunk of a tree.

"Mon Dieu." One of the men quickly stripped off his jacket and placed it around Stacy's shivering body, but she hardly noticed. Her cries had softened, almost gone. "Un ambulance, maintenaut." The second man took a walkie-talkie from his belt and called for help. Stacy still lay huddled beneath the jacket, crying and instinctively swinging out at an imagined attacker. "Stay away." The words were no longer loud or threatening, but the two men took a cautious step back. They relaxed as she began to cry.

"Elle est Americaine."

"Oui, c'est vrai. Parlez-anglais."

"Mademoiselle, we are police. We called for help." His thick French accent bent the words into incomprehensible garble as far as Stacy could tell.

She made out the final word though. "Aidez-moi," she whispered silently.

The policeman smiled to his partner when he saw Stacy noticeably relax. "Oui, je vous aide."

* * * * * *

The memory gave her more pain than the actual physical injuries she had incurred. The dark, shadowy men were terrorizing her dreams and turning them into unforgettable nightmares. Even the simplest of her imaginations were twisted and torn until they barely resembled what they had been. Instead those men would arrive and rape everyone in sight. They would not touch her. They would make her watch the ensuing scenes. She could not blink, could not turn away, and could not call for help. Even her crying sobs were soundless and unable to provoke a response.

The dreams forced themselves into reality as she spun and kicked out at nothing while she slept. It would be the same every night from now on. She would wake covered in sweat and shivering from the cool, dry air, having thrown her sheets to the floor. It was barely any different now as she lay awake, eyes trained on the whiteness of the ceiling. Rain beat against the window in a constant chorus. She listened to it, concentrating only on its presence, and soon her shaking hands calmed to a manageable degree. Her legs swung from the bed, and she planted her feet firmly on the cool tiled floor. She gathered up the sheets and blankets strewn across the room.

A yellow band of light ran across the gray tile from the doorway. Stacy didn't look up. She knew it was Carole—the one nurse who understood her pain, who knew what she was dreaming, who still felt the pain from her own attack. Carole didn't say a word. She only helped in picking up the bedspread and laying it out on the bed. Stacy climbed beneath the sheets, and Carole settled into a chair beside the door. Her eyes never wavered from Stacy's still form. Only then did Stacy finally fall into a deep sleep untroubled by nightmares.

******

Despite an exhaustive search by telephone that lasted most of the night, Arnaud came up with no news of Stacy's whereabouts or possibilities of what might have happened to her. Thus, after an hour's worth of sleep, he rose and showered. He would go out and search Paris sector by sector until he came up with something. He began with the most logical place, and that was within the sixteenth arrondissement. She had made it to the apartment; thus it was sometime after leaving there that she had disappeared. He took the metro instead of walking the relatively short distance; anything that could save him even a few minutes' time would be a help on what promised to be a long day.

The morning was clear and quiet. As it was still too early for the business crowd, only a few scattered tourists lined the streets. The various patisseries and boulangeries that could be found in any Paris neighborhood were just opening their doors. The smell of freshly baked breads filled the air outside of each. Employees from restaurants and hotels were making their ways to the shops, buying bread for the morning meals. Arnaud stepped into a patisserie on Rue Raynouard, not far from the metro at Palais de Chaillot.

"Bonjour, monsieur." A lady behind the counter, dressed in a white apron, smiled brightly.

"Bonjour, un pain au chocolat et deux croissants, s'il vous plaît."

She reached below the shelf and grabbed a single rectangular pastry and two croissants; she then dropped them into a bag and twisted the corners shut. "Huit euros."

Arnaud dropped the coins into her hand and smiled. "Merci."

The woman dropped the change into the till. "S'il vous plait." As he left the Patisserie, she then added, "Merci, bon journée."

He left the shop and continued along the same road until he reached Rue des Vignes. The pastries melted in his mouth. The chocolate provided the needed stimulant to wake him up completely. He took a left and walked up the staircase to the apartment building on the corner. After pressing the bell next to a blank card, he took out his address book and made a note in it, still eating the last of his second croissant.

"Allo?" A man's voice sounded over the intercom.

"Vincent, c'est Arnaud."

"Ah, bien." A buzzer sounded, and Arnaud entered the building. He continued straight up the stairs to the second floor. He knocked on the door at number seventeen. He was greeted by a large man with short-cropped hair and thin wire-rimmed glasses. "Bonjour, çava?"

"Non, j'ai un problem."

"Ah, oui, comme toujours." Vincent ushered him into the apartment and bade him sit down. There was never a time when Arnaud had visited without a problem.

"I have a friend that's missing. She's American but speaks French well enough to pass for a Parisian. Actually, she looks French as well. She disappeared sometime last night, most likely after five p.m. I was hoping you might be able to find out if an American had been admitted to any of the hospitals last night."

Vincent stood up and walked toward the kitchen. "Would you like some coffee? Tea?" He disappeared into the other room.

"Non, merci. Vincent?"

"Oui? Oh yes, your friend. That is difficult to say. You say she could pass for French?"

"Yes, if she wanted to, but there really wouldn't have been a reason to."

"Non, there were no Americans admitted last night." Vincent said suddenly, still from the kitchen.

Arnaud walked over to the kitchen door. "Are you sure?"

Vincent dropped a tea bag into a cup of boiling water he had taken from the microwave. "As I said, it is difficult to know for sure, but yes, I am as sure as I can be."

"But how?"

"About an hour ago, the police came by asking the same exact questions as you. I did a little checking. They were, however, a little more precise than you."

"How do you mean?"

"They asked me to keep my area of search to the seventh and eighth arrondissements."

"Thanks. I have to go."

"So soon. You just arrived. Let me make some calls and see if I can find out anything new." He moved to the phone.

"I would appreciate that. Call my office if you find out anything." Arnaud walked from the apartment, letting the door swing shut behind him.

From Vincent's place, Arnaud went back to the Palais de Chaillot and descended into the metro. He went south to Exelmans. The metro was beginning to get crowded, although he was sure the other direction, toward Charles de Gaulle, was even worse. Once back on ground level, Arnaud crossed the street and went to the apartment directly opposite where he had exited the metro. He again pressed the bell to an apartment that had a blank card.

A woman's voice answered. "Allo."

Arnaud hesitated for a moment. Although he knew Thierry had a girlfriend, she had never answered the bell before. "Bonjour, c'est Arnaud."

"I'm sorry, Arnaud. Thierry is not here." The intercom went dead. Arnaud stepped away from the door and looked up to the third floor. The shade was being drawn over the living room window. He began to wonder what was going on. First Vincent had acted a bit strange, and then this. Thierry was always in his apartment until 10:00 a.m. It was a given, and never once had he known Thierry to be gone. Perhaps it was a coincidence, but maybe not. He returned to the metro and headed across town to Montparnasse. This time he did not go to an apartment but instead to a *tabac* across from the black skyscraper. The man behind the counter was busy serving the morning crowd buying their daily *Le Monde*, *L'Express*, or *Le Figaro*. Arnaud eased himself past the line and caught the eye of the man. "Salim?" The man nodded toward the back of the store.

Arnaud knocked on the back door and entered. A man sat behind a desk with his feet propped against it. A copy of the *Herald-Tribune* was spread out, covering most of his body. "The Vikings blew it again. How the hell do you lose to the San Francisco 49ers?" He set the paper down. "Arnaud. Çava? Did you see this?" he pointed to the paper. "The coach says, 'Nobody runs against us.' Who cares; they're still a piece of crap."

"I have a problem."

"So why else would you be here? Usually I'm the one looking for you."

"A friend of mine, an American, disappeared last night. She's probably hurt. Perhaps admitted to a hospital as a Jane Doe. That's the only way I can think she wouldn't have contacted me."

"Where was she last?"

"In my place at the Champ de Mars."

"Business associate?"

"Yes, you could say that."

"So she knows the ropes."

"*Oui*, but she could have been hurt enough for that not to matter."

"ID?"

"Fake."

"But American?"

"Positively."

"Let me make one call." Salim left the room through another door behind him. Arnaud spun the paper around to read about the previous year's soccer champs not faring so well during the present season. Salim returned ten minutes later and dropped a fax over the article. There was a list of three addresses with names next to them. "I'm sure you know this is far from complete, but this is a list of

Jane Does admitted to emergency rooms in the seventh and eighth arrondissements. The names are doctors on staff who can help you. Just mention my name."

"This will work for now. Thanks." Arnaud opened the door to go out. "By the way, I agree; the 49ers are crap." He said the word "crap" with a curiously strong French accent that was in evidence only when he spoke words he didn't know. Salim laughed and said, "Like you know anything about real football."

Arnaud left the tabac and stopped on the street just below Montparnasse. He looked down at the list Salim had given him. He was halfway across town from the nearest hospital on the list. His next contact was only three blocks away. He would go there first. Besides, in a city the size of Paris, the chances of one of the Jane Doe survivors being Stacy was remote. Thus he walked north along Boulevard Raspail to the Café de la Paix. Inside the café, Arnaud recognized the mixture of French, English, and German that always could be heard coming from the various groups of people at the tables. Arnaud went straight to the bar.

"Bonjour, Arnaud, çava?"

"Oui." He said absently, glancing around the bar. "Faubert n'est pas ici?"

"Non, en vacannces."

On vacation? One surprise after another. Something was definitely wrong. "Il retourne quand?"

"Demain."

And returning the day after he needed to see him. This could not be a coincidence. Yet Salim had helped him out. There had to be a connection between the other three.

They were afraid of giving him information. Perhaps Michael would know more after he saw Gérard. Arnaud left the café and headed directly for the metro. If someone had indeed infiltrated his contacts, he might have someone following him now. In that case, he needed to shake anyone off his trail before trying the hospitals. He hated to waste the time it would take, but he couldn't risk it otherwise. He also needed to get a hold of Michael and let him know these people were better equipped than they had thought.

There were only two possibilities: this group had worked a long time in setting up this network or someone within was working with them. The second was highly unlikely. There were very few people, even inside the network, who could have made the connections with his contacts: Michael, Stacy, Lawrence, any of the others in Lawrence's group, Alain, and, ironically enough, Gérard. He could think of no one else. Thus it was reasonable to assume that one of Lawrence's group was involved.

Chapter 18

Sunlight streamed in through the clear glass windows and warmed Stacy's body. Two days ago, she would have said it was impossible, but she opened her eyes refreshed and ready to face the day. It was all thanks to Carole, who had made her understand the troubles. Stacy turned to look toward the chair Carole had settled into the night before. Sometime during the night, Carole had left, and the chair now sat empty. Stacy reached across the bed for the button that would call for the nurse. Her hand stopped short as the door opened. She heard two voices outside—one the deep monotone of a man. Her body involuntarily curled up into a ball, bringing with it the warmth of the blankets. She lay there alone, staring at the door, waiting for it to fully open and reveal who was there.

The voices stopped, and finally the door moved again. A head peeked in from the hall. "Stacy?" The voice was soft, soothing. Stacy recognized it before she saw his face.

"Arnaud." It was the first word she had spoken since waking in the hospital four days ago. She was out of bed and running across the room to him before he had completely entered. His tentative smile turned to a slight laugh. "How did you ever find me?"

"There was no help from you; that's for sure." He hugged her tightly, gently massaging her back. "They say you haven't said a word in days."

Her smile darkened, and tears formed in her eyes. "Yeah, I was ..." *How to tell him?* She wanted to get it all out, and he was the only person she trusted, but still the words would not come. Only those horrible images still floating in the recesses of her mind were left. She had felt so alive and had hoped those dreams would finally be ending. But now she knew it would be a long time before those images left her conscious thought—if they ever did.

"Yes, I know. Don't worry. I'm here now."

Those simple words calmed her more than he would ever know. She held him closer. The soft smell of Drakkar drifted up from his body. She relaxed in his arms and let him lead her across the room to the bed. He sat her on the bed and took a seat on the chair beside the window.

"Are you ready to go home?"

"I am. I don't know if they …" She motioned in the direction of the door.

"They said you can go at any time, as long as you feel ready."

Chapter 19

Stacy sat alone at a grated metal table outside Le Fouloir. It was her favorite café, even if the white paint from the tables was peeling away, revealing rusted metal beneath. The awning was faded to the point that one could barely make out the final four letters in the café's name. The sidewalk was wide and filled with tables exactly like the one at which she sat. People rarely stopped at the bar inside, and fewer still ordered a meal from its small menu. However, its location was perfect for people watching. Hundreds of pedestrians made their way past the cracked glass of the front window. It was on a direct line from Sacre Coeur to Galleries Lafayette. If Louis were willing to spend a little money in order to fix up the place, he would most likely be overwhelmed with tourists in no time. That was exactly what he was trying to avoid. He enjoyed being called Monsieur Fou by the few regular customers and making do with the small crowds that ended up at his place.

Stacy watched another group of young students pass in front of her table. They were discussing the possibility of staying in Paris another couple of days. It was so typical. Nobody seemed to plan enough time to see everything in Paris. It was so easy to chart out plans that included only the major sights, but once one arrived in the city, things changed. There was so much more to see. Who would have known that seeing Sacre Coeur at sunset was so different than at noon; and it was another sight altogether when neither the sun nor moon was in the sky.

"Bonjour, Stacy. Cava?" The voice came from the open doorway at Stacy's back. Her body froze. It was a voice she would never forget—the smooth, casual words of a confident man. But it couldn't be. She turned around, but nobody was there. She had imagined it. Yes, that was it. After all, she had been thinking about Michael a lot lately.

Arnaud come out from the interior of the café. "Stacy, let's go. We should really get back to the apartment." Without a word, Stacy got up and followed him.

* * * * * *

Michael sat alone in Arnaud's apartment, waiting for Arnaud and Stacy to arrive. He wished he had been there when Arnaud had called. As it was, all he had received on his answering machine was a short message from Arnaud stating that he had found Stacy and they were on their way. However, they would be stopping at a small café for Stacy to relax. There were no details of how or where he had found her or of what they had done to her. He did not sound overjoyed on the recorder, which could have been partly because he had slept no more than an hour over the last two days. Michael had slept little more. After his contact with the group contracting his services, he had returned to the prospective site for the hit and continued his reconnaissance. The list Josephine had provided him with was accurate almost to the minute. There were two men patrolling the area, using each road that bordered the residence as a guide. A chain-link fence crossed the area facing the park, separating the entrance to Rue Université from the area surrounding the Eiffel Tower. On the far side of the intersection was another set of residences. As they had promised, a For Rent sign hung in the window of one of the apartments. It would be his before the next day was over. The bomb could easily be triggered from there. The remote detonator with which Josephine had supplied him needed a somewhat clear path to the target to be accurately triggered. No problem from the fourth-story *chambre* that was for rent.

A car door slammed shut at the rear of the apartment. Michael went to the bathroom and looked down to the parking lot. Arnaud and Stacy were just exiting the car. She had hold of his arm but seemed stable. She glanced up, and he quickly pulled away from the window. He cautiously looked again and saw her face clearly in the entrance light below. She looked shaken up, as if someone had died. Yet she seemed physically unharmed. He had to go. The specifics of her "accident" would have to be told at another time. He had to leave, and with him his tail, before they saw him with her. He had already misjudged the extremes they would go to. He would not give them reason to again.

Michael exited the apartment through the front door just as the two were coming in through the kitchen. He was out the door and a block away before he realized he had not left a message. That too would have to wait. Arnaud would notice that the message had been picked up off the machine, and he would assume it was Michael who had gotten it. To Michael, that Stacy was safe in Arnaud's hands was what was important. Their subsequent departure and plans after that could be made tomorrow. He would run through the assassination plans with the group after he had talked to Arnaud. It was now unimportant whether he would go through with the attempt at all. He had verified the substance Josephine had supplied him with. It was not plastique but only glycerin sulfate, which would create a heavy white fog after a somewhat startling burst of noise.

Chapter 20

Arnaud led Stacy into the living room and went to his desk. "Michael," he called out once. "Odd."

"What?"

"Well, the alarm wasn't activated, and Michael more than anyone knows its importance in this flat. And the message I left has been erased. I can only assume it was Michael who got it, but I don't understand why he didn't set the alarm."

"He could be upstairs. He's a pretty sound sleeper. I'll go up and check."

"No, you stay here. I'll check."

"Don't treat me like a baby, Arnaud." She walked up the stairs, feeling for her purse. The heavy weight of her gun was no longer there. She continued anyway. There was no reason to believe anyone would be up there hiding from them.

Down below, Arnaud retrieved his own weapon from his pocket. The Beretta 92F reflected the living room light dully. He slid the magazine from its grip and verified that it contained all fifteen rounds of its 9 mm ammo. Sliding it back in place, he started up the stairs after Stacy. There were no noises, and the lights had been turned off on the upper level. One by one, Stacy checked each room with Arnaud not far behind. The den was the third room on the left. Stacy reached around the corner and pushed the light switch. A single lamp at the desk flickered on. The bedroom was unoccupied as well; the open closet showed no sign of movement or previous disturbance. The bathroom door was already slightly ajar. Stacy pressed against it slowly with her shoulder. *No one.*

Stacy shrugged at Arnaud. "He's not here."

"So I see. There's one last place to check."

"Where?"

"The attic." Arnaud went back to the bedroom and checked the control panel, which controlled a separate alarm system for the uppermost floor. The alarm was active. So Michael had either left in a hurry or someone else had gotten the message and erased it. Either way, he didn't like the looks of it.

Stacy had already returned to the living room and was starting a fire as Arnaud came down the steps. "Nothing?"

"Pas du tout."

"What do you think happened?"

"I don't know. If it was Michael who got the message, he won't wait long to check on you. He might still be worried that …" He stopped, remembering that Stacy had no knowledge of the blackmail and that he was not allowed to tell her. He still believed she deserved to know, but it was for Michael to decide.

"Worried that what?"

"That he's endangering you." It was, after all, the truth. He hated lying to her, and this was one way around that.

"That's nonsense. I hope you told him that. I can't believe that. They shot at me—not him. If there's anyone bringing danger into our world, it's me who's endangering him."

"Yes, that's true, if you look at it that way."

"You did tell him it's nonsense?"

"Don't worry; we'll discuss it all right."

Arnaud smiled. Stacy was never one to get entangled with. Her emotions tended to burst forth uncontrollably and shatter anyone opposing her. Arnaud wondered how she would react when, and if, Michael ever told her the truth. He certainly didn't want to be there. He worried, though, not for Michael, but for himself. He feared her wrath for not speaking up now. Although without knowing exactly what Michael was into, he couldn't really say much of anything. All he knew was that Michael's actions were what had caused Stacy's attack.

******

The meeting was to take place at 10:00 p.m. Michael waited outside the nightclub for his employers to arrive. He had refused their request to meet with just Josephine. If this were to progress any further, he needed answers from someone who could give them to him. The man who had tracked him down, presumably killed Gérard, and threatened Stacy's safety was not the minor player Gérard had said he was. That was evident enough now. Someone had planted the information for Gérard to find. This meant Lawrence's group had been infiltrated deeper than anyone suspected. Arnaud's contacts were shut off from him. Only one man out of Lawrence's group was still unfound, and he was presumed dead as well. Until the results of dental checks, he still had to be a candidate as the leak.

Hardly anyone milled around the nightclub's entrance. It was too early to be crowded. A single woman with a short leather skirt and a tight black blouse clicked her heels against the sidewalk. She routinely looked down the street in both directions and then to the watch again. A man who was leaning against the brick of a shop next to the club watched her. He chewed on a piece of wood that was once an ice-cream stick. Other than that, only the tall, muscular bouncer occupied the street. Michael looked down at his watch. It was five to ten. Perhaps they had arrived before the club opened its doors at nine-thirty.

Michael stepped from the alley and walked directly for the club's blue doors. He ignored the woman as she glanced at him and offered something in unintelligible French. The bouncer took no more notice of him than he had of the woman. Michael pulled the door open, and a mixture of loud music, muted conversation, and smoke poured onto the street. He blinked twice, trying to adjust his eyes to the bright lights of the dance floor. Surrounding the floor were tables and chairs, most of which were still empty. Only one couple danced under the bright lights, swaying to REM's "Personal Jesus."

Away from the floor, in the semidarkness of the furthest walls, were booths. While many of the tables remained empty, the booths were filled with the regulars who spent each and every night there. Many would not leave until sunrise—and then only because of the jobs that paid for these nights.

Josephine would most likely be in a booth with her boss—if they had already arrived. Michael wandered farther into the club, turning first to his right, where a cursory glance at each booth told him they weren't there. Then, just as he was about to do the same on the other side of the club, someone whispered in his ear.

"Would you like to dance?"

"I'm looking …" He turned to find Josephine smiling at him. "Where are they?"

Her smile turned into a sigh. "I'm to tell you that he's been detained. It won't be longer than a half hour. Do you want to dance while we wait?" She took his hand lightly and motioned toward the dance floor, once again smiling.

"I didn't appreciate the note." He shrugged her hand away, placing his into his pocket.

"What note?"

"Don't pull that on me. You know damn well what note."

"No, I don't. I sent no note to you."

"With the equipment. There was a note signed by you."

"I don't handle the deliveries. It was not from me."

Michael stared at her. Not that it really mattered, but she was telling him the truth. "It doesn't matter. You do know what they did to Stacy."

"Not exactly. I was told you eluded the tail and the necessary steps were taken. You were warned." She added the last with emphasis.

"Fuck you. I couldn't have them making my contacts, could I?"

"You could have requested a time period to contact them."

"And would it have been granted?" She stood, eyes downcast, and said nothing. "I thought not."

"They wouldn't have done anything too drastic," she said.

"Look; don't play stupid with me. You know what they're—what you're—capable of. You know what I did for a living. Don't try to pretend you're some innocent pawn in all this. You would not have been there from the start if that were true."

"So I know what's going on. I also know they wouldn't have done anything drastic. They need her. Without her, you're as good as gone."

"I have a feeling they'd find me."

"I don't think so." Josephine glanced around the club. More people were now dancing, and the tables were beginning to fill up. "Let's go and sit down. We have a booth reserved over in the back." Michael noticed how she had, without even noticing it, changed from the "they" she had been using to a "we" when the subject was no longer of any immediate harm. Yet he couldn't rate her too hard. It seemed that she had a conscience, no matter how subverted it was. Michael had done his killing directly and without remorse. Despite that, in his view, his victims always deserved it. Did it really matter that those ordering the hit were just as deserving of a death sentence?

They walked across the dance floor and slid into a booth. Black leather covered the benches while the tabletop was a glossy white. Michael stared out at the dance floor. Multicolored lights streamed down on the dancers, flashing randomly between blue, red, and green. A single ball hung from the ceiling, reflecting the light in all directions, making the whole atmosphere oddly reminiscent of a '70s' discotheque. The music was more to his liking than that era's disco. Modern rock offset by a number of ballads from hard rock wannabes kept the dancers moving.

"Do you want to dance?" Josephine asked for a third time.

"I don't dance." Michael kept his gaze on the dancers.

"What do you mean? Everyone dances."

"Not me."

Another silence fell upon them until Josephine once again spoke up. "Is she all right?"

"Who?"

"Stacy."

"I guess. I haven't seen her."

"You don't know where she is then?"

Michael stopped himself from answering. She was definitely not as innocent as she pretended to be. It was important to keep Stacy's whereabouts a secret from everyone. "Why me?"

"Why you what?" Josephine shook her head slightly.

"You know what I'm asking. You're not stupid. Why did they choose me?"

"Yes, I do not know as much as you think I do." She lit a brown cigarette, offering him one from the pack.

Michael waved his hand and took a deep breath. "You still haven't answered my question."

Josephine took a drag and let out a puff of smoke. "You were available, and you came with excellent references."

"From who?"

"Even if I knew that, you know I couldn't tell you."

"Is it such a secret?"

"It is a secret from me. I'm here in much the same way you are. As I said, I am not as involved as you think. This is a job to me. Once finished, I leave again."

"Again?" Michael prodded.

"Yes, again." The booth became quiet again. Michael pondered that answer and left Josephine to her own thoughts. There was more to this woman than she let on, but at this point, he tended to believe her when she claimed this was simply a job to her.

******

By ten thirty, Michael began to get anxious. If things were to go as planned by the next day, he needed to make preliminary preparations that night. Josephine had sensed his worry and left to make a phone call. Michael called a waitress over and ordered a Coke. He didn't like to drink while conducting any sort of business—especially when he needed to work later in the evening. Thus, he settled for a soft drink, even though it might be hours before he got the chance to ready the scene for the next night. Josephine returned only a moment after his drink.

"He'll be here in five minutes."

"So what you're saying is that it shouldn't be longer than another half hour."

"Five minutes."

Michael looked at his watch. It was a quarter before eleven. If they weren't too evasive, he should be gone before midnight. By twelve-thirty, he could be back at the apartment; and fifteen minutes later, at the site. If he wanted to use the metro to return, that left him with less than half an hour to do his work. Tomorrow he would also need to see Alain about a gun. As far as plans went, this was not his best, and it was far too risky. Still, he would make it work.

Josephine rose from the table, and Michael looked up. Two men came from the bar toward their table. Michael recognized both from the earlier meeting. He didn't get up; nor did he watch them approach. Josephine greeted them, and they sat opposite Michael. Josephine sat down next to Michael. He didn't move from the center of his bench, leaving her little room to get comfortable.

"Bon soir. I take it everything is up to your standards."

"The plastique seems a bit light." Michael sighed deeply. He hated playing games.

The man furrowed his brow and lifted his hands together. "Meaning?"

"Meaning smoke bombs don't usually kill people." Michael leaned forward with his arms on the table.

"Yes, well, death is not exactly our aim." The man smiled tightly.

"You hired me, or should I say blackmailed me, to kill a man, not put up a smoke screen."

"What is the difference to you? Besides, I thought you don't kill for a living any more. This opportunity relieves you of that duty." The man shifted in his chair and looked over to Josephine.

"There is a big difference. I'm not going to put my life on the line just to prove to you who I am." Michael's voice rose beyond the conversational tone they had been using thus far.

The man shook his head. "It seems that you were not given totally accurate information."

"How is that?" Michael asked.

"We know who you are. That is not in doubt. This is no test. We will use the attempted assassination to our advantage. You see, we want this man alive, not dead."

"You're kidnapping him?" Michael was glad to get this information. It could be useful.

"In a way, yes."

"In a way?" Michael prodded.

"That, I'm afraid, is not up for discussion. You do not need to know anything further about our specifics."

"I'm afraid I do. You need me now. If I don't play, you've lost your chance to take him." Michael knew this probably wouldn't be true, but he wanted to know just how much depended upon him now.

"First, we would only lose a chance—not 'the' chance. There will be others." The man shrugged. "Second, there is still Stacy to consider. I'm sure you know by now that our threats are not mere words."

"Someone will pay for that." Michael's eyes darkened.

"Perhaps it should be the man who brought it on? Oh, but that's you."

"Josephine here has let on to the fact that you still don't know where she is. It will be somewhat difficult to do anything in that case, won't it?"

The man shot a look at Josephine, who did not react. "Yes, if that is true." He kept he eyes on Josephine. "We know where she is, just as you do. She is with Arnaud, n'est pas? He has an apartment near the Chaillot. I believe you were there last night. I might have assumed you met with her, but I know you left only moments before they arrived. Very intelligent of you. We wouldn't want to see anything further happen to her." Sticky had said the same thing about Michael not that long ago, and Sticky was now dead. Michael vowed that this man would end up the same way.

Michael looked up as he realized Josephine had stopped talking. "Am I boring you?" she asked.

"Quoi?"

"Are you paying attention, Michael?"

"Yes, of course."

"So what are your plans for tomorrow?"

Michael wanted to say that he was leaving with Stacy on the last train to Lille, but he couldn't. It didn't matter what their plans were; his would not have to change. Michael detailed the plan.

"Good. You will trigger the charge from the room. Yes?"

"I would have preferred a longer distance, but timing is imperative. So, yes, I will trigger from there. Though I will be gone before the smoke clears."

"Of course. Now, the driver will be one of our men. If, by some chance, this is a no-go, he will sneeze once upon exiting the residence and again when he reaches the car. I do not see this as a possibility, but we must not take risks."

"Okay. What happens with the charge in that case?"

"Leave the remote in the room. We will use it at a later time if possible."

"And my payment?"

"As Josephine has already told you, it is in an account. The papers will be mailed to the American Express Office in Paris."

"And if the job is nixed?"

"It will then be mailed once the charge is confirmed to be in place, and its use is still available to us."

"It could be days before you're able to set this up again. Chances are it'll be another car or they'll find it."

"Our driver will ensure that both are taken care of. If what you say does come to pass, your payment will be cut in half."

"That's not acceptable."

"Michael, I must remind you. This payment is not a necessity on our part. It is offered because I am a businessman who likes to owe no one."

"That's understood, but I risk my neck whether you can hold up your end or not. I cannot control your failures."

"We do not have failures, Michael. But I do concede your point. How does three-quarters payment sound?"

"Accepted." Michael pushed against Josephine, who nearly fell on the floor, and then slid across to get up. "Good then. I will leave you now. There is work to be done before the night is over."

"I would say à bientôt, but I know you would prefer it to be adieu."

"Adieu." *Although I doubt either of us will be seeing god in the afterlife*, he thought to himself. Michael walked across the nightclub, leaving the man with his hand still outstretched. It would be au revoir to Michael. They would meet again, and Michael's gun would not stay in its holster.

******

When Michael arrived at his apartment, he found a message on his answering machine. It was a simple message from Arnaud. He told Michael nothing more than he already knew—that Stacy was safe and at the apartment with him. The return call to Arnaud would have to wait until later. Michael could not risk that his phone had been tapped. He grabbed the bag of tools that he had already packed earlier in the day and jogged the two blocks from his apartment to the metro and dropped down into the metro at Exelmans to Pompe, where he transferred, finally ending up at Ecole Militaire. From there the residence was only five blocks.

Michael passed the residence along the gravel path once before retracing his steps along the fence. Once both patrolmen were out of sight, he went to work. The first cut site was only four feet from the corner of the building. He looked in both directions in the park before crouching next to the fence. By this time the guards were once again coming back into view. Michael sat motionless, smelling the heavy aroma of the deep grass on the other side of the fence. The officers' heels clicked against the pavement. They reached each other at the edge of the sidewalk that had led into the park before the fence had been placed there. They spent only a moment to say something to each other and returned to their orderly march. With both their backs turned, Michael could have risked cutting immediately, yet he decided to wait until they had turned the far corner.

He then cut each link just above the notch so he could keep the fence intact yet easily push through it once he was back again the next night. He did so just above the ground, leaving the last row of links still embedded in the hard gravel. He kept the cut area under three feet, which was more than enough for him to crawl through. The actual process of getting through the fence would take less time than the two minutes he spent cutting. The guards were almost within sight as he wormed his way toward the second site. Michael once again lay still, waiting until they had passed, and then went through the same procedure at the edge of the sidewalk.

It was past one when he finally finished the job and decided to spend the night in his rented room instead of making his way back to the apartment. It took him three hours to fall asleep. The adrenaline pumped through him, as it always did the night before a kill. Of course, no one but him knew there would be a murder later that evening.

Chapter 21

Dawn crept above the even horizon; only the dullest of shades appeared between building and darkness. Michael sat alone atop the building, waiting. A cool breeze kept the air from attaining any degree of early morning heat that was always wished for during the early days of September. Only the distant sound of cars broke the otherwise silent morning. He followed the whitewashed glow of the sun as it drifted across the city until his feet were bathed in what little warmth it offered. He closed his eyes and let the sun wash across the length of his body. It was so easy for him to ease the worries away. Gone were all thoughts of pain and confusion. Within seconds, he felt the sensation that always preceded the deepening of his consciousness into a level of meditation few were able to experience. It was here that he could carefully examine the possibilities that were unavailable to him in the outside world. While it was true this meditation helped ease his mind, he often wished it could also carry over into a stronger sense of calm once he left his meditation mode. A short burst of memory brought him back to the previous afternoon. It had been raining with little chance of letting up.

******

Dark trails of muddy water ran down the streets, more than overflowing the cracks and crevices of the cobblestone. Michael splashed through the water and crossed to the open gateway that led into the courtyard of the Pantheon. He took the last few feet at a jog and started down the stairs, finally entering the mausoleum itself.

The cool interior would have been a relief had he not been soaked. As it was, the dry air made him shiver as he entered the main hall. Normally he went straight for the steps that led to the walkway around the rotunda. Yet with the rain, he knew that Gérard would be down below, somewhere within the vicinity of Victor Hugo's tomb. And sure enough, as Michael entered the long, yellowed halls of the crypts, Gérard stood with a camera affixed in between the bars of Hugo's crypt. He jumped slightly as Michael touched him on the back. A flash brightened the cell for a moment, and the whir of the camera's auto-advance motor sounded. Gérard, always the traditionalist, would never go for digital cameras. Michael was sure that the picture would not be of the tomb, as the camera had slipped up and away from the bars at the same instant the flash fired.

"Bonjour. Cava? I thought you dead."

"No, not dead yet. But I have thought myself nearly there many times in my life. And you?"

"Fine, considering, I suppose. Come; let's go above, where we can be away from the dead."

"There are dead there as well. Or do you mean to go out in the rain? Aren't you already wet enough?" Gérard lifted a damp corner of Michael's jacket.

"No, not outside. Just away from them." Michael gestured toward the numerous crypts that lined the hall. All the dead reminded him of what his earlier life was. He had caused many to end up in places just like this. They all had families—people who depended upon them. True, they were not good people, but still, he never really asked what they did to deserve the end he gave them. Michael and Gérard went through the arched doorway and into a circular passage filled with details of the Pantheon's early years and its construction. Michael pointed at it. "So what do you have for me?"

"Here? You want me to tell you here?"

"I don't have much time."

"I would have *no* time if anyone were to overhear me telling you this."

Michael looked around the passageway. No one was within sight.

Two women dressed in jeans and carrying large packs entered just then but quickly crossed to the hall of crypts, disappearing through the archway without so much as a second glance at the two men. His eyes darted back to Gérard. "Were you followed?"

"Of course not, but one never knows," Gérard huffed.

Michael pursed his lips. "That is a deceptive answer."

"As was the question. How do you want me to answer?" Gérard looked down the way from which he had come.

Michael's eyes widened. Did the man actually not know? "Were you followed?"

"No." Gérard looked straight into Michael's eyes. "I told you this."

"Okay, then give me the info. Then I will be on my way. Besides they would kill us before asking what our conversation was about anyway."

Gérard looked around the room. Still, there was no one. Yet his life depended on that. He had to agree with Michael though. Anyone of importance knew what Michael looked like. Had they seen the two together, both men would already be dead. "Sure, but let's at least go where the crowds can hide us."

"And see us. Tell me now."

Gérard stopped his movement toward the exit. He stared at the picture of the half-finished cathedral. "I heard this from Antonio, and you heard it from no one."

"Yes, yes, bien sûr."

Still Gérard did not speak. His lips quivered with a fear that would not let him. Michael slapped him once—not hard, but it was unexpected. Gérard took a step back, his hand going to his face. "I will not thank you for that, as seems the custom for you Americans."

"You can thank me later."

Finally, Gérard started, "they got to Stacy, just as you suspected."

"Bastards," Michael whispered.

"Yes, they are that."

Michael waited for Gérard to explain who they were, but he only stood silent. "Well, who are they then?"

"North African radicals. No specific country alliances."

"Why do they want Nazeem dead?"

"They don't."

"They contracted me to kill someone they don't want dead." Michael feigned surprise.

"A kidnapping."

"A kidnapping?"

"They need you to create a diversion. Their man will make the attempt during the ensuing chaos."

"So if I don't do this, they'll kill her."

"I'd say not. They need her to blackmail you into the real final job. Don't you see? They knew you would find this out. They don't need you just for this job; they need you for the one that really counts."

"I don't enjoy games. What do they want me to do?"

"There is only one person that they need to get what they want."

"So what else do they need?"

"I don't know. I only know there is a second job in preparation, with the same outcome for a second target."

"But you can make a guess."

"Truly, he's the only person I can think would affect them. He once led an organization much like theirs, before he became … how do you say … political."

* * * * * *

Michael had been watching Alain's studio since eleven thirty. It was now almost one thirty. Did the man never go to lunch? From time to time, he could see Alain through the glass of his office window. It seemed as if he were waiting for someone; every time he went to the window, he also looked at his watch. This was, perhaps, a waste of time. If Alain stayed in all afternoon, it would be another six hours before the gallery closed. Michael needed to see him, but he couldn't wait that long. He needed to risk calling him.

Michael rose from his resting spot on the corner of Boulevard de Strasbourg and Rue du Château-d'Eau. The telephones at the end of the block were out of sight of the the gallery and he couldn't risk using his cell. He hoped Alain did not choose to leave during the five minutes it would take Michael to get to them.

Michael entered the telephone booth and searched the crowd behind him for someone that slowed or stopped as well. There were very few people on the street, and none had made the slightest move to alter their movement. It would take time to develop a feel for searching for tails. He knew that, but he had no such time to learn now.

The telephone rang three items before Marsha's voice answered the line, "Allo, L'Art International."

"Bonjour, je voudrais parler avec Alain, s'il vous plaît."

"Je peux dire qui telephone?"

"Michael."

"Ah, oui, Michael. He is expecting your call." Now that she knew Michael was American for sure, she refused to speak anything other than English to him.

There was a faint click and a short pause with a Neil Diamond song playing in the background before Alain answered. "Michael?"

"Oui, c'est moi."

"Where are you?"

"Near your place. I need something from you."

"Anything."

"How about an FN Model 30-11, fully loaded?"

"When do you need it?"

"Yesterday."

"Is there something going down?"

"No, just a precaution."

"How's a rifle a precaution?"

"I've never known you to ask too many questions, Alain."

"*Oui, bien sûr*, you're right. I do have one more though. When can we meet?"

"We can't."

"How do I get it to you then?"

Michael gave him the address to his hotel. "I'll leave the door open. Just put it under the bed. When can you get there?"

"Give me two hours."

"Okay. Don't wait for me. It could cost you."

"Michael, is this something I can help you with?"

"You just did. It'll be over by tomorrow morning."

"Okay. You're not back in the game, are you?"

"No. Just a precaution, Alain."

"Oui, je sais. Je comprend."

Michael hung up the phone. He knew Alain would have the Fabrique Nationale sniper rifle on hand. He would have preferred the Galil, but it was not as readily available to Alain. He left the booth and went back to his hotel. He could wait in the café opposite the entrance until after Alain was gone.

******

Michael placed the phone card into the payphone and dialed Arnaud's cell phone. The phone rang four times before Arnaud answered. "Allo."

"Is Stacy right there?"

"Yes, one moment."

"Michael, I'm so glad you called." Her voiced sounded subdued.

Michael wanted to ask her about everything that had happened to her, to make her feel better, to make things right again between them; but he knew he had little time. "We have to leave Paris."

"When?"

"Soon. We need to make plans now."

"Where are we going? We can't leave France. There are too many people here that can help us."

"They're a risk as well. But that's beside the point. We can go to Lille. You know people there, don't you?" Michael had realized that he knew little about how much Stacy was actually involved in the business and the team.

There was a pause. It was almost imperceptible, but Michael caught it. "Yes."

"Contact someone you can trust implicitly. Tell them we'll

need someplace to stay for a short while until we can arrange for a permanent place."

"When? How long before we have to leave? Tonight?" Stacy's questions came quickly one after the other.

"No, I need two days. The sixth. We'll take the train." Michael tried to sound calm. He didn't need her thinking she could help him with something.

"When will I see you again?"

Michael thought he heard anxiousness there, and ten years ago he would have known for sure. "On the train. Arnaud will arrange everything from Paris. You just get things set in Lille. And remember: don't leave any traces."

"Michael, why can't you tell me what's going on?"

There it is again, Michael thought. *Anxiousness but not worry.* He wanted to say that it was because he was afraid she would leave him, but he couldn't say that. "I told you. Someone has tracked me down. Just trust me. Contact your friend, and I'll see you on the train."

"I love you."

He wished he could believe that. Still, he answered honestly, no matter what she might truly be thinking at this point. "And I love you more than you can imagine."

"I don't know; I can imagine quite a bit."

"I love you more. See you in two days." Michael smiled. She had a way of making him feel at ease even when tensions were high.

"Be careful."

"I always am."

Michael hung up the phone and stared at it for a minute. The next thing he needed to do was finish the attempt. With what he had planned, all hell would break loose after that. The next two days would be either a disaster or a departure; even he didn't know which one. All he knew was that he needed to make sure Stacy was on that train without a tail.

Chapter 22

Michael looked again at the list of arrival and departure times that Josephine had given him. They should be arriving within five minutes. He would then have less than forty minutes to place the bomb and return to the apartment before the man exited the residence. He lay now just outside the fence; he could see the line of cut links just above the surface of the gravel path. They had not been found. Headlights flashed, coming from the north. The car pulled up to the residence, and the driver waited for an officer to check his ID. Once verified, the man exited the car and went up the steps to the residence. He did not knock, entering through the front door. Michael glanced down the street. Both patrolmen were now out of sight.

Michael rose from his place behind the fence and slid through the cut. The wire links caught on a length of nylon fabric instead of his clothes. He left the fabric behind for use on his way back through. He went directly to the corner of the building and once again searched the streets for the patrolmen. They had begun their journey back.

Michael slid from behind the building and followed the shadows to a small niche between two garbage cans. The harsh smell of rotting fruit hung in the breezeless air around him. He shifted accordingly, trying to adjust his position so the smell wouldn't disturb his concentration. A dark figure moved somewhere in the distance beyond the car. All thoughts of the smell were immediately erased.

He waited until the figure had moved past the car and met a second black-clad figure under the street lamp some thirty meters away. He inched forward onto the grass boulevard and stopped. He looked again to the two figures under the light. They talked for a moment and then turned to resume their patrol along the streets. The second disappeared from sight past the corner bookshop and away from the car. The first made his way back toward the car. Michael slipped back between the cans. It was only a minute before the man was past the car.

Michael moved quickly just as the man's footsteps began gradually fading. He rolled from his hiding place, going directly under the car, which was only a couple of feet away. His hands went directly for the pockets on each side of his jacket. From one he pulled out a small metal box no larger than a pack of cigarettes. He reached atop the muffler and placed the box there, where it would be out of sight. A satisfying click sounded as the magnet locked onto the metal. He raised a small antenna from the box, pointing it up, away from the muffler.

A long, thin strand of wire dropped from the box, ending in a small cylindrical piece of gold metal. From his second pocket, he withdrew a small blob of a substance similar to Play-Doh weighing about seven ounces. This he gently molded to the junction between the axle and the gas tank, where the thickness of the tank was the least. Finally, he strung the wire along the muffler and across the axle to the faux plastique, fitting the golden cylinder into the soft clay.

A flash of light signaled the guard's return. Michael slid from beneath the car and retreated to the cans. Without stopping, he continued past the trees and back to the fence. After slipping back through the hole he had cut earlier, it was simple to re-form the metal links to make them appear uncut to the casual observer.

The whole episode had lasted twenty-two minutes. Michael returned to the café where he had begun the night's activities and unlocked the door. He walked across the dingy linoleum and to the door that led upstairs to his room, where he would sit and wait for the time to come. He would watch the scene below, waiting for Nazeem to leave for the conference. Then his work would be finished and he could return to Stacy with a story she would believe, along with the truth that he was finished as an assassin. The world would be without another killer. Even if Gérard was correct and they really wanted him for another companion job, he was planning on being gone before they could approach him.

Michael positioned himself in a ready posture. He took off his shoes and placed the remote on the floor. He would need both hands free for the rifle, which he picked up and slid from its pouch. He checked the ammunition. All five rounds were loaded and ready. He would be able to use only one. It was one drawback of the bolt-action rifle and the main reason he preferred the Galil over Fabrique Nationale's product. Normally he wanted to guarantee a kill with two shots, but this hit did not need a guarantee. If he injured the man, it would effectively end the ready surveillance on Nazeem.

The door to the residence opened. Michael placed his toe over the detonation button and readied the rifle, aiming at the middle of the door. The first to exit was the man he wanted. Michael followed the driver's motions, never leaving the man's chest. Following behind the driver was a bodyguard and then Nazeem. They went to the car one after the other in a single-file line. As the driver touched the car door, Michael pressed the detonator on the remote. A muffled explosion sounded in the distance, and Michael pulled the trigger just as the white smoke rose from the car. The driver reached for his chest, and his legs collapsed underneath him.

After dropping the weapon and grabbing his shoes, Michael went out of the apartment. He crossed through the back hall and exited through an open window leading to a fire escape. His feet pounded against the metal frame and shook the entire structure. He had not counted on there being so much noise. He hoped the confusion from the explosion would cover his escape. After dropping the last five feet to the ground, he stopped for a moment to slip on his shoes.

An alley led to the road. From there he went south toward the Eiffel Tower. He could already see its lit-up form above the mass of trees around the park. His feet threw up dirt on the gravel paths as he continued toward the crowds around the tower. He slowed once he reached the northeast leg, and he then sat against its concrete base. He would now need to contact Arnaud. Stacy could finally be advised of the situation. She would have to go on to Lille without him though. There was still some unfinished business he needed to complete before going on to join her.

Once he had caught his breath, he rose and walked the couple of blocks to the metro station at Passy. The night air was cool, and Michael was glad the rains had thus far held off. He descended into the metro, the warmth of its underground halls enveloping him. He could not go back to the hotel or to his apartment. He would spend the night in some back-road hotel near Pigalle, where no questions would be asked and ready cash could buy anything.

******

Michael had attempted to contact everyone but Victor thus far. All of them were unaccounted for. Not even family members knew of their whereabouts. Something dangerous was happening in Paris. The network was beginning to crumble. Sources were not only drying up but disappearing as well. Reliable information was at a premium. Reports he received, usually untainted, were becoming wild and erratic; some were completely true, some bordered on the truth, and still others held no more than gossip. Michael hoped that Victor would be able to help. Victor was the most difficult to reach, and even then it was most likely to be by chance. This also gave him the best chance to escape whatever was happening. The first three locations had turned up nothing. Michael was now on his way to a nightclub only doors away from the famous Moulin Rouge. If this did not give him any clues, he would have to consider calling for an all clear. Contrary to its code name, an all clear would send the key members of the group home. It was there that a single phone call would reach each one of them. These locations were also outside of Paris but within eight hours of their present home.

Michael approached the nightclub from the north. The street was deserted. Not even the wind, which had been so strong on the large thoroughfares that many had moved indoors, created much of a stir. The facade of the club was red brick, deteriorating with age and pollution, and wood, which constituted the lower third of the building. The wood had recently been painted a dull black with the words "La Souterraine" added above the door in neon green. A dilapidated sign hung from the corner of the building. It too was black with green letters; these were, however, faded almost beyond comprehension. Michael pressed the gold button on the doorjamb.

A moment later, a face appeared in the peep box. "Oui, c'est qui?"

Michael avoided telling the man his name. "Je cherche Victor."

"J'ai dit c'est qui?" the man asked him again.

"Il n'est pas important." And it really wasn't important; why would the man ask him that?

"Vous êtes American?"

Michael hesitated a moment. It certainly was an odd question to ask. What did it matter whether he was American or not? "Eh, oui."

The peep box closed. Michael listened for any conversation inside, but he heard nothing. After three minutes, he began to wonder if the man had simply left him, expecting him to eventually go away. He was just about to press the button again when the box opened a second time. Another man appeared and said nothing. He looked at Michael intently.

"Je cherche Victor."

"Oui, je sais. Vous êtes Jacques?" Jacques was a little-used code name that Victor had given him years ago.

"Oui, vous connaissez Victor?" Asking if he knew Victor might have been obvious to most, but Michael was to ask this if the Jacques code name ever came up.

"Oui, c'est pour vous." The man slipped an envelope through the mail slot. The peep box went shut again. The envelope fell to the ground at Michael's feet. It landed face up. The name "Jacques" had been scrawled on it. He reached down, picked it up, and put it into his pocket. He had gone by Jacques only once before in his life, and that was before he had met Cruthers. He would never forget the man who had saved his life after coast guard cutters had ripped apart his boat with thousands of rounds of gunfire. He and Caesar had jumped overboard in an attempt to flee, yet only Caesar's initiative of grabbing the tank had saved them. An hour later, after being pulled thousands of yards down the coast by the current, they dragged themselves ashore. He had never again tried to smuggle drugs. Instead he had gone north, where Cruthers had welcomed him into his family and then into his business.

******

The letter remained in his pocket until he had reached his hotel room. Even then, he put the letter on the bed and lay down. If it contained good news, such as where he could find Victor, it would have to wait until tomorrow, as Victor would most likely be out away from the city and Michael would have to wait for the morning trains. Bad news was the last thing he needed, and no length of time would be enough to accept that Victor, who was in truth Caesar, was gone. Yet, if Caesar were in trouble, Michael would be there for him without question.

Michael reached over and retrieved the letter. He tore the corner of the envelope and slid his finger along the top edge. Inside was a single sheet of paper. On it was a single sentence.

> Michael, I hope you now realize who I am and will let me go home.

Despite its simplicity, the sentence told Michael everything. Caesar was abandoning the cause and leaving his present identity for a deeper cover. There was only one way he could contact Caesar, and that was to first contact Arnaud. Arnaud was the sole person left alive with the contact numbers of the group in case of an all clear.

The telephone rang. No one knew he was there. He had even made arrangements at another hotel with loose strings. The phone rang again and a third time. A total of five rings sounded. Whoever was calling knew he was there. Michael picked up the receiver. "Ya?" He tried to sound as German as he could.

"Michael, it's Victor."

"Victor, how—"

"I followed you. Look—I'm waiting to hear from Arnaud. It's not that I don't trust you, but something has happened." His Cuban accent was as thick as ever.

"No one's available," Michael responded.

"Exactly. I can't risk being seen." Victor's voice was rushed.

"Victor, you should know that I'm the last person who would compromise you." He owed Victor a lot, and the man was one of only two or three for whom he would risk his life.

"Yes, that is true. And you do owe me." Victor laughed.

"I will repay that debt." Michael wanted nothing more than to settle this long-standing situation.

"You can now. I believe the others went home. I'm staying in Paris until I hear to do the same."

"Do you think Arnaud called for it?" Michael wondered if anyone but Victor was left to hear it if, in fact, Arnaud had.

"No. The plans were for us all to be notified within minutes. I think someone else has been drawing people out into the open and then taking them out one by one. I have yet to be contacted, and it's been almost twelve hours since the first." Victor sighed audibly over the phone.

"You are a difficult man to reach," Michael offered.

"There were provisions."

"I only wanted to ask you a question." Michael needed to change the subject and move on.

"Ask now."

"Someone is connected to this group that blackmailed me into a hit. At first I thought it was Domino, but now I'm almost positive it wasn't. Do you know?" If Victor knew, this would say a lot about who was involved.

"I should not admit to knowing what you're talking about."

"But you do." Michael held back from telling Victor off. He couldn't believe even those close to him, who were far too few, withheld vital information until asked.

"Yes. I do not, however, know the answer," Victor responded cryptically.

"Caesar—"

"Victor, please."

"Victor, loyalty was always your best quality. Tell me what you know."

"You distrust me," Victor responded.

"I don't know. Others have been persuaded to leave town without advance notice." Michael wanted to trust Victor, but it seemed no one was trustworthy these days.

"I do not know, Michael. I believe you should ask Alain." And the phone went dead.

Chapter 23

The story was not front page news for either *Le Monde* or *Le Figaro*, but each had it on page 3. The *Herald-Tribune* was another matter. Not only on the front page but also on the top line and in 36-point Times Roman, they proclaimed, "American Assassin Murdered in Paris." In all three papers, the story read just as one might expect it to. A certain American assassin who had entered the country under an alias had been fatally shot just after exiting the metro at Le Cité. Witnesses said they heard the rifle fire once but saw no one go down into the metro or run away with a weapon in hand. The shot had hit the man just below the left temple, killing him instantly. At the time, he had been leaning against a tree. His legs had collapsed, but he had fallen into a sitting position at the base of the tree. No name was released to the press.

Only after police had arrived was the man discovered to be dead. The identification found on him was quickly reported to be fake, and a subsequent search of Interpol records tied the man to the United States, but at this point, they had no name. Local informants had later verified that the man had been contracted to kill Nazeem. As was reported the day before, that assassination attempt had failed, ending in the death of his driver. The assassin's death was assumed to be a hit in retaliation, but it was unsure whether the gun was hired by Nazeem's organization or the original contractors. The article in the *Herald-Tribune* continued by relating stories of unsolved murders that could have been the work of this hit man. Only the Le Monde offered the rumor that this assassin had in fact retired from service, although it did not suggest any reasons for his doing this hit anyway.

* * * * * *

As with nearly every morning, Stacy began the day by reading the newspaper. After waking, but before making her tea, she walked to the corner and bought an *International Times* and a *Herald-Tribune*. She tucked both under her arm and walked back, enjoying the early-morning warmth. The first few days after she had been shot at near the Louvre, those few minutes were the only time she had left the apartment on her own. She felt no safer now than she had then. Arnaud was not up by the time she returned, so she went up to take a shower and get dressed. A knock came at the door only seconds after she had retreated from the shower. "Stacy?"

"Oui?"

"I must go out. I'll be back by noon. Don't let anyone in except me. I am beginning to believe there is more going on here than just Domino's work."

"What do you mean? Who else would want me dead?"

Arnaud knew he should tell her about Michael. He wanted to say, "That's just the point; they didn't want you dead. Michael killed the driver, and the blast was but a smoke screen." He couldn't understand who would want a simple chauffeur dead. Alain had supplied him with the gun; perhaps he knew more. "That's what I'm trying to find out," he finally stated.

"Okay, I'll be here."

"A bientôt."

* * * * * * * *

"A bientôt." Stacy stood looking in the fogged-up mirror. How had she gotten herself into this mess in the first place? It was so long ago, yet the memory stood out in her head above all others. Cruthers had dared her to do it, and she, being drunk at the time, had found it easy to take him up on it. After that, it wasn't so simple to carry out. Cruthers wasn't upset that she didn't do it; he just went out and found Michael.

* * * * * * * * *

Stacy was twenty-two years old and terribly in love with the wrong man—not that she knew that at the time. Cruthers had money and was handsome enough that the money made up for the deficiencies. She had grown up poor and without a mother for most of her childhood. Heroin had taken that from her. Little did she know that heroin also supplied much of the money Cruthers used to lavish her with gifts.

They were out at a dinner for Domino's thirtieth wedding anniversary. She and Cruthers had been dating for almost a year. He had seemed so classy, but perhaps that was influenced by his dad, who was kind, gentle, and extremely respectful to her. She always remembered him asking her why she didn't aspire to more. At the time, she had simply thought he was referring to her achieving more than her retail sales position with Macy's. Later she realized he was comparing her to his son. Even Domino knew the limited worth of his son as a husband. "One day he will get you to do something you'll regret only because it helps him," he had once told her.

That night it would happen. Three bottles of wine between them had gotten them more than tipsy but not drunk enough to be incapacitated. They walked out of the restaurant hand-in-hand.

"Oh, shit." Cruthers let go of her hand and reached for his notepad. He rummaged through the pages. "Shit, shit, shit."

"What's wrong?" she giggled, more from the wine than anything else.

"I was supposed to set something up for tonight. Shit. Well, it'll have to wait." Cruthers looked at his phone.

"No, can't I maybe help?" Stacy offered.

Cruthers laughed. "No, certainly not. You can't."

"I'm more capable than you give me credit for." Stacy put her hands on her waist.

"Not about this." Cruthers shook his head.

"What?" Stacy's face went suddenly serious.

"You don't want to know."

"Yes, I do." She stomped her foot on the sidewalk. "What?"

It might have been the alcohol or the rush of his girlfriend doing it, but he blurted out the answer. "I was supposed to have someone punished. It *can* wait."

"Punished, like how?"

Cruthers grabbed onto her arm with a tight grip. "You don't want to know this."

"Yes, I do." This time her stomp was punctuated with a pout.

"As in punished and they will never be a problem again."

"Killed?" Stacy took in a deep breath.

"Stacy, shut up." He looked down the sidewalk both ways.

Stacy's voice went down to a whisper. "Really?"

"Yes, it can wait. Now get in the car." He motioned toward the open door to the backseat.

"I can do it for you." Stacy suddenly thought she actually could.

"Like I said, no you can't." Cruthers rolled his eyes.

"You won't know unless you give me a chance."

"Stacy, you just aren't the type."

"I could be." Stacy pulled away from Cruthers's grip.

"I don't want you to be." This was a lie, as he was a little more than excited thinking about the possibility. She certainly was smart enough and innovative in her thinking.

"Well, I can do what I want," she said defiantly.

Cruthers laughed. "Not if I don't contract with you."

"Who is it?"

"I'm not telling you that."

"I'll go back and ask your dad."

"No!" he yelled. That would get him in double trouble—firstly for telling her and secondly for not already having it done.

She could tell that was the last thing he wanted. She suddenly had the upper hand, which was what often happened in their arguments. "Then tell me."

"You can't kill someone. It's not in your nature."

"I think you'd be surprised what's in my nature." They were both sobering up, and Stacy couldn't believe she still wanted to do this.

Cruthers thought for a moment. *What's the worst that could happen? She could die,* he supposed. There was a lot of risk. "Stanley."

"Stanley?" Stacy tried to remember the guy.

"You know. The Canadian guy. Tall, skinny. A geek."

"Why?" she huffed.

"Doesn't matter."

"It does to me." Stacy started thinking about the reasons why before he could even say a word.

"You simply can't do it if you need to know why. You want to play the game, you have to play by the rules. There's no need for you to know why."

"Okay, how much?" She rubbed her fingers together.

"What d'ya mean?"

"How much do I get for the hit?"

"Shut up about a hit. You're not doing it." He started into the car.

"Yes, I am. How much?" Stacy remained on the sidewalk.

"Ten grand."

"I'll do it." Stacy had no clue if he was shorting her or not, but she wanted to prove to him that she could do this.

"No, you won't."

"Yes, I will. I'll see you later."

"Where are you going?"

Stacy hailed a cab. "I have a job to do."

"Twenty if it's done by tomorrow night," Cruthers called after her. He fully expected this would be the last time he saw her alive.

Stacy smiled and leaned back in the cab. She was determined she would do it. She arrived at her apartment at 1:00 am with a plan in place. Drugs and suicide were always a great combination for death.

* * * * * * * *

The next morning, she bought two handguns and an assortment of pills. She still wasn't sure how she would get the drugs into him. But that was perhaps the easy part. It was having time alone with him that wouldn't be easy. Then again, it was never hard for her to get men alone with her; normally she had to say no so often she almost wanted to punch them. That afternoon she was trolling the bars for look-alikes. They didn't have to be perfect—just a close match.

It took only twenty minutes to get her "Stanley" drunk and another two to be walking with him toward the hotel elevators. His twin was drugged and silently sleeping two doors down from Stanley's room. She watched the floor lights slowly progress toward one. She had made sure the rent-a-cop had seen them together, just as she would make sure he noticed her with the twin. As they rode up the elevator, Stanley began to grope her. She pushed his hands away. "Don't."

"What's wrong, baby? You're not going to say no to me, are you?" He laughed a stupid drunk laugh.

"Of course not, handsome. It's just the cameras. They're watching." She nodded toward the security camera near the ceiling.

"Oh, yeah. Sorry." He stood up straight, fixed his tie, and then burst out laughing. "You seem like the exhibitionist type."

"Only with you alone, baby." She pushed him through the opening doors as he tried to reach for her breasts. He half walked and Stacy half dragged him down the hall. She stopped at 1108.

"This isn't my room"

"No, it's mine." She winked at him.

It took a moment for it to sink in. "Oh, okay; wherever, baby. Your room is good."

She opened the door and practically shoved him through. "Lie down on the bed and get comfortable."

He struggled toward the bed and collapsed. His last thought before passing out was wondering why there was a mirror above the bed.

Stacy shut the bathroom door before Stanley hit the bed. She splashed water on her face. What had seemed so simple only hours before and was made simpler by the man's grotesque attitude toward her was suddenly impossible. She had never harmed anything in her life, let alone killed someone. It was Cruthers. He had convinced her she could do this. She had trusted him—wanted to think she was capable of such adventurous actions. Adventurous? The word stuck in her head. Killing someone was not simply adventurous. It was a psychological decision. She was no killer. "I can't do this," she whispered into the mirror. Stacy grabbed her purse and dug out her cell phone. She dialed Cruthers's number.

"Done already?" he said.

"Can't."

"What?".

"Told you. I can't do it."

"No, I told you. Son of a bitch." He yelled into the phone. "What the fuck do you expect me to do now?"

She could feel his anger over the phone. "I don't know. They're both here in the room."

"Both?"

"Yeah, knocked out for another few hours."

"Wait a second—what do you mean 'both'?"

"Stanley and his double. It was a plan."

"Shit." Cruthers rubbed his face. "Okay, get out of there and I'll figure something out."

"You sure?"

"Yes I'm sure. Unlike you, I can do what I fucking say. Just get out. What room?"

"1108." She did as she was told. Ten minutes later she was on I-694 going north toward home.

* * * * * * * *

Cruthers threw his drink across the room. "Son of a bitch." He screamed again. "Okay, calm down. There's got to be someone." He scrolled through his contact list. "Oh, yes, this will work," he said to himself as he dialed the number.

"Sticky, what's up?" Michael asked.

"Shut the fuck up with the Sticky shit!" Cruthers screamed into the phone.

"You calling me for help, Sticky?" Michael chuckled.

"I said—"

Michael's laughter turned cold. "You're calling me for help. That means I can call you any fucking thing I want."

"Just lay off with the name, Michael." Cruthers's voice toned down. He needed this in a bad way; despite how he felt about Michael, the job needed finishing.

"What do you want?"

"I've got a mark half-cooked."

"You?" Michael asked.

"No, contract ended … abruptly."

"Couldn't stomach the job or couldn't finish it?"

Cruthers thought about lying, but Michael would figure it out anyway. "First timer."

"Shit, what are you doing that for?" Michael sighed heavily.

Cruthers grunted. "Look; it was a mistake. You got somebody?"

"Uh, yeah, sure. I'll do it."

"Seriously?" Cruthers had been hoping for that.

"Yeah, no problem. What's the fee?"

"Ten grand."

"Sticky?"

Cruthers ignored the nickname. He wanted nothing more than to get off the phone. "Twenty grand."

"So let's make it forty."

Cruthers knew Michael just wanted to push his buttons, but he once again ignored the negotiation. "Yeah, sure."

"Where?"

"Downtown Hilton, 1108. There's a mark and a twin."

"Sure. Want the twin gone too?"

Cruthers thought for a moment. He needed to clean up all the loose ends attached to Stacy, but he didn't want to get in any further with Michael. "Don't matter. You can use him or lose him. Make sure the mark looks like he did it himself and I'll owe you one."

"You'll owe me one anyway, but got it."

* * * * * * * *

It wasn't until weeks later that Michael and Stacy met, and she had no clue what Michael did for Cruthers, but after her episode with Stanley, she knew better than to ask those kinds of questions. Still, it was love at first sight. Cruthers lost his girlfriend and eventually lost his hit man.

Chapter 24

After getting dressed, Stacy went down to the kitchen to make some tea and read her newspapers. She read the *International Times* mainly because it existed. She was not particularly interested in the business news, and its dry reporting of such was in no way stimulating. Yet, just as she had so many times before, purchasing a copy was habit from when she had craved for anything in English. Thus, she always read this one first. In the time it took to heat up the water for tea, she would be through reading it. This morning was no exception. She put down the *Times* just as the teapot began to whistle. However, she ignored the pot's insistent call as the front page headline of the *Herald-Tribune*, "Murdered in Paris," sprang out at her. She felt a rush of adrenaline run through her body and disappear just as quickly, leaving her faint. She sat back down on the chair, pushed the *Times* aside, and revealed the rest of the headline. "Michael?" She whispered softly. The teapot continued its whine. They didn't give a name, but it certainly sounded like Michael, and the fact he was involved in a hit attempt explained why he might avoid her. Once again he had lied to her, and now he was gone forever. She wanted his retirement to be true more than anything in the world.

Stacy did not begin to cry until she had taken the pot off the stove. Instead of pouring the water into the waiting cup, she set the pot on another burner and turned the first off. Absently, she took the cup with its waiting tea bag and set it in the sink. Returning to the table, she was finally resolved to read the entire article again.

Her eyes followed the words, slowly taking in each phrase before going on to the next. She read until she came upon the background on Michael's previously credited kills and stopped. She wanted neither to know nor be reminded of what he had been and, through the article's direct assumptions implicating Michael in the recent attempted assassination of Nazeem, what he still was. He had not stopped. The whole story about his escape from that life was a lie.

Arnaud had suspected this. He had said as much that morning. She had thought he had sounded somewhat bothered. *Perhaps he already knew that Michael ... If Michael didn't indeed run out on Domino, then the attack on her was ...* She wanted to scream. She couldn't believe what she was thinking. Michael wasn't capable of such a thing. Would he actually knowingly allow men to be sent to do that to her? She had known that evening when they had once again run into each other in Paris that he was the last man she should trust. He had known her weaknesses and used them. He had lied to her once; why did she think that he wasn't capable of doing it again? And what of Lawrence? Was his death not so much a mystery to Michael as he had pretended it to be? Perhaps that was only the first order of business after arriving in Paris.

To him it must have been so easy to lie. His whole life was a lie. She wondered who knew the truth. Arnaud? No, never. He had proven his loyalty to her numerous times. Alain, without a doubt, played some role in the deception. She wondered about that. Was his studio only a front for something more devious?

Stacy jumped as the doorbell rang. She doubted that she would have answered the door after Arnaud's warning, but now there was no way she would open it. Instead she crawled behind the counter, out of sight—as well as out of the line of fire, if it came to that. As if echoing her thoughts, two shots were fired. The front window shattered. Another shot rang out; then all was quiet. Stacy huddled in the corner and shook. They were now going to kill her. But if Michael was dead, who was after her now?

******

As Arnaud went from home to home, he was never treated with outright hostility, but he could not blame them for being discourteous. He was alive, and husbands, fathers, and a wife had been killed. Their families could not feel the honor that they might have had their loved ones been killed "in the line of duty." But for these families, the numbers of Lawrence's group were nothing more than ordinary people. Arnaud was a stranger to them—someone who could have made the connections between their deaths and the reasons for them. Since he neither offered nor was asked to reveal these reasons, the families held him solely responsible. Not one of the families asked if he had lost someone as well. Arnaud felt betrayed by the system he had helped set up. Something—or, more precisely, someone—was now tearing down that structure. They had worked as a team. These men and women were his family. He did not help them just because it would advance his own reputation. His name was revealed to only four or five people. Two of these were still on the run—namely Michael and Stacy—and two, one of them dead, worked from within the system. Otherwise he was known only by reputation. One did not contact Arnaud; one requested something be done, and Arnaud was there. It was only a matter of time now before they would find him too. Perhaps it would be best to leave Paris and return home to Lille with Stacy.

There was only one more person to check on. Victor was the sole member of the organization unaccounted for. Victor had been Lawrence's closest ally. He had also been against letting Michael into the group so soon after he had left Cruthers's service. Since he had no specific reasons why, he had said nothing and gone along with the consensus. Victor was a loner and thus difficult to track down. He would disappear for weeks at a time, only to reappear when needed.

Arnaud sat at his desk, his feet relaxing on its simulated wood top and a copy of *Le Monde*, unread, on his lap. He had hoped the call would come before he had to go check on Stacy. It was almost noon already. If he was late, Stacy would worry. He need not cause her that kind of anxiety. There was already too much of that going on.

He started shifting through the newspaper, jumping from article to article, barely reading anything further than the headline. He could not concentrate. The phone rang.

"Allo."

"Allo, Arnaud. Victor?"

"Oui, c'est moi. Qu'est-ce qu'il se passe?"

"The group's been shut down."

"Yes, I know. I talked to Michael."

"Michael? When?"

"A few hours ago."

"But how?"

"What?"

"I'm reading the newspaper. I take it you haven't yet seen it."

"No, why?"

"It says here that Michael, or at the very least someone described as only Michael could have been, was killed last night."

"Couldn't have been. I'm sure it was him."

"That is certainly good news."

"How about Stacy?"

"She's fine. I have to see her this afternoon."

"I would go now, before she hears anything about this."

"Of course. I'm on my way now. Get out of Paris, Victor."

"I'm on my way out now."

"I would say keep in touch, but I think we both know that might not be the wisest thing."

"You will hear from me again, my friend, when the time is right." The line went dead.

******

Arnaud could not believe the news he had just received. The fifth and final member of Lawrence's group was running. Confirmed with his own words, he needed no more proof that one of his close friends had turned. The papers had said Michael was dead. He knew that at least that much was false. Michael had provided the necessary arrangements to cover his movements while they left Paris. Arnaud still did not understand why Michael didn't just travel along with them, but he had insisted that going the "back route," as he had put it to Lille, instead of the TGV was better for them all. Michael still suspected that both Arnaud and Stacy were being followed. But why? There was no evidence to support it.

Arnaud's shop near the Champs Élysées was crowded, although it took no more than four or five people to accomplish that. Yet it was still odd that there was more than one customer at a time. Usually people did this kind of "shopping" as privately as possible. Even the most uninhibited found it odd being around others while perusing the magazines and gadgets—not to mention being watched while purchasing anything overtly kinky.

Opening the front door, Arnaud took one more look inside. There was a chance that one of these men was actually watching for him to leave. If Arnaud caught sight of one of them again, he would have to avoid Stacy until he could shake the man. Arnaud stopped as he began to turn right onto the Champs Élysées. One of the men had exited his shop and was trailing behind at what might be considered a discreet distance. Arnaud froze, not knowing if he should hurry to the next block and try to avoid the man or wait at the corner and see how the man reacted. Arnaud looked up the boulevard and back down, each time passing a glance at the man. The second glance told him what he needed to know. The man had stopped as well. He had his back turned to Arnaud, but he was obviously talking into a cell phone.

The man turned, and eye contact was made. Both men reacted with basic instinct and turned away despite knowing they had been caught by the other. Arnaud wasted no time in using the split second to disappear from view. He went west and, at a full run, effectively used the brass railing to swing himself down the stairwell into the metro at George V. He did not slow down until he reached the platform. He nervously tapped his hand against his thigh, watching both the tunnel for a train and the entrance for the man. By the time the train arrived, Arnaud had moved to the far end of the platform, hoping to cover all entrances.

After stopping for less than five seconds, the train moved

forward with Arnaud in the last car. Peering out the window, he concentrated on the platform, hoping the man would arrive. If he didn't, there could have been another tail. The man could very well have been communicating with another member of his team. The train disappeared into the darkness of the tunnel, and still there was no sign of his pursuer. Arnaud immediately paid close attention to his fellow passengers. Any one of them could have been on that train for the sole purpose of keeping an eye on him. The train pulled into the next stop, Franklin D Roosevelt. Arnaud glanced up at the map of the metro line above the open door. *Where am I going anyway?* He had to think before the next stop. He eventually had to make his way back to the apartment. If he had been followed, it was very likely they knew where Stacy was as well. Arnaud thought back to what Michael had said. He had insisted that Stacy not be moved—that he had to know where she was. This, despite the fact that Arnaud was seriously considering it compromised. Michael also could have found out the identities of the members of Lawrence's group. Lawrence may have disclosed them. It would not have been odd for Michael to insist on knowing whom he was dealing with.

Arnaud could not believe what he was thinking. Michael? Not conceivable. Even when Michael was in the business of murder, he never betrayed a loyal associate. It could not be; there had to be someone else—someone involved but distant enough that he would not be suspected. The train once again came to a stop. Arnaud was at Pont Neuf. Without immediately knowing why, he jumped through the open doors the instant the warning buzzer sounded. The doors slammed shut, clipping his heels as they locked. He looked down the platform. No one had followed him off. In his haste, he had also assured himself that anyone trying to follow him was stuck on the moving train. Yet if the first man had a telephone, there would be others with the same. Arnaud found it odd to be running from a potentially nonexistent pursuer, yet he was not ready to concede himself a victory. He needed to get out of the station and away from it before someone could be sent to spot him.

He found himself east of the Louvre and facing the bridge that crossed the westernmost tip of the Île de la Cité, Pont Neuf. He walked across the bridge as fast as he could without bringing attention to himself. The sidewalk was filled with people, and he allowed himself to stop and proceed without pushing his way through the crowd. His eyes scanned the bridge traffic, but he did not look behind; he would not be able to spot anyone anyhow. Once across both branches of the river, he headed east along the Seine. There was an RER station at St. Michel. He could backtrack along that line and appear again on the surface at the Champ de Mars. From there he would have to be cautious once again. If it were true and the apartment had been compromised, by Michael or anyone else, he did not want to be seen entering it.

He hoped Stacy was still there, and if she was, that no one had tried to move in on her. As long as she kept the door shut and stayed out of the line of fire, she would be okay. The apartment had some safety traps that would help her under various circumstances. He kept reminding himself of this fact.

* * * * * *

Arnaud passed by the entrance to his apartment on the opposite side of the street. There were very few people along the road, and he was consciously trying to keep his face averted. Everything was calm. He looked through the front windows and saw the light on in the kitchen. A shadowy form was moving inside. Either Stacy was safe or some hoodlum was making himself some lunch. A man approached the residence from the north. Just after passing the line of brown brick that marked the separation between apartments, he stopped. The man glanced down the road in both directions, hesitating for a moment on Arnaud's form. Arnaud headed up the stairs to an apartment building as soon as he saw the man stop. He reached the top of the stairs and turned. The man was knocking on the front door. "Please don't answer," Arnaud whispered. She didn't. Without any apparent reason, the man suddenly broke into a run and disappeared down the street.

Gunshots broke the calm—three short bursts from an automatic rifle. Glass shattered both at the door and the living room of the apartment. Arnaud could no longer see the shadowy form that was once inside from where he was. He knew it was not because she had been shot. While one pane of glass had indeed shattered onto the bushes beneath the window, a second layer of tempered bulletproof glass had remained intact. He turned his attention from the apartment to the direction of the gunfire. It had come from ground level. Still, he could see no one. Arnaud jumped the iron railing and kneeled on the grass, searching for the hidden gunman. Two more bursts were fired. The glass held, but these shots gave away the shooter's position. Arnaud pulled his own 9 mm Glock 34. All it would take now would be for the gunman to stand up even halfway.

The man obliged him by running straight at Arnaud. Arnaud cautiously took aim at him and fired. The man took the first shot in the chest and managed another step before the second and third rounds exploded within a couple inches of the first. He collapsed without even thinking of firing a return volley. Arnaud darted from behind the stairs and landed a blow to the man's side with his foot. The limp body simply rolled over, revealing the three wounds in his chest. Without a second thought, Arnaud went for the apartment.

"Stacy, it's Arnaud," he yelled out while unlocking the door. He found Stacy behind the kitchen counter, sobbing. "Stacy, it's okay. They're gone. We have to get out of here though."

"He's dead."

"Yes, he's dead. But we have to go."

"No, *he's* dead."

"Who?" Arnaud asked.

Stacy reached up to the counter and moved the *Herald-Tribune* headline into view. "They killed him. Arnaud, they've killed him, and now they want me dead."

"No, it's not true. Michael wanted people to think he was dead. He needed time." Arnaud grabbed her arm and pulled her toward the back door.

"Not dead?" Stacy stood fast.

"Not now. Let's get out of here." He motioned toward the back.

"Why didn't you tell me? I almost didn't care whether they shot me or not." Stacy pulled her arm away from his grasp.

"I didn't know." Arnaud started toward the door without her.

She started to get up but then sunk back down as she asked, "Why didn't he let us know?"

"That's not the only question I have for him." Arnaud indeed had many questions for him, and that was the least of them.

Stacy finally rose from the floor and followed Arnaud through the back door. Gunfire erupted around her, and she felt a burning sensation rip across her shoulder. She instinctively went low and ran to join Arnaud behind a parked car. Her right hand grabbed for her left should and came back with blood.

"You're hit?"

"Yes. Nothing bad—grazed me."

They made their way south behind the cars. Gunfire continued to follow them. Arnaud stopped midway down the block.

"What's wrong?" Stacy kneeled beside him.

"It feels like they are moving us this way on purpose."

The gunfire had stopped, and Stacy looked back the way they came. The gunman obviously knew where they were but hadn't tried to actually get into a line of sight. The bullets were shattering windows on the far side of the cars. "Perhaps so. Reinforcements down the street?"

"That would be my guess. We need to get across the street here. Time is on our side. If we can delay just a while longer, the police will be here. This isn't a neighborhood used to gunfire." Arnaud pointed to a closed boulangerie just across from them. "There. Take out the glass and we can hold out in there until the police are near. Sneak out the back once we hear the sirens."

Stacy nodded. "You go first. I'll cover you. Once you're inside, cover me." She rose and took several shots in the general direction of the previous gunshots.

Arnaud ran, keeping low to the ground. He fired twice into the large plate glass that once would have displayed breads and pastries.

The window shattered into a rain of glass. He picked the cleanest section of wall and dived into the building.

Stacy heard the glass fall against the sidewalk, followed by gunshots from within. She immediately mimicked Arnaud's movements and dived through the same opening.

"How long do you think they will wait to come find us?"

"Let's hope it's longer than the length of time the police take to get here."

Sirens sounded in the distance from multiple directions. Stacy smiled. They would be there within a minute or two. Her smile disappeared as the sound of metal bouncing against tile sounded to their right. Her eyes followed the sound to the rolling object coming to a halt against a broken piece of glass. "Grenade!!!"

They moved as one through the back and down into the kitchen, diving into the room and sliding to a stop behind the metal counter in the center. The explosion threw heat and debris over them, but the steel cabinets protected them from the worst of it. The shock wave took Stacy's breath away and tossed her against the oven. Her eyes closed just as she saw Arnaud swept away in a cloud of dust and disintegrated Sheetrock.

She didn't know how long she was out, but it couldn't have been long. The sirens were just arriving outside the front of the store. She shook her head and tried to focus. "Arnaud!" she shouted, her own voice just a muffled sound.

He came out from her right. His lips were moving, but she could not make out a word. Still, he grabbed her arm, and she knew it didn't really matter what he was saying. They needed to leave.

Chapter 25

Michael woke the next morning before dawn. He had much to do before going to Lille. There was Josephine. She was the weak link in all this. If he could get her alone again, she would tell him anything he needed to know. He first needed to find her. Michael gave himself until four-thirty, when a train was leaving from the Gare du Nord to Lille, in Northeastern France, halfway to Belgium. Before anything, he called Arnaud.

"Allo," Arnaud answered before the first ring was complete.

"Arnaud, c'est Michael."

"But it can't be? What about the papers?"

Michael could hear the emphasis in his voice; Arnaud already knew the papers had it wrong. "Arnaud, you know that's not true."

"But the reports were so exact."

Michael thought for the sake of expediency that playing along was the only way to go at this point. "Arnaud, it's me."

"How can I be sure? Why aren't you on the train with Stacy?"

"She's not leaving until noon, and I'm not going with her."

"So it is you."

Michael sighed. "As I said. I have things to do here, but I will meet you in Lille."

"Michael, it's too dangerous for you in Paris. If they haven't already, they will find you."

"No, I will follow later, through the back door." For Michael, the back door to Lille was through a little town called Fourmies, where he once recovered from an accident that left him partially immobilized. Arnaud had helped him get situated there at the time.

"That is a long way to be on a train. You'll be too visible."

"They won't know I'm there." Michael hoped this would be true; he was beginning to distrust everyone around him.

"Michael, what about Stacy? What do I tell her?"

"Everything—especially that I didn't fulfill the contract."

"I don't know everything about that."

Michael heard the unspoken question. He could tell Arnaud didn't trust him either. "You know enough. Just get her out of Paris as soon as you can. Don't wait for the next train."

"When will we meet you there?"

He hated keeping more things from Stacy at this point, but until he knew whom he could trust, he couldn't afford to make a mistake. "I'll find you."

"We won't want to be found."

"I'll find you," Michael said harshly.

"Okay. Don't do anything stupid, Michael."

"I already have." He hung up the phone without explaining. Now that was done. He had nine hours to find Josephine.

The streets of Paris were still quiet on the outer rim. Tourists seldom went to these parts. There were few monuments or museums of any renown in the area. There was only day-to-day life. Michael walked from his hotel to the metro, stopping at a patisserie that had just opened its doors. The morning was cool, and the warm, aromatic air felt as good as it smelled.

"Bonjour, monsieur."

"Deux pain au chocolat, s'il vous plaît."

"Oui." The woman reached under the glass counter and picked out two pastries. She placed them in a white bag and twisted the corners shut. "Quatre Euros." She said as she placed the bag on the counter.

Michael placed a five-euro piece in her hand.

"S'il vous plaît." The woman handed him the bag, along with a single euro back.

"Merci." Michael smiled, turning to leave.

"Merci, au revoir."

"Au revoir," Michael returned.

"Bon journée," the lady added, as if it were necessary that she get in the last word.

******

Arnaud hung up the phone. He was now too confused to think. Why would Michael call with this news if he was the leak? Michael didn't know which train Stacy would be on for sure, despite his having told her to go at noon, although there were only a limited number of them. Nor did he know where to find them in Lille. Michael had insisted that he would find them, but it would be more difficult than he implied. Yet he had assumed Arnaud was going with her. That was not a part of the original plan. Arnaud himself had decided to leave Paris only the previous evening. Arnaud wished he had confronted Michael. It would be the only way to know for certain. Michael's reaction to such an accusation would be telling.

It was too late for that now. Just as Michael had things to do in Paris, so did Arnaud. If he was to leave Paris for good, he would need to send his contacts home. This would involve only one thing. He would close his shop near the Champs Élysées. Upon doing this, a list of resellers would be called, notifying them of the closing. Added to this list were names and numbers that would find the news interesting for reasons that had nothing to do with the business. This was the call to go home, just as it was with Lawrence's group. They were no longer in service.

Arnaud wondered how many would heed the call or even be available to take it. His network was already in the midst of collapse, with only a few contacts still genuine. Whether this was Michael's doing or not was still in question. Whatever the case, he needed to get Stacy out of Paris and into the relative safety of Lille. If Michael was indeed dirty, they would not be able to stay there for long. Perhaps a return to the States would be good for Stacy.

An old man sat on the curb outside Arnaud's shop. He flipped through a magazine that was crumpled from use and spotted with numerous marks that Arnaud did not want to think about. The old man rose as he saw Arnaud approaching. He waited there every Thursday for Arnaud to open, and each week he carried with him the magazine from the previous visit, which looked as if it had seen more than seven days' use. Arnaud would be glad to get away from him. The man scared him.

"Bonjour." A toothless grin from the man greeted Arnaud. The man extended a grubby hand with short fingers.

As always, Arnaud ignored the gesture. "Nous sommes fermés." The old man only looked at him with a blank stare as Arnaud told him they were closed. "Trouvez un autre magasin. Nous sommes fermés." The man took a couple steps away, keeping his gaze on Arnaud as if he didn't understand. He actually looked a little sad, but he did as he was told and left to find another store. Arnaud unlocked the door and went inside. There was over a hundred thousand euros' worth of merchandise in the small interior, but he didn't care what was done with it. Once his rent wasn't paid, the owner would most likely junk or sell it.

The lights snapped on, and Arnaud sat behind the register to write out a note to both his single employee and his patrons. "This store is closed effective immediately." Arnaud hoped Damion, who had run the shop for years with nothing but loyalty, would be able to find work elsewhere. Arnaud decided to write a recommendation letter and send it to Damion before leaving Paris. It was the least he could do for the man who had become such an integral part of his business.

After placing the message on the front door, Arnaud went below to his office. He took the photos from the walls and boxed them along with a stack of papers from the desk. Other than that, there was nothing in the store he wanted. The books, magazines, videos, and gadgets would be gone, or perhaps they would find another renter to run the same kind of business. He left through the rear exit into an alley, not even bothering to lock the back door.

One final call would put in motion the last step to his leaving Paris. He went to a phone booth on the Champs Élysées.

"Allo."

"Allo, c'est Frederique Deleau. Nous sommes fermés."

"D'accord. Au revoir." It was that simple—no questions, no wondering why. He was out of business—at least in Paris. Arnaud owned other shops in other cities, including Lille.

******

After closing the shop, Arnaud went directly to Stacy. She was expecting to leave that day, but not until noon. He was unsure how she would react to Michael's elongated absence, yet he had a feeling that she would insist on staying in Paris. She had moved from the Champ de Mars apartment into a hotel not far from Sacre Coeur. Arnaud walked up the steps that led to the basilica on top of Montmartre. A brilliant white against the blue sky, it reminded Arnaud of hope and faith; perhaps that was because of his own faith in God, but to him this building was more than that. It was God's home, but many people with no faith had found hope here. Being above the entire city did much to enhance that thought. It was, he supposed, why it had been built there.

Reaching the top of the rise, he considered going in and lighting a candle for Stacy's safety. He had no time for such displays of devotion though. He would do much toward guaranteeing her safety by getting her out of Paris. He was halfway around the basilica, the gargoyles staring down at him, berating him for such abuse of his beliefs, before he turned and went back.

The interior was serene and almost melancholy. Candles flickered their light from various points around the nave and surrounding corridor, adding what illumination they could to the sunlight streaming through the stained-glass windows. Arnaud went past the first two sets of candles, ending up before the statue of the Virgin Mary. He placed a five-euro piece in the box and took a candle. After lighting the white wick with the flame of a half-melted candle, he placed it on the rack. He knelt before the statue and prayed. Calmly, he rose from his place and returned to the main doors.

Stacy's hotel was only four blocks directly behind Sacre Coeur, on the edge of a residential neighborhood. The interior was quiet; no one sat behind the reception desk. A bell signaled his entrance. Before the owner could arrive, Arnaud started up the staircase. He had almost forgotten which room she was in, and he had to descend from the third floor back to the second. He knocked on her door twice, waited, and then knocked twice again. "Stacy, it's Arnaud."

The door tentatively swung open, Stacy's form hidden behind the door. Arnaud slid in through the opening, leaning against the peeling brown wallpaper just inside the door. "I heard from Michael this morning."

"You did?" Stacy's face lit up. "Is he all right?"

"Yes, but the news was not all good."

Stacy sighed, her eyes turning toward the suitcase on her bed. She walked over to it and continued packing the few things she had taken out to shower.

"He for sure won't be on the train at noon. And he wants us to leave as soon as possible. He'll meet us in Lille."

Stacy returned her gaze to him. "Is he in trouble?"

Arnaud was more than a little surprised by her acceptance of this information. "No, I think the trouble has passed. I have a lot to tell you in that regard, but I don't want to get into that right now. Besides, we have a train to catch. Speaking of which, if we're to make the train at nine, we'll have to hurry. It's almost eight-thirty now."

"We have to go back to my apartment."

"We can't risk that. I'll have someone retrieve your things and store them. We can return in a month or so."

"No—today. There are things there that I cannot do without."

"Stacy, it's too dangerous."

"If you don't want to go, you don't have to, but I'm going."

Arnaud sighed heavily and groaned. She wouldn't be changing her mind. She was as stubborn as Michael sometimes. "Okay. Let me make a call; we'll have to take a later train."

"Whatever." She returned to her suitcase, latching the two catches. "Let's go."

******

Arnaud and Stacy sat in a car two blocks away from her apartment. They had been there nearly an hour, and still there was no movement on the road. No one had as much as walked past the building, let alone loitered anywhere nearby. Arnaud could tell Stacy was getting anxious; she was not one for patience. They would wait another ten minutes, although even that assured him of nothing. They could be in any of the buildings facing hers or actually in the same building. They had plenty of time to set up a stakeout. The only question was whether they were willing to expend so much effort. Arnaud was unsure of that. He knew they would spare nothing to get Michael, but they knew he would not return there, and the chances of Stacy returning were slim. Michael hoped that that was what they would think. In actuality, the chances were 100 percent, For here they sat, waiting for an opportune moment.

It was time. Arnaud started the car and pulled around the block. They would go in through the rear. Her apartment was the second building in; thus they would have to cross only two sets of fences to get there. He hoped the owner was not home. The police would definitely add an unwanted presence. Although it would deter any hostility from a stakeout, it would involve too much time and the answering of too many questions for which they did not have suitable answers.

Stacy went first. The fence was only four feet high, and she easily swung over after toeing a link about halfway up. She dashed across the yard and went over the second just as simply. Arnaud followed directly behind her. Michael had always left the back door open, just in case of emergencies. He hoped it still remained that way. Sure enough, Stacy was pulling open the door just as he appeared on the porch.

"What do you need?" he asked.

"Stay here; I'll get it." Stacy went in the house further. Arnaud waited in the kitchen, counting away the minutes. He could hear her movements in the floors above. He went to the front door and peered out the small window. There was still no movement on the street. If anyone was watching the place, he or she would have seen Stacy by now.

Stacy came down the stairs carrying a box. "Arnaud, in the closet there's a three-ring notebook marked 'History Notes.' Will you grab it?"

"Sure." Arnaud opened the closet. In the back corner was a pile of notebooks. He rummaged through them. There was a red one labeled 'Literature,' a black one with 'French' written on the cover in an ornate script, another red one with no title, and finally a blue one with the words 'History Notes' scrawled across it in black letters. He took it and followed Stacy into the kitchen. "Okay, you ready?"

"I'll go first. You hand me the box. Then you go over the next fence, and I'll hand you the box." They rushed out, going over the fences and back into the car. Arnaud pulled away from the curb, and they were gone. Arnaud took them through a maze of back roads, continually checking his mirrors to ensure they weren't being followed. When he reached Rue de Maubeuge and Rue de Bellfond, he stopped the car and pulled up on the sidewalk to park. The front entrance to the Gare du Nord was to the north, only five or six blocks away.

"Okay, we wait here until ten forty-five. I don't want to be on the train until five to eleven."

"Sure. Sounds good."

"So what was so important that you needed to risk getting it?"

"First tell me about Michael and the last couple of days."

Chapter 26

Without contacts to depend upon, Michael had to work from what he already knew about Josephine's habits. This was, unfortunately, next to nothing. He had already tried the phone number she had given him for the last contact. It was disconnected. Sitting outside the nightclub held no better possibilities. She might be there later in the evening, but that would be too late. The last hope he had was to try to make her look for him. He knew they would be searching for both him and Stacy. Yet he did not want any stray members of the organization, which seemed to grow by the minute, to find him. It had to be Josephine. He decided the club would offer the best results. If he simply asked for her, she might come looking.

There was little movement on the street when Michael arrived at the club's entrance. An elderly couple was buying fruit at a stand on the next block. Two children, one of them nearly naked despite the cool temperature, were pestering a dog, who seemed to mind no more than if they had been petting it. Michael knocked on the blue door twice. After a minute and no response, he knocked again. There was a chance that no one was within. It was barely after ten in the morning. The door opened, revealing a sliver of darkness.

"Oui." The voice was feminine.

"Bonjour," Michael said, trying to do his best imitation of a tourist. "Je m'appelle Michael." He stumbled over the simple French. "Je … uh … chercher …"

"You American?"

"Yeah. You speak English?"

The door opened further. Still only a portion of the woman's face was visible. "Right."

"I'm looking for Josephine."

"Who?"

"Josephine. She is about this tall." Michael lifted his hand up to his chin. "She has red hair—long, straight. And green eyes." Michael smiled.

"Right. Josephine. She's not here. She's usually around most nights, though."

"She told me to meet her here at ten thirty. I'm a little early." He looked down at his watch.

"She's not here." The door slammed shut. Michael didn't know if it had done him any good, but it was a start. The next thing would be to call the place. He wrote down the number listed on a brass plate beside the door. The phone booth was only a block away and was within sight of the club. He tried the number and went through the same routine except in perfect French. The same woman answered the phone as had been at the door. He doubted she recognized his voice, thanks to the change in accent. *Let them think there is more than one person looking for her there.* The conversation ended on the same note as the last: "Elle n'est pas ici."

All he could do was wait and hope someone would contact her. Less than five minutes after the phone conversation, a woman exited the club. Michael couldn't be certain, but he thought it was the woman from the door. She hesitated outside the entrance, glancing down the street in both directions. Then she headed directly for him. Michael picked up the phone and decided that a German would be looking for Josephine as well. Quickly, he dialed the number. This time, just as the woman was passing by the booth, he got the answer he wanted. Someone had gone to get her. He had the break he needed.

Michael waited until the woman was two blocks away before exiting the booth. He had never trailed anyone before and hoped the woman wasn't expecting anyone. She would spot him in a second if she thought to check for tails. He followed her to the metro, moving within a car's length of her on the platform. A train glided to a stop with whistling brakes, and they both got on. The buzzer sounded, and the doors slammed shut.

The woman led him to a charcuterie. She entered and soon disappeared into the back, beyond the counters of fresh meat. It seemed that many of these small shops were more than their outward appearances implied. Michael wondered how many of these shops were indeed fronts for less-than-legal activities. It was not long before the woman reappeared. Yet Josephine was nowhere in sight. He moved to follow her but could not decide whether to continue or wait outside the butcher shop. The woman disappeared into the metro system, and his decision was made. He would have to wait there. If Josephine did not appear within the hour, he would inquire for her within.

While he waited, Michael went to a nearby phone booth. Outside of Arnaud and Stacy, there was only one other person in Paris he could trust. It was that man he called.

"Allo," a sleepy voice answered, yawning into the receiver.

"Mohammed?"

"Oui?"

"It's Michael."

"Michael, comment çava?"

"Could be better."

"What's wrong?"

"It's too complicated to discuss. Can you do me a favor?"

"Sure; I'm free."

Michael gave him the address to Alain's shop and told him to follow Alain wherever he went. He also gave him a phone number where he could be reached after four o'clock. Mohammed agreed without a question.

Michael exited the booth and returned to his bench across from the butcher shop. As he passed the shop, he glanced up to the windows above. There, standing just within sight, was Josephine. She was loading a gun with a magazine and then placing it in her coat pocket. So she had received the news. He wondered whether she was going to try to meet him or if she was running. He considered the answer obvious after a moment's thought. She wouldn't run. Her act may have portrayed her as an innocent, but Michael knew she was a professional. She would kill for her boss and not think twice. Michael knew the type; it had once described him.

Josephine exited the shop and headed his way. Michael thought about his next move. It might be unwise to do anything so close to the shop, yet he didn't want to risk having to follow her into the metro. For the moment, surprise was his. He took another step into the alley and waited. She moved by the opening without a glance in his direction. Two strides and he had her.

"Bonjour, Josephine," he whispered in her ear while taking the gun from her pocket. Once further in the alley, he threw her to the ground against the wall. "You know I won't hesitate to kill you, so don't make a sound.

"Qu'est que tu veux?" She spat the words out.

"That, my dear, was a sound, but I'll forgive it. Now, I only need to know one thing. I don't want to hear an 'I don't know' either. I won't ask who your boss is, because I know you won't say. All I want to know is if Alain is behind all this."

"Who's Alain?"

"Don't be stupid. Just answer the question."

"So I know who he is. You'll kill me, or they'll kill me if I answer. I don't know which I prefer."

"I take it that's a yes. I don't think anyone would kill you for saying no."

"Don't be so sure. You're not as bright as I thought."

"Too bad. Not that it matters, since you're dead." He fired two rounds in succession, the second making her already limp body jump. "That's for Stacy." He tossed the gun at her and ran from the alley, shoving his way through three men who had stopped to see what had caused the noise.

* * * * * *

Arnaud and Stacy ended up on the TGV, heading toward Lille at 180 miles an hour with nothing more than two suitcases and the box from Stacy's apartment. Arnaud had spent the time in the car telling Stacy what had occurred during the last three days—at least as much as he knew. He had left out only one detail. As far as he was concerned, Michael needed to tell her that it was his disobeying of orders that had caused the attack on her. On the train, he had relayed to her the unsuccessful hit as well.

"But who shot the driver then?" Stacy asked.

"I don't know. Michael rigged the false bomb. He had no reason for a rifle, and the driver was an operative of the blackmailers."

"It doesn't say that here." Stacy passed him a copy of the *Herald-Tribune*, which had an article describing the assassination attempt.

Arnaud read through the article and shrugged. "They do not know such things. It was not public information. It will perhaps never be known."

"Besides, Michael would never have missed an easy target like that."

Arnaud shook his head. "It is not good to be too proud of one's ability to kill."

"It is simply a fact," Stacy said nonchalantly.

"I've never approved of professions that thrive on the kill."

"You've never killed a man?" Stacy asked.

Arnaud nodded. "I have deemed it necessary. Yes. But I do not thrive off it as Michael does."

"I don't think he thrived off it. I don't think he ever put much thought into it—which, I suppose, is worse in some respects. Yet once it got to him, he couldn't continue. You know, he once told me, about two months ago, that he didn't know whether he could kill anyone even in self-defense anymore."

"That sounds like a man trying to convince himself of a lie. Or trying to convince you he has truly changed."

"Why do you say that?"

"Given the right circumstances, Michael would kill again. Don't get me wrong; I do not judge him on that. I am the same."

"I don't know. There's something inside him that has changed."

"He would kill to protect you. He almost did."

"But he didn't. That's just it. He left me unprotected in order to escape having to kill again. His promise to me means more than that to him." Stacy wondered how much she was saying was true. She felt as though she should be protecting Michael, but a part of her said this was all a lie to cover up something bigger.

Arnaud couldn't argue with that. "Yes, perhaps you're right. I only mean to protect you. He's not innocent."

"I don't ask him to be. I couldn't. If he killed to protect me, I would not hate him for it. How could I? Yet, even knowing this, he didn't break our promise."

"Someone did."

"But Michael didn't know about it."

"We don't know that."

"Is there something you're not telling me?"

Yes, but it has nothing to do with this, Arnaud thought. "No, not at all," he lied. "I believe you, and I believe in Michael, but there is something more than just you two going on here."

"What do you mean?"

"The network collapsing, the driver getting shot, Michael staying in Paris when he knows he should get out. And Alain heading for Lille. He never leaves Paris."

"What?"

"Alain is on this train. I saw him board just before us."

"Why is he going to Lille? And why didn't you mention that when you saw him?"

"The first is a question I would like answered. The second—I didn't want you to worry. I don't think he's personally a threat."

For the first time, Stacy wondered what else Arnaud knew that he hadn't told her. "Where is he now?"

"I don't know, but I have a feeling we'll be seeing him in Lille."

Chapter 27

Michael exited the metro at the Gare du Nord. The heavy afternoon traffic swarmed around him as he followed the blue and white signs that led him to the Grandes Lignes. His journey to Lille would begin there. A last left took him into the main platform of the Gare du Nord. Directly in front of him was a huge board that listed the departure times of the all the trains leaving within the next few hours. After a listing of three or four of the main stops was the platform number. Michael looked up to the board and found his train—Paris-Nord à St. Quentin à Aulnoye à Lille. It was scheduled to leave in forty minutes. He still had twenty minutes to wait before the platform would even be listed.

He needed to stay out of the main area. The last thing he wanted to do was be spotted at this moment, when he was finally leaving the city. He went back the way he had come and entered the tourist office. The office was not crowded. In fact, only two or three groups of students waited in line, while another five or six people browsed through the information. Only a month or so before, the office would have been packed with students and other tourists. And in a couple more, it would be empty. The tourist season had officially ended September 1, but there were still students making their way home until October. Those French who had not been able to vacation in August also used September as their getaway month.

The clock above the Eurail map read four fifteen. There would be another minute before the train's platform number was listed. He exited the office with a collection of brochures he had randomly selected from those at hand. The board rattled as the trains switched positions. He followed his train's listing as each section flipped into place. Platform 18. He stood directly in front of his train. Michael took his ticket from his backpack and stamped it at the orange *composter.* He then moved along the platform until he arrived at the first nonsmoking first-class car. There he walked up the steps into the train. His best bet was to find a compartment with two or three people already in it. The third compartment was perfect. An old lady with graying hair and a flowered dress sat next to the window. Opposite her was a young couple; the man was already dozing against the window. Michael checked the reservation listing. No one had either of the seats beside the old lady.

Michael slid the door open and slung his backpack onto the overheard shelf. He relaxed in the seat next to the door. Across from him was a little girl, who, noticing him looking at her, smiled first at him and then, when he returned the smile, at her mother. Michael looked down at his watch. They would be in Aulnoye in two hours. From there it was another hour to Lille. Alain had reservations on the TGV. If everything went to plan, he would arrive only minutes before Alain. It didn't matter though. He wasn't planning on confronting him at the station or following him. That would have to wait. He needed to know how much Arnaud knew first.

The train slid away from the station, slowly picking up speed as it passed by central Paris and then the outskirts, finally moving into the far suburbs. Open fields and rolling hills soon replaced the regular gray brick of the city. Red tiled roofs spotted the countryside, and churches rose up out of the valleys and hilltops. Michael closed his eyes and relaxed. He needed to focus on his intended plan of action.

The train pulled into the station at Aulnoye exactly on time. The one thing that was always true of the trains in Europe was that they were punctual. Michael could not remember the last time he was on a train, or waiting for one, that was late. He stepped down from his car onto the concrete platform. Normally he would change trains here, but he had lucked out with a train going straight through. The next portion of his journey would take him to Lille. The train was scheduled to leave at 6:46. He walked down the stairs, glancing at the board listing the regular trains that stopped in Aulnoye. He would not have the luxury of a compartment; that section of the train was not scheduled to continue on. Yet he was no longer worried about being spotted. They could not cover every inch of France.

"Hello, Michael." Michael spun around, his hand reaching inside his jacket. "It's only me—Victor." The man stepped from the shadows. His hair had lightened and receded from his forehead. Glasses were also another change. Michael wondered if he wore them out of necessity or just for an alteration in appearance.

"Hello, Caes …" Michael stopped himself. Even here one needed to be overly cautious. "Victor." The two men embraced.

"It's been a long time."

"Yes. You haven't changed much. Other than putting on a little muscle, I see."

"Nor have you, besides putting on a little weight yourself." Michael patted Victor's stomach.

"Well, you know. The wife's a good cook, and I no longer run around looking for trouble."

"But it found you anyway."

"That it did. I was lucky though. The others weren't."

"Dead? All of them?"

"According to Arnaud. He told me to go home."

"I thought you were going anyway."

"I was. I didn't know exactly when until Arnaud called."

Michael glanced down at his watch. It was almost a quarter to seven. "Walk with me."

"You heading to Lille?"

"Ycah, want to join mc? I'm going to takc carc of a littlc businc3s."

"No, I'm out of the game now. I'm sure you can handle it alone."

"I don't know. It doesn't look good. If I don't make it, I would like to tell you something to tell Arnaud."

"Sure."

"Just tell him it was Alain."

"Alain's behind this?"

"There's no doubt. He's the only one with the contacts—except for Arnaud. And I ruled that possibility out before considering it."

"But why? What did he have to gain?"

"I don't know. Hopefully, he'll tell me before I kill him."

"If you're right, there's more to him than we thought."

"I suspected as much years ago."

"You'd better be careful with him."

"He's not the one I'm worried about."

"There are others?"

The conductor's whistle sounded.

"Yes. Arnaud will know everything." Michael jumped aboard the train and waved through the closing doors. "Adieu, Caesar."

"Adieu, Michael." Victor returned the wave and whispered, "Bonne Chance."

Chapter 28

Arnaud waited inside the café, where he could keep the entire train station in view. The fountains in front of the station were spraying water nearly into the street. Two unsuspecting women were suddenly drenched as the wind shifted direction for an instant. It had been cold and windy for two days; the rains had come as well. Only a week prior it had been twenty degrees Celsius; now the listing above the Transpole office read ten degrees. It also showed a time of 1:36. Alain was late. However, that did not bother Arnaud as much as Alain pretending that he was not yet in Lille. Why would he want to cover up the fact that he had arrived the day before?

"Speak of the devil and he appears," Arnaud whispered to himself. Alain came out of the Gare and walked in his direction, carefully avoiding the fountains. He was smiling and tossing a small package back and forth between his hands. Arnaud thought he had never seen Alain look so happy—certainly not in the last couple months—although it was true he hardly ever saw the man. *Business must be good.*

Arnaud rose and greeted Alain as he entered the café. "Bonjour. Le voyage se passe bien?" Arnaud didn't actually think that he could trick Alain into a slipup by asking how his trip was, but it was worth a try.

"The TGV is certainly a luxury compared to how we used to have to travel to Lille. A three-hour trip into less than an hour isn't bad."

"Monsieur?" A waiter stood before them.

"Ah, oui, let's see." Alain looked at the menu, shaking his head a couple times. "Okay, moules et frites. Et un Heineken."

"Merci." The waiter walked away writing the order down on his pad.

"I haven't had a good clam-and-fries meal in months. What are you having?" The smile still played prominently on his face.

"Nothing. Je n'ai pas faim."

"I can tell you're all business. What can I do for you?"

"Do you know where Michael is?" He really wanted to ask why Alain felt it necessary to hide the truth about his arrival, but Arnaud wasn't ready to get into that.

"No. I saw him a day or two ago. He said he was leaving Paris. I presumed with Stacy, but you said she's with you." If Alain was hiding anything, he was certainly casual about it.

"Yes, she's with me. Michael is in Lille though."

Alain's smile disappeared, and he sat back in his chair. "He is?"

"Oui, but I do not know where." Arnaud suddenly became cautious. The truth was that he didn't know, but at that point he would not have said had he known. "I don't know what's going on, but he's become very secretive lately." Arnaud began to wonder whether he could trust Alain or Michael. He doubted whether either would do anything to him, but they were at odds and refused to admit it.

"Would you like me to try to find him? I don't know many people here, but they might bring something up."

"Sure. Just let him know Stacy's trying to find him. Don't, under any circumstances, let on that she's in Lille as well. In fact, imply she's in London or something. We do not need the others getting involved."

"You don't trust him."

"I don't trust your sources to keep quiet."

"I won't even mention her name. If I find him, I will talk to him personally."

"I appreciate that."

"However, I do know that they are not in as much danger as we suspected. Domino has not ordered any sort of hit on either of them."

"But then who …" He stopped the question midway. If Alain

knew the answer, he wouldn't tell. It would betray his involvement. The truth was that either Alain was lying or Michael had some answering to do. Even Lawrence had been caught up in this mess. If Cruthers's men weren't looking for Michael, who was?

"Shais pas," Alain answered, despite the aborted question. It was the only answer he could have given. He ate in silence while Arnaud drank his tea. They were each hiding secrets the other needed to know, yet neither felt hostile toward the other. It was the nature of the business. As they said in the spy game, everyone was on a need-to-know basis. No one had good friends, and no one took unnecessary risks. Even in the European world of socialist democracies, capitalism was alive and well. The private sector had latched onto its ideals. The huge EuroLille complex that stood between the Gare Lille Flanders and the new Gare Lille Europe was a tribute to that. Money was power in all aspects of life—even the illegal one; especially so, perhaps.

They sat in silence once the waiter brought Alain his food.

"I need to go over to my office by Place République. Want to walk over there with me?" Alain finally said after finishing his meal and slipping cash under the glass.

"Yes, I can stop by the UGC theatre."

"You're going to a movie?"

"Sure. *Pulp Fiction*." Arnaud smiled. He loved the Quentin Tarantino film, which had become an American classic in France.

They walked out of the café, crossing Rue Faidhube, and continued west toward the Cathedral St. Maurice. "Aren't there other things that need to be taken care of?"

"Not until I find Michael; besides, it's for Stacy. She's been kind of down—for obvious reasons." Alain nodded. "I think she'll enjoy it."

"She'd probably enjoy it more in English."

"That's true. Perhaps the Gaumont has it in English."

"Sounds like a plan."

"Thank you. I'm sure Stacy will appreciate it."

"De rien."

******

Michael had watched the entire conversation from his seat at the Place de la Gare. The fountains had continually sprayed him as well as the woman that Arnaud had approached. Michael had donned a long black wig and a motorcycle jacket to go with his leather pants. Dark sunglasses, despite the cloudy sky, covered his prying eyes. He wished he could have heard them as well, but his disguise would work only at a distance with these two.

He followed their movement across the road and past the cathedral. Another block and they were on Rue de Béthune, where Arnaud quickly ducked into the theatre to buy his tickets. Michael risked moving into the lobby with him, overhearing Arnaud buying two tickets for the 6:50 showing. He would have wondered if the other ticket was for Alain or Stacy had the sign out front had not proclaimed the film to be in the *version originale*.

If he were to confront either man, he needed to do it soon. The meeting with his team was in another hour. It would take him thirty to forty minutes by metro to get out to Lambersart. He almost considered returning at seven to meet Arnaud and Stacy at the movie. However, he was not ready to see Stacy yet. He needed to clear up who was involved before talking to her. Besides, he couldn't even imply an accusation toward Arnaud with her around. She would never forgive him if it were untrue. He was sure Alain was running the show, but he still didn't know how much Arnaud knew. If Stacy trusted him, Michael tended to think Arnaud was safe, but all he knew for certain was that Arnaud wouldn't harm Stacy.

He knew that the end was near for him in this world. He needed to truly disappear; otherwise, he would not last much longer. The secret to making it as far as he had was selfishness. He could not afford to care about anyone else and continue. It had already forced him to bend his luck. They had let him get away once; he could not chance it happening again. Still, that's exactly what he was doing. He should show up at the movie and tell Stacy he was leaving, and it would be her decision as to whether she wanted to go with him and be gone forever. But he couldn't do that. Revenge was still on his mind.

* * * * * *

Michael waited until they separated, Alain going north along Boulevard de la Liberté and Arnaud to the east, back into the center of Lille. He would contact Alain, who would be the easier of the two to find, later. Arnaud walked through the small park along the Boulevard and onto the Place de Béthune. Michael wondered whether he should let him lead and find Stacy as well, or if it would be better to stop him here. Arnaud entered the McDonald's on the north side of the square. It was just after noon, and the restaurant was a mass of slowly moving people. It would be more than a half hour before Arnaud got through the line. Michael instantly regretted not following Alain. There was little he could do now but wait. Taking a seat in the café opposite the McDonald's, he kept watch on the entrance.

"Monsieur?" A waiter appeared.

"Le plat du jour, s'il vous plaît." He might as well eat as long as he was waiting.

"Oui, monsieur. Et comme boisson?"

"Du thé." The air was cool, and the tea would do him some good in warming his insides. Autumn had suddenly shifted into winter. The rain had stopped earlier in the morning, but it looked as if it could begin again at any moment. He was one of the few to risk the outdoor tables on such a day. The waiter brought a cup and a pot of steaming water. Michael poured the water over the tea bag and absently stirred the mixture.

As sure as he was about Alain's departure from the group, he began to doubt again. Victor had been right in questioning how it would profit Alain to do anything so dramatic as collapsing the network. He profited as much from their information as any of them. Besides, they often sent business to him. There was no reasoning behind it. And deliberately sending someone after Stacy—that wasn't like Alain at all. But Victor had also suggested there was more to

Alain than one suspected. As Alain was always on the fringe, it was possible he was doing some dealing behind a second personage, as Michael had long suspected. Even then, how was he to profit from this mess?

"Monsieur." The waiter placed a plate in front of Michael—the *plat du jour*: *moules et frites*. Michael did not particularly enjoy clams, but he ate them regardless. The fries were nearly worth the cost of the meal anyway. He would have to remember this place. He glanced over his shoulder. He could see Arnaud moving through the line, coming toward the entrance. Michael reached into his pocket for money just in case Arnaud had gotten his meal to go. But Arnaud headed to his left and up the stairs. Michael placed some euros on the table and finished his meal.

What role did Arnaud play in all this? Perhaps he had been too quick to dismiss the possibilities. He had known Alain for almost ten years; Arnaud only a little over that. Yet he couldn't find any motive for Arnaud either. They were in relatively safe positions that would allow freedom of movement without worry about potential threats. This was really just the opposite position of the one he himself was in. There had to be another player involved. Perhaps this man who had blackmailed him had more to do with all this than he originally thought. It would not be the first time a terrorist group spent months setting up one hit. He needed to find out who that man was important to. That would lead him back to this new group and Josephine's boss.

Arnaud exited the McDonald's just as Michael was pouring the last of the water into his cup. Michael rose from the chair and followed him. Arnaud continued along Rue de Béthune past the cinemas and another one of Lille's American by-products, the Disney Store. Michael wondered how well its operations were doing compared to EuroDisney, which had had a very difficult start on the continent. At the end of the Rue du Sec-Arembault, Arnaud headed for the cathedral doors. *Where is he going?* Michael thought.

The interior of the church was dim, and the combination of candlelight and sparse sunlight shining through stained-glass windows gave the nave an ancient look that went beyond its stone pillars and wooden chairs surrounding the altar. Arnaud was picking out a candle and placing it among the others; soon he was carefully lighting it with one of the others. Michael followed in behind him. This was as good a place as any to talk. He took a candle from the box and went to kneel beside Arnaud.

"You must put two euros in the box for one that size," Arnaud informed him without looking up.

Michael smiled. He should have known that he couldn't follow Arnaud without being detected.

"Bonjour, Arnaud." Instead of paying for the candle, Michael replaced it in the box.

Arnaud shook his head. "It's not worth two euros to make a prayer for someone?"

"It's not worth one penny if you don't believe." Michael remembered a time when he did believe and considered that perhaps one day his faith would return to him.

"I always thought you were a religious man." Arnaud rested a hand on Michael's shoulder.

"I have an interest in religion. My pursuit of it is purely academic."

"I see." Arnaud reflected on that a moment before continuing. "Am I to assume you have completed your business in Paris?"

Michael nodded. "As far as I am willing to go at this time."

"Stacy is anxious to see you."

"As I am to see her. But that must still wait." Michael looked Arnaud in the eyes. "Arnaud … How well do you know Alain?"

"Not well enough, I think."

"Do you think he's behind this as well?" Michael asked.

Arnaud smiled. "It is either him or you."

"Or you."

Arnaud's smile increased, and he turned to Michael. "Yes, I see your point. It is not me. And you? Where do you fit into it all?"

"Exactly where you do—on the wrong end." They sat kneeling next to each other in silence, Arnaud with his prayers and Michael without the answers he needed. The more he wanted to end it all, the more complex it became. "Why is Alain in Lille?"

Arnaud sighed. "That is a question he would not answer for me."

"When did you and Stacy arrive?"

"On the same train as Alain."

Michael studied Arnaud's face. The man loved to play games. "You assume I knew which train he took?"

"I do not assume; I know you."

"Why not earlier?"

Arnaud looked down at his hands. "Stacy retrieved some things from the apartment."

"You went back there?"

Arnaud paused. "Yes. I know it wasn't wise. She insisted."

Michael took a deep breath. He didn't like this. "What did she need so badly?"

Arnaud shook his head. "Some history notes."

"History notes?"

"Do not ask." Arnaud raised a finger toward Michael. "I do not know their significance."

"You know there's one person we've forgotten about in all this."

"Who's that?"

"Stacy." Michael had a hard time believing there was even the smallest of possibilities of this, but he also had a difficult time removing it from his thoughts.

Chapter 29

The phone rang once, and then twice, and it then went dead. Alain glanced over at the man who sat opposite him. The man's hair was dark black—almost blue in the fluorescent lights of the office. His eyes were hidden behind reflective sunglasses. They had been discussing the plans for the next two days. The phone sounded again—once, twice—and again went dead.

"Will you please excuse me?" Alain gestured toward the door.

The man rose from his chair and stared at Alain and then the phone. "I will be in the theatre."

The phone rang a third time just as the door swung shut. This time Alain waited for one, two, three rings and picked it up. "Bonjour, Michael."

"You're alone?"

"Of course."

"How long have you been in Lille?"

Alain considered the question. He had lied to Arnaud about his arrival, but Michael knew things that he shouldn't. If it was a trick question, a great amount could be lost. "Yesterday. Late afternoon." The truth in this case was a much better solution. He could always explain why he had lied to Arnaud.

"Good. Have you any news about Arnaud and Stacy?"

"No. I know they left Paris. I thought you were with them."

"I had to make sure someone wasn't around anymore. She caused me and Stacy more harm than you can imagine." Alain immediately thought of Josephine. It was quite a shame losing her. She had done some wonderful things for them, not to mention what she had done for him personally. “Do you think you will find them?”

“I don’t know many people here.”

“More than I do.”

“Yes, that might be true. I will try. Where can I contact you?”

“I’ll get back to you.”

Alain could only think of one way to get Michael to come to him, even if Michael didn’t realize that’s what he would be doing. “I have some news for you.”

“Yes?”

“You aren’t going to like it.” Alain smiled. The phone was a wonderful invention. Using it, one could easily hide the truth from being revealed. “Your extortionist is in town.”

“What?”

“Oui. Nazeem is giving a speech here. They are planning the abduction. Tomorrow night.”

“Where?”

“Place de Génèral De Gaulle.”

“Do you know any specifics?”

“No. I just heard they were in town and that something would go down that night. They are very elusive, these people. I would be careful with them.” Alain had to keep from chuckling. He loved to give himself compliments.

“I need to find Stacy.”

“I’ll do my best. Call tomorrow morning.”

“Okay, salut.”

“Salut, Michael, bonne chance.”

******

Alain had for years lived by a rule that had never failed him: whenever you need something done—not just anything but something more important than life itself—do it yourself. This, he told himself, was an exception. He had neither the time nor the energy to find Michael and eliminate him. There were too many objectives that required his presence. However, there was one person who could devote all her time to finding him. Stacy was his only chance. He knew Michael would again try to stop the kidnapping. The only question was how. Stacy would conveniently provide him with that.

There was the matter of finding Arnaud and Stacy. They would have used her normal channels to secure a safe house. That was traceable. Michael was on his own, not trusting anyone—not even Stacy, it seemed. Thus Alain turned to Stacy's sources in Lille. They would provide him with the address, and she would provide him with Michael. Fréderique Deleau owned a sex shop not far from the train station. If Stacy and Arnaud had gone to anyone, it would be him. Alain stood outside wondering what his best approach was. He was waiting for two of his men who could provide for necessary treatments in the case of unwilling informants.

To question politely and reveal his identity was one way of dealing with the situation, and depending on what Stacy had told this Fréderique, it might work. However, that also meant risking Stacy finding out that someone was searching for her. That someone would then be identified as Alain. That could send both Stacy and Arnaud deeper under cover. As it was, they were probably in an apartment that remained vacant and ready for use in these "emergency" situations.

Alain spied his two associates coming up the street. They would go in first. He could not risk being seen.

"Salut, qu'est-ce que tu veux?" the first man asked. He towered over Alain's short frame and was almost as wide as Alain was tall. The second man looked small in comparison, yet he too was both taller and wider than Alain.

"J'ai besoin d'information."

"De qui?"

"Il y a un homme, ici." Alain pointed to the shop where they could find Fréderique. "Il s'appelle Fréderique Deleau."

"Quel information?"

"Je cherche cette femme." Alain handed him a photograph of Stacy. "Elle s'appelle Stacy, eh, Stacy …" He realized he had never gotten her last name. All these months and never once had her last name been spoken around him. "Je ne sais pas son nom de famille."

And come to think of it, Arnaud was also nameless. That was a definite mistake he would not make again.

"Cava. Il peut mourir ou pas?" The question of leaving the man alive or making sure he did not survive was not a difficult one. Alain had no qualms about killing Fréderique. Stacy would not find out until it was too late. Even if she did, a few rumors would place Michael at the scene and would give her more desire to find him.

"N'importe." He really didn't care one way or the other.

The two men crossed the street and entered the shop. Alain stayed only for a moment. They would contact him with the address when they were through. Other worries needed his attention, such as who was expendable enough to put on stage. If the kidnapping went awry, they would be the first to go.

Chapter 30

Michael hung up the phone. How had Alain known that it was not an attempt on the man's life? He had never told him. Once again Alain seemed to know more than he admitted to. There was a connection here that Michael was not making. Alain had to fit in somewhere, and the only place Michael could think of was the top. Alain had to be orchestrating the entire event. Still, he needed some proof of that before he condemned a man who had been so loyal to him over the years. Trust was not purchased overnight, and neither should it be tossed aside so lightly.

Michael picked up the phone and then returned it to the cradle. He needed help, but he wasn't sure whom he could trust at this point. Any one of the people who were after him could have hired those he would call. They were all professionals, and despite any good relations with Michael, they would follow through on a contract hit without hesitation. He needed distractions, and he needed at least two people with enough guts to get arrested and know how to get out of it. So he decided to turn to two who were retired. Neither had been out of the game for long, so perhaps they would be anxious to help out. Besides, he knew they would love the chance to get back at someone that tried to blackmail a fellow assassin. That just wasn't done.

The call was picked up on the first ring. "Markus?"

"Yes. Who is this?"

"Michael."

"Ah, you are in trouble, my friend." Markus chuckled.

Michael wasn't sure if this was a good thing or not. "You've heard something?"

"Yes. No worries, though. I wouldn't take the job. Retired, you know?"

"I heard. I'm trying to get there myself. Want to help?"

"Normally I would tell you the same I told them, but I wouldn't mind a little action if it means helping out an old friend."

"Old friend? Markus, I wouldn't exactly go that far." Michael was beginning to get a little suspicious.

"Okay, Michael, I don't like that they used someone against you to do this. It's not acceptable. We may not be old friends, but we've always been professional with each other. I will help. Besides, I could use a little extra cash."

"Good. And yes, you will be paid. I don't have much cash right now, but you'll get a good sum."

"I trust you. We understand each other perfectly."

"Great. Lille, tomorrow morning. The boulangerie near the train station." Michael hung up the phone and sat back in his chair. He still wasn't 100 percent sure that he could trust Markus, but he would have to take him at his word.

Antonio hadn't heard the news and obviously had done a better job than Michael of completely retiring. However, he was just as eager to help for the same reasons. Michael had heard the phrase "honor among thieves" many times before, but he had lived according to "honor among assassins." They might not all have been good people, but most believed in a code of conduct.

******

Alain stepped into the apartment. The walls were bare of any photos or paintings. The only furniture was a brown leather couch, which had numerous rips along each cushion, and a small gray card table with four chairs situated around it. He closed the door and went farther into the room. He glanced into the bedroom. There was only a single queen-size bed. A gray-and-white comforter lay strewn across the mattress, revealing no sheets or pillows. The bath was next to the kitchen. It too was bare. A bottle of shampoo, two toothbrushes, and a tube of toothpaste were the only evidence of habitation. He went to the refrigerator, which was as empty as the rest of the apartment. A single open can of Coke Zero sat in the middle of the wire shelf. He took the can and drank from it. The carbonation had been lost, and he spat the drink into the sink, pouring the rest of the can there as well.

He hoped they would return soon. Only three hours remained before his next engagement. If all went well here, there would be little need to make that appointment. Otherwise, he would have to make sure Michael understood the gravity of the situation. Alain sat on the leather couch. He sank into the spongy cushions. A key, inserted into the lock, sounded at the door. Alain stayed seated. The lock turned and the door swung open. "And then what did he say?" Stacy asked.

Arnaud didn't answer. Instead he stared into the apartment and then nodded toward the interior. Stacy turned, and the plastic Match grocery bags pushed the door open further. Alain smiled and waved to them. "I hope you're going to get new furniture."

"What are you doing here?" Stacy asked, casually bringing the bags into the kitchen. Arnaud followed her in. He, unlike her, kept his gaze on Alain. Since talking with Michael, he trusted neither him nor Alain any more.

"I thought you might like to know I spoke with Michael. He is in Lille just as you suspected, Arnaud."

"Yes, we know. Arnaud—" Stacy stopped, and Arnaud shook his head slightly—"told me that's what he thought."

"You've talked to him?"

"No, I just told her what I told you."

"Oh, well, you can lie; it doesn't matter. I do want to tell you something of importance. I hope this doesn't offend either of you—especially you, Stacy, considering your relationship with Michael." Alain paused, moving to the card table and sitting at a chair there. "You see, Michael came to me with a request two days ago. For a gun. Not just any gun. It was a sniper rifle made by Fabrique Nationale."

"He has to protect himself. Why should that offend me?" Stacy placed a liter of Evian into the fridge and shut the door.

"First of all, you know that one doesn't use a sniper rifle for protection. Second, have you read today's *Voix du Nord*?" Alain took a paper from his jacket pocket. Stacy and Arnaud looked at each other, shaking their heads. "Here. It's on the front page."

The headline read "Gun Found in Apartment Linked to Chauffeur Slaying." Arnaud scanned the article and then handed it to Stacy. "This seems hard to believe. Are you saying Michael fired those shots?"

"It looks that way. Either that or someone with whom he's involved did."

"Michael wouldn't have missed," Stacy simply stated, tossing the paper back to Alain.

"I'm not saying he did." Alain retorted quickly.

Stacy's eyes narrowed. "What are you saying then?"

Alain shrugged. "That the driver was the target."

"That seems unlikely. What would be the point of that?" Stacy countered.

"To scare him. Killing him would only make him a martyr. They might want to force him to adjust his views."

"You sound like you know who they are."

"No, not at all. Not that I haven't tried to find out. They are very elusive."

"Michael said he never went through with the hit." Stacy turned to Arnaud, half questioning him with the statement.

"Oui, exactement. But this changes things."

"I wouldn't believe it. He gave me his word."

"As he has done before." Alain retorted.

"That isn't fair. He's not like that anymore!" Stacy went to the door and left.

"It seems I was a bit out of line." Alain frowned, still looking at the closed door. He did not trust himself to look at Arnaud.

"No, it was something she must consider."

"So where does this leave us now?"

"Do you know where Michael is?" Arnaud wanted to talk to him alone again anyway. He was still not sure if he could implicate Michael solely through Alain's testimony. He needed to find out why each of these two men was playing Arnaud and Stacy against the other man. Neither was giving him a complete story.

"No, I talked to him on the phone," Alain lied.

"Find him. I'm going to find out what he's doing in Lille."

"Okay, good luck." They left the apartment together.

******

A single man dressed in a black business suit sat outside the apartment. Another had just followed after Stacy. The second waited for Arnaud. Two minutes after Stacy had come out of the house, Arnaud and Alain came as well. The man in the suit dropped in behind them as they reached the far corner. His instructions were to take the shorter man with black hair once he was on his own. He would meet the first man later, hopefully with Arnaud joining him consensually.

Two blocks down the road, Alain took a staircase down into the metro. The tail heard his final "*Salut*" to Arnaud as he made up the distance between them. Before Arnaud had reached the intersection, the man had his hand on Arnaud's shoulder. Whispering into his ear, the man pointed back the way they had come. Arnaud looked at the man and nodded. Without another word, they started off.

******

Almost ten blocks down the same road, the first man was having trouble keeping up with Stacy and not looking conspicuous. He did not want to spook her. He had been assured that she would come without a hassle if he explained the "circumstances" to her. The problem was that he couldn't get near her to explain.

Stacy stopped running just outside the Gaumont Theatre. The lobby was full of people. *Pulp Fiction* was being rereleased that day. She would not be alone in the theatre; that was assured.

The tail reached the cinema just in time to see Stacy walk up the stairs to the interior. He could not confront her in there. He had to follow her in. After buying a ticket, he went up into the theatre. He sat down two rows directly behind her and waited.

* * * * * *

Stacy exited the theatre onto Rue de la Riviérette. Her mind was still on Michael, and the changing action of the movie, especially the last half, had been lost to her completely. She had not paid attention to the film for longer than five minutes at a time without again returning to Michael. She needed to find him in order to ask him to his face what the truth was. Just as he knew her weaknesses, she knew his. The slight smile that attempted to be a frown but more often than not failed was a sure sign that he was lying. Even Arnaud had laughed when she told him this, he had detected this in Michael's visage as well. She could remember him saying, "But I haven't known Michael to lie." Sarcasm was not his strong point, but on this he had was directly on the spot.

The night had grown colder, and an intermittent sprinkle fell. In her haste, she had forgotten an umbrella—a necessary accessory in wintertime Lille. She did not know where she was heading. Who would know where Michael had lost himself? She hoped Arnaud had not worried at her absence. He really was too kind to her. He would have expressed himself in Michael's favor much better than she had. Why had she left so abruptly? It was not like her to run from such accusations. A thought crossed her mind that she would never have imagined possible. In the smallest way, she considered what Alain had said to be true. Arnaud had once suggested the possibility. The gun was far from foolproof though. Who was to say that was the same gun, or even that Michael actually got such a gun from Alain? It was not his normal weapon. He preferred a semiautomatic; the Galil was his favorite. She hated knowing these things. She hated remembering the hours she had spent listening to him talk about guns and ammunition and sight lines. At the time, she had thought them to be nothing but a hobby. Once she knew the truth, she no longer recalled those times fondly. Michael had lied to her before.

She found herself outside a bar. The rain had done little to dampen her clothes, but she was still cold. The warmth from inside, as well as the soft music, drew her in. She could think better after a cup of hot tea. She opened the door and made her way to an empty table near the back. Above her, the burnt wood of the ceiling and the length of worn oak of the bar made it look rustic—almost foreign to the area. She had been in there before, years ago. The place had seemed so much more polished.

"Bonsoir."

"Bonsoir, du thé, s'il vous plaît."

"Oui, merci." The waiter walked away, returning no more than a couple minutes later with a cup and a small pot of water. Stacy put the tea bags directly in the pot and stirred it with a spoon. After the water had turned a deep brown, she poured herself a cup. The tea warmed her insides, instantly soothing frigid muscles. *Now, where to go*, she thought. *Who in Lille would be the most helpful to me.* The name came to her from out of the past. *Toulouse.* He would have heard if someone were looking for a place to stay, no questions asked. Michael had to be staying somewhere.

She waited until finishing her tea before again going out into the cold. The rain had stopped, but the coolness it had brought remained behind. She considered taking the metro to the Gare but decided the few blocks wouldn't kill her. It would eventually get colder. As she walked through the crowded streets and across the Place de General DeGaulle, she thought about nothing. She forced herself to relax and forget about her troubles for the short time before she reached Toulouse's apartment. It lasted for thirty seconds before thoughts of Michael returned, reminding her that he had lied to her before.

Chapter 31

Michael couldn't hide forever, and if he was a part of the upcoming hit team, he would need hardware. Alain vowed not to provide him with such; thus Michael would have to go elsewhere. Stacy would find him if and when that happened. They were now in her city. Her contacts either knew nothing of or were not affected by whatever had happened in Paris. Most of them knew only her, and she meant to keep it that way. It was convenient that she and Arnaud had gotten split up. She would have felt uncomfortable telling him she didn't trust him, even if she really meant anyone, with her contacts. Toulouse had sent her to another friend from the past—one who reminded her a lot of Arnaud in more ways than one.

Stacy got on the metro at Canteleux. From there she transferred at Porte des Postes and exited at the train station. She knew neither Arnaud nor Michael would believe where she headed next. Two blocks from the metro, along a quiet side street, the blue painted glass of Ciné Sex Shop stood out against the otherwise dingy gray brick of its neighboring shops. Stacy entered the shop and began to browse. Two minutes after she arrived, a man came up from the back stairs. His thinning hair was slick against his head. The green button-down shirt he wore hung half out of his torn jeans.

He approached her while she tried to keep her eyes averted from the photos that came at her from every direction. When she did find a line of sight away from the magazines, she found herself staring at the shocked expression of a blow-up doll, its mouth fixed open in a never-ending "Oh"—or perhaps it was a "Wow."

The man stood over her. "You looking for Freddy?"

"Who, me?" Stacy took a step away from him.

"Oui, vous."

"Yes, I am"

"He's gone. Be back by ten. You can stay if you want." The man grinned. The teeth that still occupied his mouth were a grayish yellow. Stacy took another step back.

"No, I'll come back." She turned to leave. "Ten?"

"Oui, c'est ça."

"Au revoir, Merci."

"De rien. A bientôt." The man smiled again.

Stacy left the shop and returned to the metro. She glanced at her watch. It was almost eight thirty. She had just enough time to make the trek out to 4 Cantons and back before Freddy, as the man had so affectionately called him, got back. She would have to remember that when she returned. It was the first time she had heard anyone call him anything other than Fréderique. It was also the first time she had seen that man—and, she hoped, the last.

Stacy relaxed against the stainless-steel pole that lined the door to the train car. Alain had made it quite clear that he had not yet passed judgment on Michael. None of them could. No one but Michael knew the whole story. She knew that Arnaud still had his doubts. He believed Alain knew more than he was telling, and what he himself was telling was but half-truths at best. There was only one way to find out, and that was to confront Michael; however, she knew better than anyone that that didn't necessarily mean she would get the truth. First she needed to find him. Lille was a big city and getting bigger by the minute, but Michael couldn't hide forever. If he was as involved as Alain had implied, Michael would need things to prepare a plan. If not, Michael would not wait long before contacting her. The result either way was going to happen soon. There was a distinct possibility she would just have to wait it out.

Stacy left the shop, bumping into a man on her way out. "Pardon."

"De rien, Stacy," the man replied.

Stacy stopped and looked back at the door, which had now

closed behind the man. Did she know him? She couldn't picture the man's face. He had glasses and a large nose but nothing else specifically noticeable. She debated entering again to find him. She felt uncomfortable about him being so near and her not knowing who he was. She reached for the door again, but it opened before she could touch it. The same man she had bumped into came out.

"Je te connais?" she asked, still not recognizing the face despite getting a better look.

"Non, mais je te connais." How did he know her? Stacy glanced around the street. There were people near enough to be able to hear her scream. "I am asked to give you this." He handed Stacy an envelope. She opened it and read the short message inside.

"Where?" She didn't know who had sent it, but the note implied this was someone she should trust.

"Follow me."

"Where?" She stood where she was.

"Je ne peux pas dire."

"You can't say, or you won't say?"

"Je ne peux pas dire," he repeated.

"Okay. Arnaud's already there?"

"Oui."

"Can we call him and verify this?"

The man looked at his watch. It reminded Stacy of 4 Cantons and then of Fréderique. The first was now out of the question. The second was still a necessity. "Can I be back here by ten?"

"Shais pas." The man shrugged. "On peut téléphone."

"Good. Do you have a cell I can use?"

The man shook his head but said nothing. She felt lucky that despite the influx of cell phones into the system, the French still liked their pay phones. Instead of searching the streets for a booth, Stacy returned to the train station, where there would be plenty. The man took a slip of paper from his wallet and picked up the receiver. Inserting his télécarte, he began to dial. Stacy watched him dial 20. So it was in Lille. The man had stopped and was staring at her.

"What?"

"S'il vous plaît."

"Oh, you don't want me to see." Stacy chuckled. There was more than one way to accomplish such things. She took her compact from her bag and turned around. Through the mirror, she noticed the man still staring at her.

"S'il vous plait," he repeated a little harsher.

"Désolé." She put the compact back.

"Allo. C'est moi. Elle est avec moi. Elle veut parler à Arnaud." The man waited for a moment in silence. "Eh, oui. C'est ça?" Again he paused. "Oui, bien." He tapped Stacy on the shoulder. "Here, talk to him."

"Arnaud?" The receiver was warm against her ear.

"Oui, c'est moi."

"Cava?"

"Oui, cava bien. It's okay; come on in. I think they work for Michael."

"Okay, where are you?"

"I don't know. Look; I have to go. I'll see you soon."

"Okay. Are you sure it's all right?"

"Oui, à bientôt." The phone went dead. The man reached over her shoulder and retrieved his card. Stacy still wasn't sure whether to trust the man or not, but she had a feeling she didn't have much of a choice.

****

Stacy had followed the man as far as Wazemmes. They exited the metro and headed east. The area looked faintly familiar to her. She had been there before, but couldn't remember when. The feeling was strong enough that she knew it had been fairly recently. They crossed a small park where children were playing on a swing set despite the cold weather. The sun had not been out for days. As if this reminded her how cold it was, she wrapped her arms around her body and shivered. It was almost dark. The apartment complex before them was spotted with lights through open windows. The mixture of odors in the air reminded her that she had not eaten in hours. Perhaps they would have something where Arnaud was.

The man led her into the complex and past a soccer field. They entered the complex on the far side of the buildings. The hall was dim and dirty. Paint peeled away from the walls with the slightest rush of air. A pile of paint fragments lay along the hallway. A single bulb hung above them from a wire just outside the elevator. Her guide pushed the button, and the door immediately opened. Stepping inside, Stacy immediately wondered if the stairs wouldn't be better. The strong odor of urine invaded her nose, and she coughed. First holding her breath and then taking a cautious breath through her mouth, Stacy attempted to control her feeling of nausea. They went to the third floor. Stacy exited past the man. He grabbed onto her arm and then relaxed his grasp, almost as if he thought she was going to run. Something odd was happening here. They followed the hall to the last apartment. The door was slightly ajar, and the man simply pushed it open, letting Stacy go through and turning back down the hall once she was inside.

Another man appeared from around the corner of the entrance. "Ah, Stacy, I presume." His accent was English. He took her purse from her shoulder and tossed it to a man behind him, who, in turn, quickly looked through it and placed it on the table in the center of the room.

"Oui."

"It is a pleasure to meet you. Come in and have a seat." Stacy went further into the living room. Arnaud was seated in a chair, his hands behind his back. He smiled slightly at her. The man pointed to another chair next to Arnaud. She moved to sit down, but the man who had searched her purse grabbed her roughly, did a quick frisk, and finally pointed to the chair. She narrowed her eyes at the man but said nothing and sat down.

"What's going on?" she whispered to Arnaud.

"I didn't know."

"What didn't you know?" She glanced nervously at the men on the other side of the room.

"They are not friends of Michael."

Stacy rose from her seat.

"Now, you're not going to give us any trouble, are you?" His English accent suddenly seemed a little off.

"Who are you?" she asked, unsure of her status.

"Let's just say some friends of yours would like you to spend a couple days here with us. It really is comfortable." There it was again. Stacy noticed that while he was good at the accent, it was too forced.

"I want to know what's going on." She moved toward the two men.

"We're not going to have to handcuff you as well, are we?" Stacy turned to Arnaud, who rose slightly and revealed his shackled hands.

"No, of course not." She returned to her seat. It was better to remain free than to argue a point she wouldn't win anyway. There were only two of them. She had her gun down the front of her pants; rarely did men search anywhere near there. It was uncomfortable, but she was glad she had taken the precaution. She wondered if she should dare try to get it out. "Do you mind if I smoke?"

"Non, please make yourself comfortable." The two men moved into the dining area. Stacy reached down to get her purse and then rummaged through it.

"Damn," she whispered.

"Something the matter?" The first man turned toward her.

"No, I just don't have my lighter." The man reached into his pocket and threw a lighter at her.

"Thanks." She returned to her purse, and feigning to reach inside it again, she instead grasped the grip of her gun. It would be all timing. It had been a while, but she knew how to shoot. The small gun carried only six shots, but she felt she could get them both.

She looked over to Arnaud. He was trying to arrange himself into a comfortable position. The handcuffs continually restricted him from sitting back. She decided it was best he didn't know what was going on. The gun felt heavy in her crotch. She took a deep breath and stood up, letting the purse fall away as she pulled the gun. Both men turned toward her. Stacy lifted the weapon, firing before it was level. Two shots exploded into the wood floor, tearing up splinters.

She continued the barrage, firing twice at one man and moving to the next. Two shots rang out, one immediately after the other. The second man doubled over after the first. The final shot caught him in the back of the neck.

Stacy stood frozen. The room had become quiet again. Both men lay motionless on the floor. Her gun was warm. She let it fall to her side in one hand. Only then did she look back at Arnaud. He sat upright, his hands firmly enmeshed into the cushion of the chair. Eyes still wide, he smiled. "Très bien," he uttered softly.

Stacy slowly walked over to the two bodies. They had to have the keys to his handcuffs. She looked back at Arnaud, who had stood. She then looked back at the two bodies. *Why am I here?* She shook off the confusion. *Of course, the keys,* she remembered. She had seen only one dead body before, and certainly none that she herself had murdered. She leaned over and took a deep breath. *Don't deal with this now. Let it be; deal with it later.* She was relieved when she found the keys in the blazer pocket of the first man.

Arnaud rubbed his wrists, trying to get the circulation moving through his hands again. He walked over to the fallen bodies and retrieved the gun from the second man's holster. "Just in case."

Stacy took the gun that had fallen at the feet of the second body. She had been that close to getting shot herself. "Are there any more in the building?"

"Shais pas." Arnaud shook his head. "I only saw the one, but there could be."

They followed the short hall to the door. Stacy peered through the peephole. There were three or four people milling in the hall, all looking at the door. None of them strayed far from their own open doors, ready to make a quick exit from the hall if necessary. Stacy ran into the hall, firing her gun once at the floor. Concrete sprayed up from the divot. It accomplished just what she had hoped. Those in the hall were back in their own apartments, doors slamming shut almost at the same time, before Arnaud exited from the apartment with her.

She led the way through a door marked "Sortie" in white letters against the green plastic. Their feet pounded against the stairs, throwing echoes of footsteps in all directions. After running down three flights of stairs, Stacy took the last three steps with a single leap. She pushed the door open and headed for the entrance. The soccer field was filled with children beneath the lights. They were staring up at the building. All eyes shifted from the building to them. They ran through the center of the field, amid a wave of children backing away. The police would not take long to arrive. If the kids had heard the shots, so had everyone else in the complex.

Stacy tried to remember where the metro was. She went west and recognized the park. Cutting across the gravel pathway, she led Arnaud down another road and within sight of the metro. Sirens sounded, coming immediately closer. As they crossed the street and stepped onto the sidewalk, Stacy saw two police cars coming directly for them. Taking the steps three at a time, they entered the recesses of the metro. Stacy hoped the police had been too busy watching the road to pay them any attention. The horn announcing the leaving train sounded just as they reached the platform. Stacy jumped into the train, pulling Arnaud in behind her. The doors squeezed shut, and the train began to move. Stacy sighed. "Cava?"

"Oui, cava bien." Arnaud laughed. They were all right for now.

Stacy slid down onto a green plastic seat and sighed heavily. The adrenaline had faded, and she could feel the energy drain from her body. It had been a long time since she had fired a gun. The noise still rang in her ears. She had forgotten how much emotion was tied into the act—especially when the result was two motionless men left behind. She needed time to relax, yet there was none. She would find Michael. It was more than coincidence that this happened not long after he and Arnaud had met. And it would not be long before he discovered the recent events.

Arnaud put his hand on Stacy's shoulder. "Cava?" He smiled as he gently massaged her shoulder.

"Oui, cava."

"Merci."

"For what?"

"For getting me out of there."

"Sure. I wasn't planning on staying anyhow."

"What are you going to do now?"

"Find Michael." Arnaud nodded. He had suspected as much. "And you?"

"Find out why Michael and Alain are in Lille. It is not a coincidence."

"Funny."

"What?"

"I was just thinking that these men coming after us so soon after you met with Michael. Was that a coincidence?"

"Remember: It was Alain who was at the apartment. We have no proof that Michael even knows the place exists."

He was right. Why had she been so quick to condemn Michael? It was this wild flux of emotions that altered her perception. Once thinking clearly, she would be able to explain everything—even the gun. Yes, the rifle was an important issue. If she could reason that out, she would feel much more comfortable. Still, she needed to find Michael—now more than ever. Besides, nothing said that Michael and Alain couldn't be working together on something nefarious. It wouldn't be the first time; of that she was sure. The metro pulled in to the next station—Rihour. "Shit." She whispered. Arnaud looked at her questioningly. She nodded toward the doors. On the platform, ready to board, were five or six men, all wearing the same pin-striped lavender jackets.

Arnaud repeated her oath. "Merdre."

The men came on the train, spreading out in their car. One of them came up to Arnaud. "S'il vous plaît." Arnaud made a weak attempt at trying to find his ticket, pulling several old ones from various pockets. He finally shrugged his shoulders. "Désolé."

The man only shook his head and retrieved a book from his pocket. The fine was forty euros, over thirty times the cost of a single ticket—and over that if bought in a carnet of ten. The train arrived at the Gare Lille Flandres just as the man was handing Arnaud the ten euros in change. The lavender-clad men exited the train, and Stacy sighed in relief. The time it had taken the man to give Arnaud his fine had been enough to cause him to miss her.

Both Arnaud and Stacy exited the train behind the metro inspectors. "You should pay me half," Arnaud whispered to Stacy.

"Never," she giggled. The escalator brought them to the surface between the old station and the EuraLille shopping center. "So where will we meet?"

"Tomorrow, at the McDonald's. Vers midi."

"Okay, Place De Gaulle?"

"Oui. Bonne chance!" With that, Arnaud started in the opposite direction.

Chapter 32

Michael knew what it would take to complete his end of the events. Alain, on the other hand, knew nothing. Michael needed only to stay undercover for another twelve hours, and he could then go his own way. However, there were things that needed to be done. Arnaud and Stacy had to be found. If Alain no longer trusted him, he would not trust Alain either. Against better judgment, he was going to have to ask someone to find them for him. It had been his habit to never rely on others when he himself could do the same job.

He watched the clock above the Place Général DeGaulle. His team would be there within the hour. People were moving about the plaza, but the square was, for the most part, empty. It would not be long before crowds began to appear as well though. The routine traffic would keep things busy until that night, when people would start showing up for Nazeem's speech. He would be back then as well—but not on the ground. He would have a much better view of the events from his room in the Bellevue. How appropriate that name was.

The McDonald's was just opening when the first of his associates arrived. The woman said nothing; instead she sat along the brick retaining wall of the fountain. Michael waited in silence as well. Two minutes later, a man came from the north, and Michael stood. The woman followed his actions, and they went as a group toward Place Rihour. Michael led the way, while the other two walked some ten to twenty feet behind him. He went through Place Rihour and around the monument.

They came together just outside the entrance to the *office du Tourisme*. Michael glanced out from the alcove. No one was within sight. “Thanks for coming.” Michael extended a hand to each of them.

“No problem. Where you need help, that’s where we are.” It was the man who spoke with a thick New York accent. He looked to the woman as he said it, and she nodded.

“I know this isn’t your city, but I need to find a couple people.”

The woman smiled. “We’ll do what we can.”

Michael handed them each a photo of Stacy and Arnaud. “They’re here in Lille, and they’ll most likely be at the speech tonight.”

“Speech?”

“Nazeem Basrath is giving a speech at Place General DeGaulle.”

“That’s what the stage is for.”

“Yes, I need to get this message to one or both.” He handed them each an envelope.

“These are the same?”

“Exactly. If you find one of them, give it to them and your job’s complete. If you haven’t found them by this time tomorrow, there’s no need to continue looking. Whatever is going to happen will occur before then.”

The man smiled and let out a small chuckle. “You’re giving us one day?”

“I know. You’ll be lucky to hear from them, let alone find them.”

“No problem, Michael. It’s a fait accompli.” She elbowed the man.

“I won’t be found again, so you guys take care.”

“You’re disappearing for good?”

“That’s the plan.”

“Good luck.”

“Thanks. And to you too.”

Michael waited until they had gone from sight before leaving the alcove. He went straight for the metro at Place Rihour. Now the only thing left to do was wait for the evening’s activity. For this he left Lille and went out to Lomme in the suburbs. He changed lines at Porte de Postes and was exiting at St. Philibert less than an hour and a half later.

******

Arnaud listened to the man's description of his inquisitor. The portrait he painted was not that of Michael: longish black hair, gray eyes, height not overbearing but above average. It was the man's hands that he remembered best. "His fingers shook. It is why I noticed them. Black smudges ran down their length, but only on his right hand." The man pointed along the insides of his fingers. "At first I thought they were just dirty, but then I realized they were discolored from some kind of burn. He winced from time to time when they touched each other."

Arnaud sighed deeply. Michael had had no such marks on his hand when they met in the church. That is not to say that something could not have happened between then and his meeting with this man. The burns would leave scars at the least. He would know the moment he saw Michael. "Merci." Arnaud left the tabac and went north along Rue Nationale, stopping at a nearby *presse* to buy a *Herald-Tribune.* This man had been one of the fortunate ones. Two others were missing, and one had been verified as dead. Witnesses described the same man that the last had. Either Michael was having someone do his legwork or he was not involved. As well as he knew Michael, he was sure Michael would not send others to do this sort of job.

Yet who else would be looking for them? Alain fit the description even less than Michael. But Alain would not go out questioning himself; that he would leave to others. There was a chance that a third party was involved. Still, Arnaud could think of no one who would simply want them out of the way for a few days. And getting at his informants indicated this was more than just an average hoodlum. This man, or woman, whoever he or she was, dealt with an elite organization. The only man Arnaud could think with that kind of power was Alain. However, Alain retrieved his information in a much subtler way. Never had he known Alain to kill for information.

The only alternative was that this man had not heeded his boss's instructions and had become more violent than was dictated.

The next stop on his list was the Manhattan. It was a small brasserie tucked into the buildings just after Printemps. The black wood of its facade distinguished it from the surrounding buildings. As Arnaud approached, he realized that the entrance was closed. He walked up to the windows and peered inside. The interior was dark; even the back lights behind the bar, which normally remained on all the time, were off.

"C'est fermé." The voice came from the tabac next door. Arnaud went over to the man.

"Où est Fabian?" The owner had known Fabian for over thirty years. Their two businesses were almost as one.

"Il est mort." Dead. Another one of his contacts had been killed. It was beginning to look as if informing for Arnaud was a mortally dangerous career.

"Quand?"

"Hier soir." Only the night before. If he had been only a day earlier, he could have warned him to be careful.

"Qu'est-ce qu'il s'est passé?"

The man went into a full description of the events that led to Fabian's ultimate demise. The characterization of this assailant was of utmost attention. It was not the man from earlier attacks. Instead he described a tall, dark-skinned French man. Gold-rimmed glasses had covered the man's eyes with dark lenses. The last identifying mark told Arnaud everything. The red scar that marked the man's throat from jaw to shoulder could mean only Alain.

******

Michael sat alone on in Place Vendôme. He waited for his messenger to arrive, watching people walk past the monument made out of cannon captured by Napoleon. Not that the man knew he was going to be a messenger. They had met only once before. Each had a chance to kill the other, but neither took advantage of that opportunity. Michael knew his reason; at the time, Michael killed only scheduled marks. Michael also knew now that this was a very weak attempt at justifying what he had been doing. Still, that was his reason. He was taking a risk in assuming that the other man's reasons were no longer valid.

"I should have killed you when I had the chance."

The voice came from behind him, but Michael forced himself to not react. "If you had tried, you wouldn't now be alive."

The man laughed. "I have forgotten. They told me you were confident."

"I should kill you." Michael sat on the park bench, offering the other man a seat next to him.

"But you're not going to."

"No. I need you to do something for me."

"For you?"

"It's quite simple, really. I won't ask you who you work for. That question has ended in no answers and too many dead."

"Then what?"

"Give a message to your boss."

"I think I can handle that."

"He won't be happy about it."

"He has yet to take out punishment on a messenger."

"Okay. Tell him it won't work. I know what's going on, and it will come to the same result as last time."

"He'll know what you're talking about I assume."

"That's a stupid question."

"That's a dangerous response."

"Just tell him. I'm through playing games."

The man rose from the bench, looking to Michael with an odd grin. "You really don't know what you're up against, do you?"

"It can't be all that bad."

"It is. It is." He walked away from Michael, his shoes slapping against the wet pavement as he crossed the street.

Michael watched him go. He was taking a huge chance in letting him know of the plans. Yet Michael knew the man. He worked for Alain. If anything happened that night, he would be assured of Alain's involvement. Still, the result may be that he would simply find out and go to his grave knowing for sure Alain was behind everything. It was a risk he was willing to take. If he were to disappear with Stacy, they would need at least one contact on the outside. Alain had to prove that Michael's trust in him had not been in vain.

******

Arnaud watched the man go as well. He fit the description witnesses had given. The meeting was an amicable one—no guns, no threats, and not even any wary looks. One piece of the puzzle had been put together. Michael was involved with the disturbances. And so was Alain. Now having seen the man in person, he recognized him. This man worked for Alain. Arnaud intended to find out why they would start to use deadly force and how these disappearances and deaths would help Michael. But he would not do so by going directly to the source. Michael was there, only one hundred feet away, with all the answers, but Arnaud couldn't trust him. Michael would hide the truth. That much was clear. He was keeping something from Stacy and thus, as was necessary, from him as well.

Arnaud backed out of the park, keeping his eyes on Michael. Fear now accompanied that uncertainty about the retired assassin. If Michael was making people disappear, there was little to stop him from making Arnaud go as well. There was no proof that all his contacts were dead, but the precautions had not been held to. No word from them in days pointed to just that. As long as Arnaud knew Michael to be involved, for Stacy's sake, Arnaud hoped that they were not all dead and the couple deaths were merely the result of men who enjoyed their work too much—not Michael's orders. He did not want to have to tell Stacy that Michael had once again turned to killing those who got in the way.

******

Arnaud left the tabac with his copy of *La Voix du Nord*. He went north along Rue de Paris. The gray stone of the cathedral rose up from the street on his right. Cars lined the road, and horns blared in impatient haste. *The French are so fond of their horns*, he thought to himself. One could never imagine spending a whole day in a French city without hearing them at least ten times an hour, and this only when it was totally unnecessary. He crossed the street through the unmoving traffic toward the cathedral. Sitting on a bench in the plaza before the western facade, he opened his paper and waited.

The photo was on page 4 underneath its accompanying article. Gérard's face was somewhat blurred, and it was only of his left profile, turning away from the camera. Arnaud had no doubts about who it was though. The headline "Disguise Foiled Identification Attempts" confused him. Why would Gérard be wearing a disguise? Arnaud read through the article with growing amazement.

The dead man who had first been identified as Michael at the Cité metro station was in fact Gérard. The authorities had not thought to look for a disguise, and it was not until the autopsy that the man's real face was revealed. The article continued, but Arnaud set the paper in his lap. *Gérard dead? Why was he following Michael? Michael met with the ex-spy, but that is no reason for the disguise.*

Arnaud glanced back at the paper and noticed another article next the photo of Gérard. This was as compelling as the first. Arnaud unfolded the paper to read the entire article. Nazeem Basrath was going to be in Lille. Arnaud knew instantly there would be an attempt made on his life, or perhaps another false threat. It explained Michael's presence in Lille and his desire to stay clear of both Arnaud and Stacy. It did not offer any clues as to why Alain was here as well. Except if Michael was right and Alain was somehow involved with the group now most likely attempt an assassination of Nazeem.

With Gérard's death obviously somehow tied to Michael, and Alain's attempt at blaming everything on Michael, as well as Michael doing just the opposite, the whole situation was becoming more complex by the minute. Arnaud had a feeling he might never know the whole truth.

Chapter 33

On the other side of the city, Stacy was reading the same paper. She too had noticed both articles. The first convinced her that Michael was lying about something. He would have recognized Gérard, disguise or not. The second gave reason to his secrecy. He was here to complete a contract after he had failed the previous one in Paris.

Stacy rose from her park bench and headed toward Place Général DeGaulle. The speech was to take place in three hours. She would be there and find Michael. Arnaud would be there too. She knew he was most likely thinking the same way as she was.

However, he would not feel as betrayed as she did. Michael had done nothing but lie to her since the beginning. She believed nothing of the story Michael had told her. If he had not retired, perhaps Domino was behind all this. It would make sense. He had ties to the same group. They would have reasons to want him alive. It was finally beginning to come together. She needed to find Arnaud and Alain. They would both be in danger—especially Alain, who already knew of Michael's involvement. He too would probably make the same connection between Michael and Domino. That would make him dangerous to Michael as well. If that's how Michael wanted it, that's how he would get it. It would be him or them, and right now they outnumbered him.

Now she needed only to find those involved. Everyone seemed to be running for the hills for different reasons. Still, she knew more people in this town than any of them, so it was finally to her advantage. In the end, the only one she truly cared about was Michael. He had a lot of questions to answer. And answer them he would, whether she had to get someone to professionally "interrogate" him or not. She deserved answers, and despite the fact that she was finally at the point of no return with her trust in him, she wanted to know the complete truth. He owed her that. His betrayal had gone beyond just killing again, despite his promises to her. No, she had been abused physically and emotionally because of his actions, and if she found out that the whole "I was blackmailed into it" line was false, then he was not only responsible for but also complicit in that abuse.

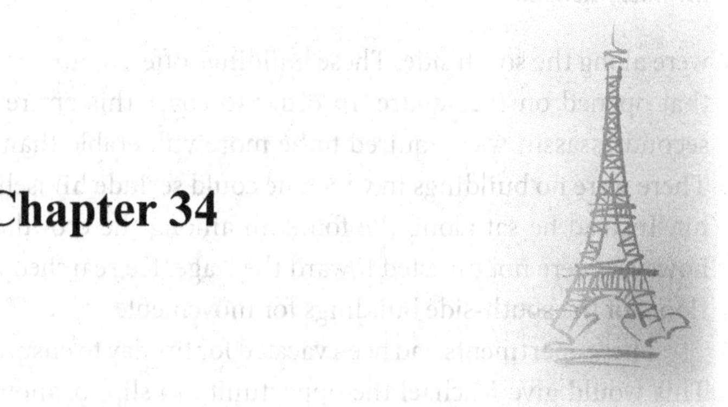

Chapter 34

There were two of them, each carrying the same exact model of rifle. Alain had wanted no doubts that Michael was dead. The money mattered little to him now. This would be his last decisive blow for the cause. Nazeem would be abducted, Michael shot, and finally Stacy killed. He regretted the last. She had done nothing against them. Yet he understood the reasoning. She would not let Michael's death go unavenged. It was not so much that she posed a threat to their lives as it was that she presented a risk to the secrecy they held so close. It was for this reason that the kidnapping would be claimed by no one. The reason for its occurrence would be obvious. And then he would be done. The money we would receive for his services in all this was enough to keep him going for decades. He didn't need to live lavishly, but only in comfort, and that was his plan; he would go somewhere far away from France, where no one knew him.

Thus two assassins moved through the crowd, which was already forming to hear the speech. One headed behind the stage, carefully avoiding the security teams that closely patrolled the area. He entered the FNAC Gallery and headed straight up the stairs to the offices of *La Voix du Nord*. It was from there he would make his attempt. If the shots came from any of the buildings on the southwest side of the square, he would be responsible. Firing from directly behind the stage would offer him the best view of the intended victim.

Alain had made one assumption; he did not believe Michael would risk his own life to stop the abduction. The only available locations where someone could target those on or near the stage were along the south side. These buildings offered numerous rooms that opened on the square. In order to cover this entire area, the second assassin was required to be more vulnerable than the first. There were no buildings in which he could seclude himself after the hit. Instead he sat along the fountain among the crowd. His eyes, however, were not directed toward the stage. He searched the upper floors of the south-side buildings for movement.

These apartments had been vacated for the day to ensure security. This would give Michael the opportunity to slip in unobserved to the normally occupied flats. The assassin, too, had an advantage here. Any movement in those windows would immediately gain his attention. Only someone secreting past the security teams would be there. His eyes scanned the buildings floor by floor, never hesitating, in a distinct and repeated fashion. The sun, hidden behind the clouds, cast an even light across the square. The assassin looked down to his watch, stopping his search only for a moment. It was 7:45. The speech was scheduled to begin at 8:05. Twenty minutes. Michael would need to be set soon. He could not risk the kidnapping taking place before the speech.

There! Just above the Foret du Nord, one level below the top floor, a curtain had shifted aside. The assassin fixed his gaze on the room. It was perhaps too distant a target for his partner. No matter. If they both fired, there was a much better chance at success. He felt down to his bag. The rifle was in three pieces. It would take him no longer than six seconds to place them together and fire. He needed to do this the instant a face appeared in the window. There could be no hesitation. The only chance for escape was an ensuing panic that caused the crowd to disperse. If instead they went down, he was ready to take a second shot from the gun he had holstered under his jacket. Dying for the cause at his own hand was something he had faced before. Sometimes he had even willed it to happen. This, however, was not one of those times. He said a silent prayer that the crowd would run madly in every direction. He would disappear with them. Another movement. This time the window swung open, only slightly—perhaps just wide enough for a barrel to sneak between the two frames. Still, he could see no one. He considered moving across the square to a better position.

******

Michael surveyed the scene below his window. The crowd was beginning to increase. There were still fifteen minutes before the scheduled appearance, but Michael was ready. The barrel of his gun slid between the wooden frames of the two windows. He sighted various points on the stage as well as the stairs leading up to it. There were several people with signs that hid the actual stairway from his sight. He would have to wait until they were on stage. He hoped they would wait until the mess after the speech to make their move. According to his sources, that was their plan, but Michael knew how these things changed.

The man and woman he had working for him were milling through the crowd. Michael spotted two of them moving toward the stage. They stopped and talked to the people holding signs and moved them away from the stairs. "Good job," Michael whispered. Music began to play through the loudspeakers. It was the French national anthem. They were not afraid to make a show of it. The crowd began to get settled and pressed toward the stage. There were more people than Michael would have imagined. He knew the topic was controversial, but he had thought there would be less of a following. This man, after all, preached harmony and common cause—not so popular in these days of polarized political rhetoric.

Michael sighted the first of Alain's men as he moved onto the stage. The man held a hand out to help Nazeem up the stairs. Following directly behind them was the second of Alain's men. Nazeem took his spot before the podium, and the two men stood on each side of him and back a couple of feet. The man on Nazeem's right was hidden from sight. It would be a difficult shot. He put his sights on the other man first.

The crowd quieted, and the speech began. Michael did not pay attention to the words. Darkness had come, and the lights on stage seemed to glow even brighter. Several cheers, as well as some boos, erupted from the crowd with each point the man made. Still Michael concentrated on his target. A final shout from the speaker gave rise to the crowd's voice, and applause filled the square. The man turned to walk off stage. It was now or never.

Michael fired twice and moved to his second target before the first had fallen to the ground. He fired twice and dropped the gun. He spent no time in verifying his hits. He was out of the hotel room and into the stairwell when he heard additional shots behind him. Before the door to the stairwell closed, he heard glass exploding into the room he had just left. Another shot, this one farther away, rang out, and the door slammed shut. He ran down the stairs, aided only by the green light of emergency exit signs pointing their way down the stairs.

The alley was dark, and the lights from the nearby street angled only partially into the blackness. Michael slowed his steps and exited onto the main street. He glanced quickly toward the hotel entrance. Police were surrounding the entrance, and more were within. He turned away and headed north along Rue J Roisin. He was no more than ten steps away before he heard feet pounding on the pavement. Someone was running in his direction. He turned and recognized the man who had threatened to kill him. Michael took off without hesitation.

He ran onto Rue Nationale, which was a maze of people heading away from the main square, under the length of the Printemps sign. Crossing the street as the traffic slowed to a crawl, he continued west. He did not know where he was headed, but as long as they were behind him, he kept moving. He turned right on Boulevard de la Liberté. His legs ached, and his momentum slowed. Then he was across Avenue Mathias Delobel and into the Bois de Boulogne.

******

The hit man in the Voix du Nord offices saw his partner go down before he heard the shots echo across the crowded square. The crowd panicked almost instantly. He drew his rifle to the window and aimed in the general direction from which the noise had come. The second set of shots was fired. He could see nothing. Then he spotted a movement in the Bellevue Hotel—top floor. A curtain moved back across the window. He could see no other movement. Still, he fired twice. He saw the glass shatter, falling into the room and out of sight.

He heard another shot come from the ground. His associate was aiming once again. He never got the chance to fire, as a succession of bullets ripped through his body. He stood, rocking backward against the retaining wall of the fountain. Blood spread across his chest in three red circles. The rifle fell from his grasp. His body continued backward, finally falling over the wall into the water. Another dead in the name of their cause. His name would be spoken of with reverence.

He looked again to the hotel wall. There were two windows shattered along its facade. He had shot one out. The other, two stories below, had been his associates' doing. He wondered which one was the correct floor where the man they called Michael was. Without knowing why, he knew there would be no body found in either place that matched the description of that man.

He rose from the window and took a seat at the desk. They would be coming for him soon. They would be able to charge him with nothing. The shots that had been fired were not from his gun—at least not those they cared about. He took the gun apart and began the routine cleaning job. They would confiscate the weapon, and no one would think to keep it clean until he once again was able to retrieve it.

A commotion of people sounded outside the glass door. He could see the blurry images of four men making their way across the press room to his office. He placed the pieces of the rifle into the case and shut it. The door opened, and four French police entered, guns drawn and concentrated on his form.

"Bonjour."

They looked around the room and moved toward him. He did not move. There was no need to end up in the same heaven as his associate. Without a word, they surrounded the desk.

"Levez-vous." He rose at their command.

"C'est quoi?" Another of the policemen pointed to the case. "C'est une carabine." He did not need to hide the existence of his gun. They would find it anyway.

"Ouvrez-la." Again he did as they asked and opened the case. Upon seeing its contents, the man behind him grabbed his wrists and locked them behind his back with cuffs. The second officer closed the case and took it out of the room. The hit man was led out as well, past the office workers who stared in amazement at the whole scene. The man smiled and knew that he would become famous soon. He was in a newspaper office; did not anyone want an interview?

The flash of a camera began the noise. Reporters appeared from every corner of the office, asking questions he would gladly answer. More pictures were taken. He posed brilliantly for these. He would no longer be useful as an undercover man, but he didn't care. He would be famous.

******

As for the cause of the commotion, Arnaud had no idea. There were still people hiding behind trees and doors, looking out only cautiously. The square itself was empty. Not even the stage crew was still present. The sole occupants were two policemen standing over a motionless man. The barrel of a rifle rose out of the fountain's pool of water just beyond the body. The body itself was soaked, and Arnaud assumed that it too had been in the pool. He moved no closer to the scene. Detainment by the police for whatever reason would mean delays. At the far end of the square, just below the La Voix du Nord sign proclaiming its seventy-fifth anniversary, another group of police appeared with a rifle case. The man who was among them in cuffs was smiling and answering any and all questions the reporters, who kept within reach of the group, could ask. Flashes of light marked the photographers.

A single policeman surveyed the scene from a window in the Bellevue. The glass from the window had been shattered. Arnaud noticed that another window two floors above had also been broken. He immediately thought of Michael. Had he been at one of those windows? Perhaps his body still was. Either window would have provided an excellent view of the stage. Had someone been shot? He looked back to the group near the fountain. Someone had been; that much was definite. He backed away toward Rue Nationale. He would wait until things calmed down and then find someone who knew what had happened.

The crowd along Rue Nationale was heavier now than usual. Arnaud assumed this was attributable to the overflow of people who had been on the square. They were slowly filtering back there despite the police blockade that had been hastily put up around the area. He began to turn down Rue J Roisin but was greeted by another scene with police. There was no reason they would detain him, but he could not take the risk. They were, in fact, randomly stopping people and asking for their papers. An ambulance stood outside the hotel, and just as he was about to continue on, two paramedics wheeled a stretcher out. The man laid out on the white sheets was still alive and was most definitely not Michael. *A third hit man?* A couple next to him answered his question by way of their conversation. The man was a cameraman for a new underground online publication. He had been shot by the man who now lay beside the fountain.

Arnaud waited until the ambulance rushed past and headed south on Rue Nationale. He finally turned on Rue de l'Hôpital Militaire before turning again toward Place Rihour. The huge monument dedicated to the dead of the world war came up on his left. The metro station was on his right. He walked between the two and sat at a table at the café.

A waiter appeared almost immediately, "Monsieur, bon soir."

"Un café, s'il vous plaît."

"Oui, monsieur."

The waiter disappeared back into the café. Arnaud looked over toward the stage. The yellow band of police tape surrounded the stage. *So two hit men, one dead; one cameraman shot; someone on stage shot, presumably; but still no Michael or any sign of where he might be.* The second broken window in the Bellevue suggested he might have been there. They had supposedly emptied the hotel some time before the speech was started. Had he been shot or just shot at?

Or perhaps had there been no one there? Michael was the only one who could provide any answers. He wondered, too, where Stacy was. She would most likely have been at the speech. Where was she now?

* * * * * *

Arnaud sat among a crowd just outside the McDonald's. Normally they would be indoors, where it was warm. However, the activity surrounding the stage kept them where they were. He was talking with two women as they relayed the story of the events directly onstage. Neither could say where the shots came from, but both assured him they would never forget the looks on the two men's faces. One described the moment as awkward and silent. Both men fell within seconds of each other. There was no blood until after they hit the ground. Arnaud listened intently to their stories. The two men were on either side of Nazeem, each at least three feet away. Once again, Michael had been aiming at two of the sideline players. He had no doubt it was Michael this time. The two shots at each man, the second as they were going down—that was his trademark. But what was their importance? If only he could answer that.

The last of the police cars moved away from the scene, and the spectators also began to move away and find the warmth of heated night spots. Arnaud remained where he was despite the offers for free drinks from the two women. He needed to find Stacy. Alain's story was beginning to make less and less sense. There had to be a connection somewhere, either between Alain and the men who had been shot or between Michael and some unknown party. What he really needed were the names of the two dead men, but that couldn't be found out until morning, if even then. He had very few contacts left in the city. Perhaps Stacy would be doing the same thing as he was.

Arnaud finally rose from his seat, leaving only two couples at the tables. He wrapped his overcoat tighter around his body and headed across the square toward the stage and farther to the metro. Police tape still lined the stage, as well as a portion of the square. He had noticed the same tape near the fountain, where barricades held up the yellow band. That man had not been killed by Michael though. The police had done that. Arnaud had seen the man's gun before they took it away. It was a sniper's weapon, specially designed for portability. It could be assembled and disassembled in a matter of seconds.

Descending into the metro, Arnaud felt the warmth of its interior rise up the escalator. The weather had turned cold suddenly, and even though it had not rained, the ground was still damp from the previous evening's showers.

"Arnaud." The voice was a harsh whisper coming from the bottom of the escalator. Arnaud reached inside his jacket. "It's me, Michael."

"Michael?" Arnaud took the rest of the way down at a run. "What are you still doing around here?"

"I needed to talk to you. I thought you were never going to leave."

"I was listening to what happened, but I suppose you could have told me that." They continued into the metro together and down toward the platforms. Michael revealed all that he had found out about Alain and the group. "I still don't understand why Alain."

"I was trying to make the same connections."

"I'm going to Paris in the morning to find Alain."

Michael did not offer any explanations to Arnaud. They both knew why. Michael went on to explain everything that had happened to him over the previous few days. It answered a lot of questions for Arnaud, who still wasn't sure whether to trust Michael or not, but it all made sense.

"Be careful. He will not hesitate to kill you. You know that now, don't you?"

"Yes. It's either him or me. Tell Stacy what happened. I'll be back tomorrow. We can leave France then."

Chapter 35

Once Arnaud found out Victor was dead for sure, he realized that left only him alive out of the five. They had died, ironically enough, in the same order as they had joined the small fraternity. The last was the only one left. Arnaud wished he could believe all that Michael had told him. Who could? Alain had nothing to gain. Still, why would Michael seek him out and tell him all this? It would have been simpler and less risky to just kill him. Arnaud reminded himself that there was Stacy to consider. The more Michael convinced Arnaud, the better his chances were of convincing Stacy.

Arnaud moved into the next train, which appeared and headed out toward Lomme. No matter what the truth was, he needed to find Stacy and tell her all of what Michael had said. He could not wait long at their apartment, but it was the only place he could think of reaching her. He tried to make some connection between Alain and Nazeem. Even if Alain was involved with this group, what benefit did they have in kidnapping him? He could think of no answers to either question.

The distinctive feminine voice announced the next stop as Canteleux. Arnaud stepped toward the doors. The train slid to a stop, and he exited the car. Going to his left, he stepped onto the escalator and finally went across the station to another escalator, which brought him to the surface. The whole time, he continued trying to reason out the situation. For Stacy's sake, he wanted Michael's story to be true. Yet the main connection was missing.

He turned onto Avenue de Bretagne and continued straight,

past the sign announcing he was leaving Lille and entering Lomme. The streets were lined on both sides with weathered brick houses. Children played in the street under a single lamp that stood above a telephone booth. Arnaud unlocked the door to 3 Rue Galliéni. The house was quiet and dark. Stacy had either not returned or had left again. Arnaud went into the kitchen and retrieved a baguette from the cupboard and a package of sliced ham from the fridge.

Rain sounded on the skylight, and Arnaud looked above his head. He had gotten in at the perfect time. Of course it meant that he would need an umbrella before going out again. Stacy was somewhere in the city. He could not risk her coming across Michael alone. Hopefully Michael had taken one of the last trains out to Paris instead of leaving in the morning. Stacy's feeling shifted so dramatically when it came to Michael that she would not be thinking straight. The rain stopped as quickly as it had started, but Arnaud knew it was not over. Once the weather turned as it was now, there would be few dry sunny days before spring.

He placed a cup of water in the microwave and set the timer for a minute forty-five seconds. The machine buzzed, and he watched the cup turn on the plate within. Stacy knew Alain even less than he did, which meant there was little hope of her finding a connection. Tomorrow Michael would confront Alain, if indeed Alain had returned to Paris. Michael's story explained Alain's presence in Lille. Arnaud also remembered that Alain was surprised to hear Michael was in Lille and that Alain had left more nervous than he had arrived. The only thing Arnaud knew beyond a doubt, though, was that there was a newfound tension between Alain and Michael. Michael had said it was "either him or me." Personally, Arnaud saw Michael leaving Alain's gallery alive. That did not answer any questions though. Neither Michael nor Alain was the controlling force here; there had to be someone else.

******

Michael had, in fact, waited until the morning train to return to Paris. He arrived at the studio before noon. He watched from across the street. Alain's office was dark. Marsha sat below, filing her nails. No one had even glanced into the gallery in the twenty minutes since his arrival. His legs were tired, and the rain had soaked through both his jacket and the sweatshirt beneath. There was no reason he couldn't wait inside. He would need to take care of Marsha somehow. Alain would not stay long if she informed him of Michael's presence. Perhaps Alain had even assumed Michael was dead. The gunman had killed someone.

He crossed the street and entered. Marsha looked up and smiled. "You're all wet."

"Yes, the rain is coming down pretty good."

"Let me get you a towel. I'm sure we have one in the storeroom." Marsha left the room. Michael took the opportunity to take the stairs to Alain's office. He touched the button at the bottom of the stairs, and lights flickered on above.

"Michael?" He heard the call from below.

"I'm up here," he yelled down. Michael looked around the office, spying a key in the closet door. It was a walk-in closet almost five feet deep. She would be safe enough in there.

"I don't know if Alain would want me to let anyone …" She stopped, as Michael had turned around with his gun out.

"Come here, Marsha." She hesitated, looking back to the stairs. "Marsha!" he shouted. She jumped at the sound, dropping the towel. "Come here," he continued, softer. She began to walk toward him. "The towel, please." He motioned to the towel with the gun. She retrieved it and continued forward.

"What's going on?"

"Do you know what your boss does for a living?"

"What?"

"You heard me. Do you?"

"He's an art dealer." Her eyes watered, and she bit her bottom lip.

"Not exactly. In his spare time, he gets to do things that are a lot more fun." His sarcastic tone was not lost on even the French woman.

"What?" She tried to hold back the tears, but they began to fall.

"He can order people to do lots of things. Do you know what he did to Stacy?"

"No." She reached him and handed him the towel. He took it and waved her into the closet.

"He had someone beat her up."

"Alain?"

"Yes, Alain. They beat her up to scare me. They threatened to rape her next time, and Alain told them to."

"No. He wouldn't."

"He did. And now he's going to pay for that and for killing Lawrence and Vincent and anyone else that got in his way."

"Lawrence ... Vincent?" She had backed into the closet and stood next to some coats. "I don't know them."

"No, you wouldn't. They died before you could meet them. Your boss is responsible though."

"I can't believe that."

"It's true. Now all I need you to do is stand, or sit, in here quietly. Someone will let you out after I've gone. But if you make any noise while Alain is here, or if you tell anyone who was here, I'll find you and you will be responsible for those things just as much as your boss. Got it?"

She nodded.

"Good. Don't worry. Nothing is going to happen to you otherwise. If you listen carefully enough, you'll even hear Alain admit to those things." He shut the door and locked it.

******

Michael sat in Alain's office. It was almost too warm in the spacious room. He could feel a light drowsiness fall over him. The heat always did this to him. It made him feel lazy—sometimes a little light-headed. Perhaps this was why he preferred the warmth. Within its effects, he could blame his inactivity upon something. Michael got up from the chair and began pacing the room. This was not a time to feel lazy or, for that matter, light-headed. Alain would return before the end of the day. He hoped that Marsha's absence from the front desk wouldn't scare him into running. Michael had neither the time nor the energy to chase him any further. They would end it here in Paris, where it had all begun—where their friendship had begun. *Too many years ago*, Michael thought, *to end like this.* He wished there were some other way. Yet the attempt on his life had resolved him to this fate.

He kept from the windows while he paced, but from time to time he strolled to the tall glass walls and looked down. There were hundreds of people along both sides of Avenue Turbig. Each time, he scanned the crowd for Alain's face. He never stayed long at the glass though. He could not risk Alain seeing him. Alain thought he was dead. At least that was what Michael hoped. Perhaps seeing Michael would give him a heart attack. That would save Michael the necessity of killing him. Michael could then simply let Marsha out of the closet and leave. Such fantastical wishes rarely came true, and Michael knew it would be necessary to use some sort of violence. Alain would not accept his fate as readily as that.

Michael returned to the chair, relaxing against the cushioned back and putting his feet atop the desk as Alain so liked to do. He had seen him thus so many times before. In fact, the first time they met, Alain was in just such a pose.

****

"Bonjour."

"Bonsoir," Alain replied, half-correcting Michael. "I understand you can help me find some rare pieces."

Michael found the pun a bit melodramatic, but as a code word, it served its purposes.

"So I can." Alain took his feet from the desk. He withdrew a couple of sheets of paper from a drawer to his right. "What are you looking for? Something exotic or perhaps modern?"

"I don't need anything fancy. Just something that does what it's supposed to do." Michael moved his weight from foot to foot. His hands continually found themselves in his pockets and then out again.

"Sure. I believe I have just what you need." Alain took the papers and rose from the desk. He crossed the room to a large filing cabinet and opened the top drawer. He retrieved a Beretta Model 92F.

"Perhaps something a little less dramatic," Michael offered before Alain had shut the drawer.

"That I can do." Replacing the weapon, he retrieved another. This one was a 9 mm MAS. "It is a standard weapon for the French." He handed Michael the weapon. It was light in his hand, and he liked the feel of it. "There is a drawback. The ammunition is a bit scarce outside of France."

"No problem. I'll only need it a few days. I'll need two magazines, fully loaded."

"Veronique can handle that. Just give her this slip." He handed Michael a small scrap of paper with a number written on it. "She'll give you a box in return."

"Great. How much?"

"That has already been taken care of."

Michael smiled. Cruthers had planned ahead. It just might be enjoyable working for him.

******

Michael heard the door open below. Alain called out for Marsha. Again he called. Michael heard footsteps on the stairs.

Alain entered the office with a cautious first step.

"Bonjour, Alain." Michael stayed in the chair.

"Ah, Michael. Où est Marsha?" Alain remained in the entrance.

"Come in. After all, it's your office."

"Oui, so it is." Still he remained at the top of the stairs.

"Surprised to see me?"

"Perhaps I shouldn't be, but yes, I am."

"Your hired guns were not good enough. Although one did actually did shoot someone before getting it himself."

"They were not mine."

"I can't believe that now. Why, Alain? I thought I could trust you."

"I've told you a thousand times before, Michael: trust no one. Not even Stacy."

"Don't try to pin anything on her. She doesn't know what's going on." Michael sat forward at the desk. He may have only suspected that Alain had something to do with Stacy's incident, but he wasn't about to let him take her situation lightly.

"Exactly. She thinks you've betrayed her. And you have, haven't you?" Alain smiled.

"Bullshit. Don't try to stall for time you haven't got."

"She's prepared to kill you."

Michael had known Alain a long time, and he wondered if Alain knew something he didn't. "What? Based on what you've said? Never."

"She already believes me. I told them about the gun you bought from me."

"It proves nothing." Michael stood. He didn't have time to deal with Alain right now.

"It doesn't need to. You've lied to her before, Michael. All I needed to do was push her in that direction."

Alain had a point. Stacy hadn't exactly been in "trust Michael mode" lately. "What did you say?"

"Wouldn't you like to know. I told them the truth—or at least what I wanted them to believe was the whole truth."

Alain might have thought he had something to sell to Michael, but Michael wanted nothing but vengeance at this point. He needed only confirmation—something that even hinted that Alain knew of the assassination blackmail before Michael asked him for the gun. "It doesn't matter. It can't change what you've done to me or to Stacy."

"Yes, Stacy. That was unfortunate, but it was not my decision. That was out of my control. They went too far, in my judgment."

"And Lawrence?"

"Lawrence played the game and lost."

And there it was; both Lawrence and Stacy were of his doing. "And did you plan on winning?"

"No. I have forfeited my spot. I'm retired."

"Why, then? What does all this do for you now?"

"Two reasons. One, there is no one left who can identify me. Two, your ex-boss pays well. I'm surprised you ever left his employ."

"Domino is behind this?"

"Yes and no. He gave them you and asked me to make sure it happened the way it was supposed to. And my last project is now complete." Alain reached into his suit coat. He never finished the draw, as Michael took one step forward and fired. The first shot sliced through Alain, shattering the mirror behind him. The second caught him in the neck. Michael walked over to his fallen form. He dragged the body behind the desk. "You are indeed retired."

* * * * * *

He had the gun pressed against her ribs. They were heading for the exit. The train would be at the station in less than ten minutes. Stacy glanced around. None of those seated had noticed his rough handling of her. A train going in the opposite direction passed by, jostling them. The man looked up at the train. Stacy took the opportunity and turned the gun against him. She pressed his finger against the trigger, firing once. The muffled pop of the silenced gun was further deadened by their bodies.

A blank expression appeared on the man's face as he collapsed into her arms. Through the glass door, Stacy saw that no one had reacted to her actions. She opened the door to the lavatory and relieved herself of the burden. The train slowed noticeably. They would be in Paris soon. She had never gone back to the apartment and decided to head to Paris to confront Alain herself. She figured she would be back in Lomme before Arnaud knew she was missing. How this man had found her, she didn't care; but she knew now that Alain was the only man who could help her unravel the truth from all this. She might have to virtually kill him to get it, but that was something she was willing to do. After all, Alain—or Michael, she supposed—had driven her to kill two men already. She hadn't liked the feeling, but she needed this all to be done. She felt now that with either Michael or Alain around, she would never be safe.

The only voice she heard was that of a man who dialed a number on his cellular phone. The conversation was one concerning his business interests in Morocco. A "Allo, âllo?" was immediately followed by a soft sigh. He dialed the number again. He apologized for such an occurrence and continued the conversation. The scraping of brakes against tracks signaled that the arrival in Paris was drawing closer. The vast fields of green and small towns had been replaced by tracks of houses and commercial sites. Trees lined the tracks from time to time. A small open field covered with metal shacks came into view. People walked among the shacks, where clothes hung from strings attached between the metal structures.

Trains situated along the side came into view, and then the TGV sped past a slower RER train, both coming into the heart of Paris. It was six minutes before their arrival. All the passengers packed up their belongings and readied themselves to get off. The conductor announced the impending end of the line, as if no one knew it was coming. He did this in both French and English. They would be coming into Paris Nord. High-rises now marked the city along the tracks; Technics, Sanyo, and Panasonic advertised their names atop offices.

And then Sacre Coeur rose up in the distance, though only for an instant. Its white brilliance stood out against the gray skies and even grayer buildings. Graffiti-marked walls of dingy black replaced the view of the basilica, and the train slowed further. The low squeal of brakes sounded again. The station was in view, and the aisle filled with passengers ready to hurry off the train. A woman and her son were beside Stacy. The lady's husband had abandoned his attempts on the phone after two more ended with premature disconnections.

Stacy froze at the door, seeing the blue of the French *policier.* There were three of them: one woman and two men. Their gaze was one of observation, not an intensive search. Stacy relaxed. They weren't there for any particular reason. She took another step down from the train.

Chapter 36

Arnaud stopped his car outside his apartment and sighed heavily. There was no telling what Stacy might do. He needed to find her before she found Michael. He supposed Michael could explain for himself, but there was a good chance she wouldn't believe him. Or worse yet, she might not even give him a chance to explain. He opened the door to his Peugeot and stepped onto the sidewalk. Leaves crunched under his feet as he walked up to the front door. He could smell the mixture of aromas that drifted from neighboring buildings. It was lunchtime, and the thought made him hungry. There was nothing in the fridge; that much he knew.

With so many numbers running through his head, it took him a moment to remember the code number. He flipped the switch just inside the front door, and a series of lights brightened the hall. One light was fixed above each portrait that lined the wall; there were ten faces—five on each side. He paid no attention to the artwork and continued into the kitchen. A search through the cupboards and the confirmed empty fridge produced a box of pasta, two bars of white chocolate, and a box of Brun Petit Extra. Not a nutritious lunch, but it would have to do.

Arnaud put a pan of water on the hot plate and proceeded to open the chocolate and cookies. He let each morsel of chocolate melt in his mouth, following it with a Petit Extra. The water was soon boiling, and he added the box of pasta. He checked his watch and let the pasta boil, going into the living room. The room was dark, and he did not turn on a light. The brightness from the kitchen was enough to afford him sight to get to the couch without bumping into the television or table.

He snapped his fingers and turned before sitting down. He was always forgetting to check his messages. Sure enough, a red glow produced a "1" on his answering machine. He pushed the message button and returned to the couch. The machine whirred for a moment and then clicked to a stop.

"Arnaud, it's Michael." Arnaud half-stood as if Michael had appeared. "Um, I hope Stacy isn't with you at the moment. I'd rather explain to her in person. Alain's dead. I'm going back to Minneapolis. There's one last person to take care of. Domino's behind everything. He used me, Arnaud. I don't know if Cruthers is really dead, but they used Alain to get to me. Well, I have to go. Tell Stacy where I'm going but not why. I'll explain everything fully when I get back." The background noise was undeniably that of an airport.

Arnaud rose from his seat and returned to the kitchen. *Domino?* It was truly a necessity to find Stacy now. If Michael was in Paris, Stacy would have followed not far behind. He looked again at his watch. There would be a TGV leaving for Paris soon. He took the pan of pasta, dumped it into the sink, and turned off the hot plate. He needed nothing.

He got into his car and sped away from the curb. He only hoped he was in time to catch her. He could think of nowhere else but the gallery to find her. He wondered how long it would take her to find out Michael went to Minneapolis if she wasn't at the gallery but had been.

Chapter 37

Stacy stepped down from the TGV. She stared down its length for the man who had been with her captor when they took her before she could even sit in her seat. She was sure he would have found his partner dead by now. There were too many people to see clearly. She took a step back on the train to raise herself above the crowd, and she looked again before realizing doing so exposed her to anyone searching for her. After jumping to the concrete platform, she hurried her way out of the station and straight down into the metro. Her first order of business was to find Alain. He would have seen Michael or soon would be seeing him.

The metro was crowded with noontime traffic. Stacy squeezed into the first car on the tracks heading away from Le Gare du Nord. Alain's studio was, in fact, not far away. She would be there before twelve thirty. At once, she wondered whether the studio was open during the lunch hours. She tried to remember whether she had ever been there during those times. So many places closed down for lunch. No, she hadn't. It had always been in the morning or late afternoon. Still, even if it was closed, that did not mean Alain wasn't there.

She exited the metro at Passy and walked from there. As she approached the building, she began to feel an odd sense of doom fall over her. She quickened her pace almost to a jog. Reaching the building, she glanced into the main gallery. The lights were on, but Marsha was not at her desk. The hours were painted in white on the door: "Lundi–Samedi, 9h à Midi, 14h à 19h." They were closed for lunch. "Damn," she muttered. Stacy took a step back from the building to look up into Alain's office. The lights were on up there as well. She went back to the door in search of a bell. Finding none, she knocked. The glass rattled, and the door edged open slightly. Stacy glanced up and down the street before pushing in on the door. It opened without resistance.

Stacy slipped into the gallery, turning to lock the door behind her. Something was wrong. If they had been open, Marsha would be at her desk. If not, why was the door unlocked? Even the ring of the bell upon her entrance did not bring anyone to the front. "Marsha?" She called out, regretting the disturbance immediately. But she received no response, good or bad. The floodlights above the multicolored steps were off, but she could see the light coming down from Alain's office. There was no sound of talking or movement.

Taking each stair with a light step, she made her way into the office. Halfway up the stairs, she noticed a red light embedded in the wall about two feet above the staircase. Remembering the bell at the entrance, she assumed this was much the same device. She didn't want to risk the chance that it was instead an alarm. She stopped before it, wondering whether going over or under it was better. At first she ducked to go beneath, but she changed her mind and went over instead.

The rest of the way up the stairs, Stacy paid close attention to both walls for any additional triggers but found none.

The door to the office was open. She took the gun from her purse and cautiously slid the magazine from the grip. After confirming it was full, she slipped it back into place and then burst into the room. She covered the entire office with a sweep of the gun. She stopped her scan just before the desk. A pair of legs stretched out from between the wall and the desk. She walked over to the body.

The red stain that covered Alain's neck and chest told her everything she needed to know. It was Michael's mark: two hits—one to the head and a second to the neck or chest. Though any random killer might end up with the same results, this was far too much of a coincidence. Michael was on a killing spree. She thought he was maybe trying to tie up loose ends before leaving. Even if he knew she wouldn't believe him, she was sure he wouldn't want anyone telling her the truth.

* * * * * *

Arnaud rose up the escalator from the metro into the Gare du Nord. He circled back around the stairs and headed toward the front entrance. He could see the fountains outside, and beyond that the midday traffic along Rue du Priez. The sight of the cafés along the far side of the road reminded him that he had not eaten anything other than a couple pieces of chocolate and a cookie or two in quite some time. Just to the right of the main entrance, he went through a glass doorway and then a sliding glass door.

To his right, an information booth sat in front of a row of *guichets.* He took a number from the dispenser. He looked up to the board above the desk. There were five people in front of him. He sat in the chairs along the wall facing the EuraLille shopping center. He hoped only that he would arrive in Paris in time to catch Stacy. She would not listen to reason from Michael; that much he had decided. With Alain now dead, there was no one but himself who could corroborate Michael's story. There was always a chance she wouldn't be able to go through with it. She still loved him; even he could tell that.

The next number clicked onto the board; below it a flashing "5" corresponded to the "5" flashing above the counter. Arnaud was next. He would be in Paris within two hours. He reminded himself he needed to figure out where Alain's studio was located. In all his years in Paris, he had never had the need to go there. Even if he found the place, there was no guarantee Stacy would be there. She could still be in Lille. That was a hope, he knew—that Stacy would not let what she believed to be another lie go unpunished. Michael had not exactly lied. Arnaud was as guilty as he was. Where a half a truth would do, he made it so.

Arnaud's number flashed onto the board, and he went to the flashing "6."

"Bonjour."

"Bonjour."

"Je voudrais un billet pour le prochain train à Paris."

The woman punched a series of buttons on her keypad. "Treize heures trente-trois." Arnaud looked at his watch. It was a quarter after one—twenty minutes away. There was more than enough time to get over to the new station.

"Parfait."

"Il départ de Lille Europe."

"Oui."

"Aller-retour?"

"Non, aller simplement. Deuxieme classe."

The woman printed the ticket and showed Arnaud the times of arrival and departure. "Deux cent vingt-cinq."

Arnaud gave her the forty-five euros and took the ticket. "Merci, au revoir."

"Bon journée."

Crossing the Place des Buisses, he followed Rue le Corbusier past the red-and-gray complex that served as hotel, shopping center, and apartments. Once past the construction that still occupied the plaza in front of the building, he saw the station. He hurried across the walkway and entered. A board above the main corridor listed his train as track 46. To his right were tracks 49 and 50. On his left, a stairwell descending below his present level led to track 46. "Voilà." The train was already at the platform. He climbed into car nine and found his seat. He would be in Paris in an hour.

* * * * * *

She was too late. Alain was still warm, and his body had not yet begun to stiffen. She closed his eyes, which stared open as if he were still in shock. Where would Michael go from here? He had no one to turn to in Paris. Everyone was dead or missing. Michael had brought that on himself. The only explanation she could think of was that Domino was somehow behind it all. Cruthers wasn't really dead, and he had sent Michael over here to end some sort of blood feud, including killing off those who were helping the unfortunate ones within his control. It was his type of power play—kill those who were more powerful in any way and worry about the consequences later.

Stacy stepped away from the body. She wanted there to be a way in which Michael was not a part of all this—not willingly at least. He was in Paris, and she didn't know where. A muffled sob came from the other end of the office. Stacy swung around. There was a knock against the door to the closet. She walked over and pressed her hand against the knob, turned the key, and took two deep breaths. She swung the door open, letting it slam against the wall, and swung the gun toward the small space. A scream erupted from within, and a lone figure went deeper behind some coats. Stacy nearly squeezed the trigger but then stopped. She recognized the frightened face of Marsha peering from within.

"Marsha?" Stacy took a step into the closet.

"No, please don't hurt me." Her eyes were red, and mascara ran down her face, bleeding into the rouge.

"I'm not here to hurt anyone."

"I didn't see it. I can't say anything."

"What? Marsha, who did this?" Stacy motioned to Alain's body.

Marsha followed her arm and started crying again. "I don't know."

Stacy hoped for an instant. Certainly Marsha would have recognized Michael. "You don't know? It wasn't Michael?" She wished harder than she had for anything else in her life. *Please say no.* Marsha only stared at her, wiping away tears and further smudging mascara across her cheek.

"Marsha—was it?" She needed to know the truth.

Marsha struggled with the answer. She looked to the body and again at Stacy. Finally, she gave a nod. Stacy stepped out of the closet. Marsh knew it was Michael. If he could do this to Alain, there was little doubt in her mind that he had killed Lawrence as well. The whole story about an assassin had been a hoax. Was Cruthers still alive? She looked down at Marsha, who still sat against the back wall of the closet. "Come on. Let's get you home. You don't need to be here when the police come." Marsha hesitantly stood, pushing aside the coats.

"Will you do me a favor?"

Marsha stopped, looked at her, and again nodded.

"When the police ask about this"—she waved her hand again at Alain—"say you don't know a thing … that you were at lunch. I'll take care of it myself."

"Why?"

Stacy wondered if she was asking why Michael killed Alain or why she wanted to take care of it herself. "Why what?"

"Why did he do it?"

"I don't know, Marsha. Perhaps for money."

"He was a good man. What made him do it? He had the money already."

Again, Stacy didn't know which man she was talking about. But she supposed it had to be Alain. Michael was never a good man.

"You're sure it was Michael?"

"Yes, I heard only them talking. Two shots were fired."

* * * * * *

Marsha calmed down after returning to her apartment, and Stacy finally felt ready to leave her alone.

"What were they talking about?"

"I wasn't really listening that closely. Something about betraying friendship and trust. I don't know."

"I'm sure that was it. Michael has betrayed a great many people in the last few days. I need to find him. Did he say anything about where he was going?"

"No. I mean, I'm not sure. I couldn't hear very well. I was afraid of making any noise. He said that if I …" She trailed off as tears came to her eyes again. Stacy handed her another tissue.

"I thought I knew him. I didn't think he was capable of such threats."

"He did say he wasn't going to hurt me." She could sense Stacy's confusion.

"He threatened you and then said that?"

"Yeah."

"Well, that's a new one. One of the two was a lie. He can't seem to stop telling lies lately. Ever." She added the last word as she thought of the first lie he had ever told her—the one lie that made her leave him. Now more lies took away any possibility of her loving him again.

"He did say something about Domino."

"Domino?" Stacy came out of her daydream with a start.

"Yes, do you know him?"

"He was, maybe still is, Michael's boss."

"Alain seemed to know him too."

"Did you hear anything about that?"

Marsha struggled with her memory, which was a daze of fear and muffled voices. "Only that he was doing it for you. He told me that before he locked me in the closet as well."

"He was doing it for me?"

"Yes, after all that Alain did to you."

"Alain? He didn't do a thing to me. More lies."

"Maybe." Marsha shrugged.

"Are you going to be all right now if I go?"

"Sure. The police will be here soon, I suppose. They'll wonder why I'm not at the gallery."

"You're at lunch, right?"

"Okay. I can try. I don't want to see Alain again."

"You don't have to."

"Where are you going?"

"To find Michael."

"You still love him, don't you?"

Stacy saw tears form in Marsha's eyes and felt hers follow them. "I can't. I won't let myself. I knew when I saw him again in Paris that he was the last person I should trust, and I won't let that happen again."

"You do love him. And he loves you."

Stacy said nothing in return. She would find Michael and do what must be done. She doubted she could hurt him physically, but at the least she would let him know how she felt—how he had abused her trust too much to ever reconcile that with her. He would pay for what he had done. Even if she couldn't do that, the authorities could. She would make sure they showed up at a time when he would be with her. They would take care of the rest for her.

Chapter 38

The conductor's whistle blew, and a hiss of air released from the train. Still the train did not move. Another whistle. Michael looked down at this watch. A slight movement—or was it just his imagination? Then it moved; there was no doubt now. The stone walls of the station moved away, and the train clattered into the rain. The conductor announced that the train was traveling from Paris to Lille Flandres with a stop in Tourconing. He also notified the clientele that there were bathrooms located in cars four and thirteen, as well as a bar and dining car between each section of first and second class.

The rain fell against the window as the train picked up speed, leaving Paris behind. Michael wanted nothing more than to forget what had happened there. Only he couldn't—not yet. He still had one more thing to accomplish before that part of his life was over. Alain was gone. Everyone in the network was either dead or had gone underground. He knew Stacy needed to be told what had been happening—the whole truth. It was her decision as to whether she accompanied him to Minneapolis to finish his work.

The block apartment buildings on the outskirts of Paris's Banlieu were just sliding past, and single family homes followed immediately afterward. The train had already been moving for over ten minutes, and still they were within range of people who called Paris home. The homes finally gave way to fields, still green in mid-November. Villages dotted the landscape with red roofs and churches. The train banked sharply to the left and once again straightened out. The rest of the journey to Lille would be a straight shot.

Michael hoped the rain would not be falling in Lille. He did not look forward to trying to find Stacy in the cold rain of November. He once again wondered how much Arnaud had already told her. His loyalty to her was, of course, stronger than to Michael. If she knew what truth Arnaud had been able to give her, his disclosure of the rest would do little to change her mind from whatever decision she'd already made about their future. Killing Alain would not help matters either. He had considered telling her everything but that, yet there was no one else who would have killed him. She would know instantly upon finding out about his death. Michael was sure Arnaud would have told her that he was in Paris. Besides, Marsha had recognized him. She most likely wouldn't keep quiet for long, despite his threats to her.

He could not resolve himself to the fact that although he did not lie to her, through Arnaud he was able to tell her only partial truths. What Arnaud didn't know, he couldn't say; and if Michael didn't see her, she couldn't question. There was some sort of deception in all that. Stacy would consider the whole mess a lie, and he really couldn't blame her. He was in for a long lecture at the very least. At the other end, it was quite possible that she would leave without a word, never to be seen by him again. He would have liked to give her the chance to decide what to do about Domino. If she asked him not to, he would concede. They could be gone within the hour and never look back. New lives awaited them both somewhere. What use were those possibilities now? He had no time to talk to her. If he lost her because of this, at least she would be safe.

* * * * * *

Arnaud watched as Marsha entered the gallery. He was not sure if she was a customer or not until she sat down at her desk and picked up the telephone. She replaced the phone on its cradle and took a deep breath. Something was not right. Arnaud crossed Rue Turbigo and entered the gallery. Marsha rose from her desk. "Je suis désolé, mais nous sommes fermés." She crossed the marble floor to lead him out.

"I'm looking for Alain."

Marsha stopped midstride and anxiously looked up to the office. "He's …" She had no idea what to say to him.

"Yes, I know he's not there."

Marsha smiled, tears crowding her eyes.

"Or is he?"

"No … I mean … I don't know."

"I'm a friend of Stacy's. Was she here?"

"Stacy?"

"Yes. Was she here?"

"Oui. I just left her."

"Where?"

"From my apartment, but she's not there."

"Where did she go?"

"I don't know. To find Michael."

"And where is he?"

"I'm not sure. Stacy asked me the same thing, but as I told her, I couldn't really hear. On my way back to the studio, I remember that she did say something about mini apples."

She mangled the name of the city, but Arnaud knew what she meant. He was going to Minneapolis. That meant Michael was returning to Domino. There seemed to be no stopping him. He meant to clean out the entire nest of hornets, including the queen bee, unless it was true that he was still working for Domino. If Stacy was headed there too, she meant to accomplish the same thing. Yet she might have the wrong top man in mind. He hoped she wasn't too desperate. Michael was as unsafe as Domino, and neither of them knew it. How could Michael ever expect that Stacy would be going after him?

"What did she say?" He returned to Marsha.

"I don't know. I mentioned that Michael had mentioned the name Domino, and she said something about it being related to home."

"You were here when Michael was?"

"Yes. He put me in the closet. He killed Alain."

"I was told it would end like that."

"Do you know why? Alain was always so kind to me."

"Alain was not the man you thought he was. He's ended the lives of a great many people in the last week."

"That's what Michael said. He had Stacy beaten."

"He told you that?"

"Oui, and Alain admitted to it. He said it was regrettable."

"Did you tell Stacy that?"

"No. I didn't want to bring back any bad memories. Stacy said that Michael had lied all about it. I wasn't sure what to say to her."

"Normally I would have agreed. However, in this instance, it could have saved a lot of pain." Arnaud walked away from Marsha. "Is Alain still here then?"

"Oui. I called the police."

"I wasn't here."

"There are a lot of people who weren't here."

"Yes, I suppose that's true."

"You will keep all the confidences?"

"Even Michael's? He killed Alain."

"Even Michael's. He's not as bad as it may seem."

"Stacy loves him."

"Yes, I know, and if I don't get to her first, she may kill him."

Chapter 39

Michael relaxed against his seat on the 747. They would be landing at Kennedy within half an hour. He did not know what to expect upon his arrival either there or in Minneapolis. He had used his real passport, not any of those manufactured by one of his associates. There were no associates left. He knew no one in Paris anymore, and his short search in Lille for Stacy or Arnaud led to nothing. He still did not want to believe that Alain was capable of all that had happened, despite Domino's obvious involvement. No matter what, he needed to get to Domino before he heard about Alain. Once Domino knew Alain was dead, he would know Michael was after him next. Domino knew him too well to think otherwise.

He paid little attention to those around him. Michael felt the plane shift its momentum into a lower speed. A moment later, the plane also dropped in altitude. The New York skyline would be visible within a few minutes. He had been gone from the States for only ten months, but it seemed as if a lifetime had passed by. His retirement had caused, in the end, almost as many deaths as all those he had been a part of in his life up until then. He wondered where Stacy was at that moment. *Perhaps back in Paris.*

If Arnaud had explained everything to her, she would be looking for those simply missing and hoping to find some still alive. Michael suspected she would not find many. Domino had really gone overboard in his attempt to gain more control. What he had, in fact, accomplished was throwing the entire network into disarray. It would be years before anyone involved with Domino would be able to function in Europe. One thing Domino had forgotten in his attempts was that the structure must remain in order to control it.

The pilot was just announcing their impending arrival. It was a balmy fifty-two degrees in New York. Winter had not yet arrived to the Northeast. *There could be snow on the ground in Minneapolis*, he reminded himself. The weather in one part of the country in no way dictated what it was like at the same moment in another. He still needed to pass through customs, which would be impossible had the police in Minneapolis tied him to either Marta's or Cruthers's death.

Marta was another matter altogether. Before he returned to Europe, he would see her mother. Any questions that needed answering would come from him. He knew she would not have gone to Domino or Cruthers. She would have no more trusted their responses than those of the devil. It was likely she would offer him the same respect, but it was in Marta's memory that he would try to explain to her mother what had happened.

In actuality, going to her gave him the most risk. She would be more likely to inform the police of his probable connection with Marta's death. That was a risk he would take for Marta—the one person who had understood why he left and who had understood that he could only love one person: Stacy. If only Marta were alive now, she could explain it all to Stacy. He would not have to hope she believed his half-truths. The killing would remain a secret that only the deceased and he would know. Blaming it all on Domino would not be a lie.

******

There could be no doubting it now. Alain was dead—the two hits had been, after all, successful—and now Victor, whom Michael had known in Florida. No one else knew that. Victor would have tried to contact Michael. He would have done anything—including, it seemed, risking his presence on the platform at Aulnoye. Who else could have even suspected such a meeting would take place? And then there was this Josephine woman, whom Michael had killed in cold blood. All these deaths, and not a word from Michael in a very long time. No matter the explanations, Michael could never again convince her that he was retired. She needed to confront him and end it once and for all. She would then disappear and live without any semblance of her old lives.

Even the Michael she knew was capable of murder would not have done what happened to Victor. He had changed, but it was not in the way Stacy had imagined. Killing had become even easier for him. Friends were no longer safe from his gun. If there was a threat, Michael would eliminate it. It had been his career for ten years and had finally become a lifestyle. She wondered what he would do now. There were no more ties to hold him in Paris. Had this all been a scheme devised by Domino? Had Cruthers's death been a convenient ruse?

If this were true, there was only one place Michael would be heading, and that was Minneapolis. Marsha had all but confirmed that. Domino must have offered him quite a large sum to go along with such a complex and lengthy plan. Perhaps Michael was ready to retire, even if for reasons other than those he had given her. Chances were the money he would receive for single-handedly tearing apart the network and killing its two most important members was unimaginable.

Thoughts of his retirement brought Stacy back to their relationship. He might very likely return to Paris with a story that somehow explained everything. With the money, he would want to take her into the country and buy a house, just as she had always wanted. She wouldn't give him the chance to masquerade as a reformed man again. She would return to Minneapolis and confront him there. As far as she was concerned, there was only one thing that remained to be done between them. That was for Stacy to stand before him with a gun and try to kill the only man she loved—or could ever love. Was it possible that hate and love could be so real at the same time?

The lights of Paris below her were beginning their daily routine of bringing life to the night. On the distant horizon, a violet glow edged the few clouds remaining from the morning storm. It was somewhere past those clouds that she would find him. She wondered whether snow had fallen yet in Minneapolis. It was the one thing she missed most about Minnesota. Nothing compared to waking up to a brilliant blue sky above a new carpet of white snow. The thought brought tears to her eyes. It had been eight years since she had seen such a sight—eight years since Michael had refused to give up his profession for her. She had so many good memories of the city, overshadowed by that one decisive moment in her life that even now played its part. She would return and act out another scene that would shadow even that. There would be no returning to Minneapolis again, no matter how much she longed for the snow and bright blue skies.

The Eiffel Tower shed its dark exterior and was bathed in a shower of yellow light. She stepped away from the window in Montparnasse. A train below would bring her to the airport. She would spend the night there, waiting to return home. It still was home; not until tomorrow had come and gone would she refuse even that.

Chapter 40

In the darkness of night, the air was cool. Michael shivered, drawing his coat tighter around his body. Clouds covered the stars with masses of swirling, dark black cotton. The wind buffeted against his coat, finding its way up the sleeves and down his back. Michael clenched his teeth and closed his eyes for a moment, thinking of warmth, willing his body to respond. It had always worked before, even if only for an instant. A rush of warm tingles would spread across his body, leaving in the wake some semblance of relief. Despite the thoughts, no relief came now—only the bitter cold that was now added to by the first drops of rain.

It was not long before his hair was soaked, despite his cap, and his jacket was wet through. He shifted his position under the tree. It offered little protection against the rain. The winds blew the stinging wetness in all directions. However, his back was against the trunk and was dry. He tried to think of only that. A large drop of rain collected on the leaves above and splashed against his neck, the cold liquid moistening his collar. Michael shifted his Minnesota Twins cap so the brim faced backward. At least it would cover his neck. The rain slackened so that the furious pounding of water against puddles became only an occasional splash. *Thank God for brief showers*, Michael thought.

With the rain nearly gone, the cold remained behind. Michael unclenched his hands. Stiffness gradually gave way as his joints cracked with the simple effort of opening his fists. He pulled them back up into his sleeves. He wondered whether it was worth sitting there with his entire body shaking, his legs straining, the cold sapping away their energy. What had he to gain from all this anyway? Was it his pride or, worse yet, his ego? He knew of many men who had said that no one would get away with harming their loved ones. People paid dearly for such abuses. Revenge was a way of life for many. Did the act justify the fact that another murder would be committed? Did killing Domino change what had happened to Stacy? To Lawrence? Had killing Alain or Josephine done it? He only knew that neither death had given him any pleasure. The detached emotion of his days as an assassin had left him months ago, yet even then he had never found any pleasure in killing. He knew now that there would be no pleasure in what he had to do tonight. No matter; it was something he had to do. There was no denying that either.

Michael shook the water from his hair. Stray drops of liquid rolled down his back. He was already so cold he barely noticed their presence. By the time Domino returned home, he would be in no shape to do anything. His hands were once again locked in the embrace of the cold. He should have known to bring gloves. His ears tingled, and he could barely feel his toes. It would have to wait. There would be other days. Yet if he left now, he knew he would not be back. The edge of his anger had been lost. Revenge was no longer an immediate concern. No, he would stay. Even if it were his last day on Earth, he would stay. He reminded himself that in the condition he was in, it very well could be the last day for him.

He again stretched his fingers away from his palms, this time pulling them all the way back through his sleeves and under his armpits. It would not do to get caught off guard like that, but he needed his hands to function. He could feel the grip of his gun against his elbow. It served as a reminder as to what he was there to do. Domino had controlled his life for too long. Even when he had thought the man was gone, it wasn't the truth. Michael did not know how long Alain and Domino had been working together, but they were no longer in business. With Cruthers, Domino, and Alain gone, there would be a multitude of men killed and injured while the others fought for control. It was now not money, but power, that mattered.

Money could buy some power, but it was not enough. There was someone out there like Domino who could convince others that it was in their best interest to back him. Money would further his cause, but influence and persuasion would be more powerful at first. Michael looked up to the house. A light flashed on in the living room.

He was home. It would happen tonight. There was no turning back now.

******

"Hello, Domino." Michael entered through the same door through which Domino had just come. Domino, never one to let the spontaneous reaction to a surprise get the best of him, simply smiled. He completed his circuit through the dining room and sat down on a love seat.

"Come in, Michael. You know, I've been wondering when I might see you again."

"You mean *if* you would see me again."

"Yes. You disappeared so suddenly just before my son's death. I can't imagine you had anything to do with it." Domino motioned to the empty chair to his right.

"I was gone before he died. It's not that I didn't want to kill him. But you knew that." Michael sat, keeping his gun trained on Domino.

"You don't happen to know who was responsible for that Moroccan deal?" Domino glanced to his right, where the windows looked onto the backyard.

"I never handled those things. I didn't even want to know they existed. But I'm not here for idle chitchat or a discussion about your miscreant of a son."

"No, I suppose not. Why have you come back? I would like to think you were comfortable in Paris."

"I was for about two minutes, until you decided to intervene."

"You must choose your friends more wisely next time." Domino shrugged. He again looked to his right.

"I've come to settle the score, Domino. I can't let you get away with what you did to Stacy."

Domino stood, facing Michael for the first time. “I had nothing to do with that. I didn’t even know it happened until much later. You must speak to your friend Alain about that. You know how I felt about Stacy. She was like a daughter to me.”

“I don’t see it that way. I always figured you’re responsible for the garbage you hire.”

“Michael, this won’t work. You can’t leave here alive.”

“Neither can you. I only want to know one thing. Why?”

“Why what? Why come after you? You were responsible for my son’s death. Just as you’ve come after me to avenge Stacy, I went after you. You have to understand that.”

“Why Lawrence? Why Victor? Why everyone else?”

“That was not me. It seems Alain wanted out and nobody left to identify him. I only needed to pay off my debts—the debts you caused me to have. I sold you out to someone who could use your services. I knew this would not end well for you.”

“That simple?” Michael shook his head.

“That simple.”

“There’s nothing left over there. No one you can count on. The network may have supplied Lawrence with information, but they were your sources as well.”

“A short-term inconvenience. I am being watched a little too closely here. I’ve had to temporarily scale back the operation. As long as I was doing that, I decided to clean house.”

“So you used me.”

“You provided me with an opportunity. I took it.”

“Alain is dead.”

“I suspected as much.”

“He deserves the same fate as you. You know I killed him with a weapon he sold to me—one that you paid for.” Michael took his hand from his pocket. “Do you remember this?” Michael showed him the Beretta 92F that Alain had given him years prior.

“You still have that? I never thought of you as being sentimental.”

“It comes in handy. I even bought this to go along with it.”

Michael produced a silencer from his other pocket and tightened it to the end of the weapon. "Have you ever thought of retiring?"

"Michael, wait; we can work something out." Domino took his handkerchief out and wiped away perspiration from his forehead. He began to realize the truth of Michael's words. Neither of them might survive the day.

"Funny … you know, Sticky was sweating just like that the last time I saw him." Michael raised the gun to fire, but a shot rang out just before he could pull the trigger. Michael's gun went flying into the center of the room. A second shot entered the back of the chair, and he felt the impact against the vest he was wearing. The chair had softened much of the force, but he still fell forward.

Michael reached behind himself and pulled a second Beretta from the small of his back. The window had shattered, and the backyard was dark. He wasn't sure where the gunman had come from. Perhaps he had arrived with Domino. He needed to take care of Domino and then the gunman—no witnesses.

Domino was gone from the chair, taking the momentary distraction to go farther into the house. "Domino, you can't hide. You know I'll take care of both of you."

"Go fuck yourself. I've called the police. I'd rather deal with them right now," Domino called out from the kitchen.

Michael crouched low as he ran from the chair to the dining room. He glanced through the shattered window and saw a flash of light that was followed almost instantly by the whoosh of a bullet tearing past his ear. The china cabinet exploded into a mass of dishes and glassware. Michael swung around and fired twice in the direction of the flash. He rolled into the kitchen and stood. Domino was just pulling a gun from a drawer, and Michael fired twice. Domino's face went white, and a deep intake of air was followed by his body going to the floor. Michael calmly walked over, and for the first time in his life he fired a third shot, making sure this man would never be a problem again.

Michael made his way to the front door and glanced through the side windows. His two shots at the guy in the backyard might have bought him time, but he would have been lucky to hit him, let alone kill him. He wondered whether there was just the one. Domino never had much protection around him at home, but with his son dead, he may have increased that. He didn't see any movement and opened the door, pushing it toward the wall with his foot. Michael inched around the door frame, gun first. *Nothing.*

Just as he began to step into the opening, two shots rang out. One shattered the mirror behind him. The second sliced through the door frame and went on across his thigh. He collapsed, with his hand reaching for the wound. He lay sprawled across the tiled entry, raising his head just enough to look at his leg. It had just grazed him, but it hurt like hell. Well, that answered his question. There were at least two of them—both with rifles. Michael backed farther into the house. He needed to get out—and fast. The police would be arriving any minute.

A small rock rolled forward in front of the doorway. Michael rolled behind the half wall that separated the foyer from the living room. There were windows everywhere in the place. He grabbed the leg from the loveseat and pulled it to cover his back. If they came after him inside, he was confident he could take them out before they got him. Yet he couldn't wait for them to do that. Just then he saw the shadow of a figure pass the far window. Michael trained his weapon just above the windowsill, a couple feet from where the figure had crouched below the bottom of the window.

He gave the man five seconds to look; if he didn't by then, Michael would take action. It took only three, and Michael fired twice. The figure jumped up slightly and fell backward. *One down and one to go.* It was time to take it to the second. He wondered if the man out front was still where he had knocked the rock. It was as good as any place to start his search. He wondered no more as gunfire ripped into the half wall, throwing splinters up over his location. Michael curled up against the stone at the base of the wall. He held his breath as the gunshots stopped. There were no sounds. And then, in the distance, he heard the sirens. They would be here within a minute or two. He needed to be gone.

His car was two blocks up the street, and he decided to make a run for it. Michael rose up from his hiding spot, his gun trained on the open doorway. He kicked against the wall and got the response he wanted. The man immediately entered the doorway to fire again. Michael fired twice, and the man's eyes went wide. A spasm clenched the man's hand and forced his finger against the trigger. Bullets followed up the wall, spraying Michael with dust and Sheetrock. He felt the bullet graze his left shoulder, and he went down again.

The sirens were louder still as Michael crawled out through the doorway, where the man's body was twisted backward against the stone walkway. A single bullet had torn through the man's face. Michael shook his head and whispered, "I missed."

******

It was nearly eight o'clock by the time Stacy arrived at the hotel. She sat on the bed, listening to the same station she had always had on so many years ago—KQ92. The DJs had changed, the songs had changed, but the format had stayed the same: a few songs and a lot of commercials, again and again. It was almost as if she had been gone for only a few weeks. She was worn out from the trip, and sleep tugged at the corners of her mind, but she resisted the urge. Finding Michael would not be easy. There was only one place she could think to look, and that was Domino's. It was a dangerous prospect. If Domino was there to greet her, it would not be with a warm hug. Of course, he would act cordial, probably even invite her in for a drink, but she would not last long after she left. In fact, she wouldn't put it past him to plant a bomb in her car while she was there. There were no rules when it came to upsetting Domino. She got up and retrieved the keys to her rental car. Domino's place was not far from where she now was. Despite how she might feel now, Michael's sins would be her sins in Domino's eyes.

She turned left out of the parking lot and went past the Ikea, which sat on the same lot as the old Met Center. She had fond memories of going to North Stars games when she was young before they moved in the early nineties. She turned right onto Eighty-First Street, driving past the Mall of America. Lights burned against the tan brick of the front entrance with a red, white, and blue sign proclaiming its name. It spanned the distance across four blocks from Cedar Avenue, easily encompassing the site of the old Metropolitan Stadium and its parking lot.

From there she crossed Cedar and continued west until she reached Queen Avenue. She was a block away from Domino's place, and already she knew Michael had been there. Police cars lined the street on both sides. An ambulance stood in front of the driveway, but no one seemed in much of a hurry. Paramedics were loading an empty stretcher through the rear doors. One stood talking to an officer. Stacy pulled behind a police car and watched. She wondered which one of them had ended up dead. The feelings that mixed inside her gave her a headache. If Domino had killed Michael, she would not let him get away with it. However, there was a part of her that knew she would be relieved that she herself would not be faced with that decision.

Michael had gotten away, though. The sixth sense that existed between them told her that Michael was still alive. He could be anywhere. The one chance she had at finding him easily was gone. A policeman walked toward her car. He came over and motioned for her to roll down the window. "Can I help you, ma'am?"

"What's going on?"

"Just an accident."

"Anyone hurt? I'm a nurse," she lied.

"No. We have things under control."

"Sure. Okay, have a nice day."

"Thanks. You too."

Chapter 41

Arnaud went straight from his gate to the taxi stand outside the main entrance. He needed to track Stacy. She would have gone to a hotel. He moved down the line of taxis, showing each driver a photo of her. She would have arrived sometime around 5:00 p.m. No one recognized her. He received a few lewd remarks but nothing else. The cold wind was making its way through his light jacket. He couldn't stay out in the cold much longer.

She might have met someone, but that wasn't likely. She had been gone too long to still have contacts here. The only other thing he could think of was a rental car. He crossed the street that served as the taxi queue and went into the parking ramp. Luckily the traffic was light, and he had no trouble finding a clerk at each desk ready to help him. It was at Avis that he got his first clue.

"Sure I saw her," a woman told him. "I think Shirley helped her. Shirley, come here." A tall blonde woman in her early forties came over to them. "You helped this woman, didn't you?" She handed Shirley the photo.

"Yeah, I remember her. She was in quite a hurry."

"Did she say where she was staying?"

"Can't help you there."

"Try to remember anything she might have said."

"Look, there might be a local address on her contract, but we're not allowed to give that information out."

"It's important that I find her soon. Seriously, it is a matter of life and death."

Shirley rolled her eyes. She started to smile but then stopped. "You're serious, aren't you?"

"Yes, I am."

"Okay, I'll get her contract." She leafed through a pile of rental contracts. "Here it is. But she left no local address."

Arnaud sighed. What was he going to do now?

"Wait a second. She did leave something. She was in such a hurry. Now, where did I put it?" She went into the back and came back a moment later carrying a magazine. "I really don't think she would come back for it, but you never know."

Arnaud took the magazine. It wouldn't help him much. He set it back down on the counter. Then he saw the number penciled on the margin of the ad on the back of the magazine. "Do you have a phone I can use?"

Shirley pointed to a pay phone in the back of the office. Arnaud went to the phone. He stopped halfway there. He didn't have a single penny in American money, let alone a quarter for the call. He didn't have a cell phone that worked in the United States. He looked back to the counter. Shirley had returned to the back room, and the other woman was helping a customer. He continued to the phone and dialed the operator.

"Operator. This is May. How can I help you?"

"I would like to make a collect call, please."

"What number, please?"

Arnaud gave her the number. The phone rang twice, and a woman answered with "Holiday Inn Metrodome." Arnaud hung up before the operator could even ask for his name or if they would accept the charges. He pulled the phone book up from beneath the phone, searched the yellow pages, and found the address.

"Hi, I would like to rent a car."

"Did you find out where she is?"

"I think so."

"That's great."

Now he only hoped he was in time to find her.

* * * * * *

Stacy waited for Michael high above the plant's floor in the manager's office. She knew the message she had left through his old contacts would get to him—especially after Domino's death. No matter which door Michael chose to enter through, she would see him—that is, if he came at all. It was not just to confront Michael that she came here. She knew now that killing Michael was the only way to stop him. He couldn't stop killing, no matter what he might have claimed. She needed to end this—end him. For all these months, she had believed in him. So many lies, and he would regret every one. How many people knew? Alain? Was that why Michael killed him—for telling her the truth? Could Arnaud have known? He had withheld things from her at Michael's request. What else had he hidden?

Outside, the sun passed behind a cloud and the windows dimmed. Shadows appeared throughout the plant floor. Printing machines sat cold and unmoving. Plastic was still spooled through the presses, and the machines had been shut off in the middle of printing. Those who normally ran the machines had left them as such the previous afternoon. Demands for a raise and better working conditions had not been met. Thus, a strike had ended the work. Stacy wondered if they were asking for as much as the athletes who had once walked out years ago—first baseball, and then hockey. Money was what made the world turn, and it caused Michael to betray just about everyone he knew.

He had forsaken their relationship and lied to her for money. What had he told her once so many years ago? "They deserve to die, and they will. I might as well be the one who pockets the cash." She could remember it clearly. That was the day she had left him, nearly eight years ago. He had changed. That much was obvious. He was even a colder killer. Not even friendship affected what he did.

Stacy heard the first drops of rain fall against the roof. They would normally be lost in the roar of the presses, but today they echoed into the farthest corners of the building. She looked down at her watch. He was late. How long should she wait for him? He could ignore the message. After all, he had no doubts that Alain was dead. It wasn't like him though. He was too curious, wanting to know how everything came to be and what was to come. It would nag at him if he didn't show up. She had known that when she sent the telegram. He also now knew she was privy to his secret, so wouldn't he need to take care of her too? She wondered whether he had it in him to kill her, and not for the first time, she wondered whether she had it in herself to kill him.

The echoing sound of a door closing broke her from her thoughts. She glanced at the entrances below. No one was there. She had missed him. "Damn." Concentration had never been her strong suit. Stacy slid the window above the plant floor open further. She listened for any sound. Anyone other than Michael would make some noise. *Nothing—not even a footstep.* It was him, and it was time to confront him. Her hands began to shake, and tears formed in her eyes. She only hoped she could follow through with it. Otherwise she might be the one ending up on the floor with a bullet wound.

She stepped through the door and quietly moved down the stairwell. The sound of her feet clicking against the metal steps reverberated in the narrow space. The door below was open. He would hear if he came near that doorway. Stacy stopped and took her shoes off. Trying again, she made it to the bottom without another noise. The wide-open space beyond the door was clear. She wanted to meet him there, where he couldn't duck into a hiding place.

"Stacy?" Michael called out.

"Michael, I'm over here." She waited until he came fully into the open, and she then twisted from the doorway, raising the gun toward him. "Drop the gun, Michael." He did as he was told without hesitation.

"Stacy, it's me, Michael." He took a step away from her.

Of course he didn't really believe that she didn't recognize him, but what else could he say. There she was with the gun Domino had given him for a Christmas present. She wondered if he recognized it and maybe wondered how she had gotten it.

"Who are you?" Stacy rubbed the tears away from her eyes. She had promised herself not to cry, but there she was, facing Michael, ready to kill the man she could never stop loving—not even now.

"What?"

"I don't know you." She stumbled over the words, hardly able to control the shaking that had begun.

"Yes you do, Stacy. I love you."

"Menteur!" The word sprang from her lips and echoed in the silence. "You've never loved me."

"I always have. Why don't you believe that?"

"What kind of gun did you use on those two men in Lille? Was it the same gun as the one you used in Paris to kill that driver? Did Alain supply you with another one of Fabrique International's bolt-action sniper rifles?"

"I … no … I don't know where to start."

"What do you need, more time to think up your lies? No good on the spur of the moment, are we? Too bad; you don't have any more time. And how about Josephine? Did she deserve to die too? Did they all deserve to die?"

"What? Josephine? How do you even know that name?" Michael raised up his hands in defense. He looked around the plant. The nearest machine was almost fifteen feet away. She would have no problem getting him before he could reach it.

"How do I know her name? That's all you have to say? I don't want to hear any more lies. I've already fallen victim to you too many times before. I'm too naive when it comes to you." Her tears no longer fell. The shaking had stopped. She realized she was truly going to kill him. No matter what he said, no matter how much he pleaded, she had become the executioner's executioner.

"I did it for you."

"For me?"

"Yes. They were blackmailing me. Alain, his friends, Domino—they wanted to get rid of us all."

"Alain and Domino? Why would they be working together? Alain was just an art dealer."

"He was not just an art dealer. He dealt weapons. How do you think he sold those rifles to me?"

"Of course he's a dealer. What, do you think I'm an idiot? You can't tell me one truth and think it's going to make up for all the lies. It's not good enough. I can't believe you anymore. I won't believe you." She kept saying this to herself. She had not come this far to back off now simply because of more words.

"It's the truth. Ask Arnaud."

"Arnaud already told me everything. If he could, I'm positive he'd be here in my place. I've never doubted his word."

"Or Alain's?"

"I don't care about Alain. You lied to me and continued killing. Lies I could have walked away from. Your easy manner of killing, even your own friends, I—"

"Stacy." Michael dived for the floor, spinning toward the opening on his left. She heard the shots and saw their impact. The first ripped into his shoulder; the second, his chest.

Chapter 42

Arnaud ran through the same door where Michael had entered. He couldn't believe he had heard gunshots. Stacy had told him to wait outside and said she needed to talk to Michael alone, but he never suspected she would actually be able to kill him. Yet there she was, leaning over his sprawled bloody body on the plant floor.

Stacy didn't even look up as Arnaud arrived at her side. "Arnaud, he's dead." Tears streamed down her cheeks, and she could barely speak. "What have I done?"

Arnaud bent down and grabbed her wrist. "We need to go. Someone had to have heard the shots."

"We can't just leave him here."

"We can't take him with us. Stacy, he's dead. They'll take care of him." He tried again to pull her away from Michael.

"No, I'm staying with him. I'm not a cold-blooded assassin like he was. He may have deserved it, but I shouldn't have been the one to end it. We should have turned him in."

"Stacy, you have the gun in your hand. If you stay, they'll put you in jail. I'm not going to spend the rest of my life making weekly trips to the local prison to see you."

Stacy bent over Michael's face, letting tears drop against his flushed complexion. She kissed him lightly on the cheek. "Je t'aime," she whispered, and while that may have been the truth, she knew this would have been it for them no matter how it had ended. She had now killed three people, including someone she loved. She was no better than him. She had become him in a way. A door slammed shut somewhere in the complex.

"Stacy!" Arnaud whispered harshly.

"Yes, I'm coming." She finally let Arnaud pull her away and toward the back exit. He pushed open the fire exit and the alarms erupted, adding to the rushed confusion just coming alive at the other end of building. They went down a stairwell and through a back alley to Arnaud's car. Stacy dragged behind Arnaud, his hand still grasping her wrist. She had stopped crying but could not turn away from the building behind them. Arnaud pushed a button on his key chain. The lights of his car flashed twice, and the doors unlocked with an audible click. He put Stacy into the passenger side before getting in himself.

He turned the ignition and looked at Stacy. She was still looking back down the alley toward the factory. Suddenly, Arnaud looked in the backseat and then to her again. "Stacy, where's the gun?"

"I left it back there. It was his gun—a gift from Domino."

"Merdre. Why did you do that?"

"He used it to kill others. I couldn't keep it."

"But your prints. They'll think you killed them both."

"Nope." Stacy raised her hand and gently peeled away a transparent layer from her hand. "Michael taught me a few useful things."

"Still, it wasn't the wise thing to do."

"They'll never think of looking for me anyway."

"That's beside the point. Let's find somewhere to lie low."

Arnaud started away from the alley. Michael would still be resting on the concrete floor of the factory. She envisioned a number of striking press workers standing around him, wondering who he was. The American assassin supposedly shot last week in Paris would now be found dead in Minneapolis. The newspapers would have a lot of fun with that.

"Where's a hotel near here?"

Stacy watched the University of Minnesota campus roll by with the Mississippi in the background. It had been too long since she had been to Minneapolis. So many things had changed. Perhaps she would stay for a while. Maybe she could head back to Paris or begin a totally new life in a new place. She had options; that was all that mattered. She was in control of her own life. She could go anywhere.

"Stacy?"

She shook her head. "What?"

"Where's a hotel?"

"Oh, just keep going straight. There's one just north of here, I think."

About the Author

Michael J Reiland grew up in Fridley, MN, and graduated from the University of Minnesota with a bachelor's degree in English creative writing. He has published poetry in an American anthology and has lived in France, Florida, and Las Vegas. Michael, who still enjoys traveling to many foreign destinations, currently resides in Virginia. Pursued is his first novel.

Printed in the United States
By Bookmasters